"It is a suspenseful and action-filled novel that promises to thrill crime and murder mystery enthusiasts who appreciate imperfect heroes. **A spectacular story!**" *-Susan Sewell for Readers' Favorite*

"It's rare that all the elements work together in harmony to make **a perfectly entertaining and delicious novel** such as this one." *-Literary Titan*

"He manages his multiple plot threads with panache as the action races to a sad and yet hopeful conclusion. **This is a stunner.**" *-The Prairies Book Review*

"Mike does a great job with setting, characters and plot. His descriptions of West Virginia, her land, people and events are spot on. **The plot is full of twists and turns.**" *-Author Amy Deal*

"**Surprises add to a strong, scary story** filled with questionable characters." *-Kirkus Reviews*

"It is the kind of book that **is impossible to put down**, and when I had to I longed for it!" *-Red Headed Book Lover*

In The Country Dark

Mike Mallow

Cressen Books LLC
Gerrardstown, WV

Cressen Books LLC
Gerrardstown, WV

Visit our website at www.cressenbooks.com

The characters and events portrayed in this book are fictitious. Any similarity to real persons, living or dead, is coincidental and not intended by the author.

ISBN 978-1-940249-18-6

Library of Congress Control Number: 2020941995

Printed in the United States of America

Table of Contents

Dedication

For Travis, Clay, Uncle Michael, and all the Upper Tract men who never had the chance to see the far side of adulthood.

Dedication

It's funny how people don't really think about certain friends unless that friend happens to be right in front of them. Cabel Walsh was no exception, not putting a lot of thought towards his friends, or much of a focus on anything, during his long drive home from the office. Instead, his thoughts danced around from the mundane to the ridiculous, but ended where they often had – work.

Although the newspaper industry was dying, the work made Cabel feel alive. Interviewing and investigating were not so much his forte. There were officemates that made a mission of raking up everything short of muck that could be counted on to crack the nut of a story wide-open. But that wasn't what Cabel was about, even though he loved to write. Honing and chiseling away at words until they were their sharpest was his passion. The click-clack sounds of the computer keyboard soothed him when he was carefully crafting the perfect paragraph.

Cabel was contemplating an upcoming writing project while he traversed from Baker County, through Stonewall County, to reach his home in O'Brien County. But even those thoughts could only hold his attention for so long. During the cross-county journey through the rural West Virginia countryside, he ceased paying mind to his work and turned his thoughts towards what his plans were for the oncoming weekend.

It was Veterans Day and the autumn sky gradated from blue to orange, the colors sagging below the horizon during the hour-long commute. The rugged Appalachian hills silhouetted against the darkening quintessence and soon it would dip into an unrelenting shade of black that only the unpopulated vacuum of the country could supply.

As he contemplated his options for the weekend, he remembered something more pressing. It was the recollection of date plans that evening which forced Cabel to accelerate. The wheels of the black SUV began turning faster as the race down the desolate two-lane began. He sped not to reach his destination faster, but to find a patch of earth that intersected with the ever-elusive cell service for the area.

Cabel's left leg started to bob anxiously while he kept one eye on the road and another on the signal strength of his cell phone, which displayed on the center console navigation screen of the newer-model vehicle. A glimmer of excitement shivered along his nerve-endings when a single bar of service strength illuminated on the panel, presented as the shortest single line in a row of increasingly taller lines that were grayed-out until the signal could grow stronger.

"Call Miranda," Cabel commanded, slowing the vehicle to help maintain the signal. The console screen transitioned to black and displayed the single word "DIALING" in a font unimpressive for the times. After a pause, a ring tone could be heard.

"Hello?" a poor cell service distorted woman's voice answered.

"Hi Miranda, it's Cabel."

"Cabel? You got to tell me about that name some time," she responded, her tone chipper through the static.

"Would love to, but my cell service isn't great where I am," he evaded. "Just wanted to let you know that I'm running behind. Can we meet at the tavern rather than me picking you up? I don't want to keep you waiting."

There was a brief lapse before a voice crackled back over the static. "Um, yeah, I guess that's fine."

"I'm so sorry," Cabel apologized, recognizing some disappointment in her voice. "I got caught up on an assignment and lost track of time."

Miranda laughed. "That's okay. As long as you buy me a drink, and tell me about the name thing, I'll let you slide this time."

* * *

Troy Mason was engaged in a fistfight with an 83-year-old dementia patient from Ward D, the nicer of the sections of the nursing home. What the gentleman lacked in mental fortitude he made up for in physical fitness, and was possibly recalling the memories from his youth when he was a bare-knuckle boxer.

Troy was overconfident and allowed the gentleman a free punch, brandishing the twisted grin of displaced confidence as he lowered his guard. It proved foolish. A swift left hook to the jaw put Troy to the floor. He spun and dropped to his knees while the rattle of the impact gave him a lightheaded sensation. Once his knees impacted the floor, the rest of his body followed in a crash. His head, the last to take a turn, hit hardest and bounced off the white tiles.

The spritely gentleman danced gleefully over Troy and hooted to himself with two arms raised in victory.

A man dressed in nursing scrubs that Troy knew as Dave, rushed into the small room, eyeing the situation. The aged gentleman paid him no mind and continued to spryly bobble and dance. Troy remained motionless on the floor with the broken pieces of his ego.

"Were you just fighting?! You shouldn't be fighting with the residents, Troy," Dave chastised from the edge of the brightly lit room, his tone heavy with indecision of whether he should engage any further.

Troy rose enough to turn onto his side. He responded slowly, "Reckon in this particular moment, I concur." Troy slowly stretched his pinned arm from under his body and rubbed his jaw, grumbling unintelligibly when the painful area was discovered. He tasted the coppery flavor of blood, but fought the urge to spit the confirmation onto the pristine floor.

A fellow Certified Nursing Assistant, Carl, arrived soon after and ushered the old man away while the standoffish Dave seemed to decide it was safe to help Troy get upright again. Dave crouched down, slipped both hands under Troy's shoulder, and yanked upwards. Troy stubbornly refused to budge at first, but yielded after recognizing Dave's relentless need to make things right.

Once in a sitting position, it took both palms flat to the floor to keep him upright. Appearing to recognize that he had accomplished all that he could, and that Troy wasn't getting to his feet any time soon, Dave stood and moved in front of Troy to reestablish eye contact.

"This is bad," Dave stated grimly before his eyes drifted away. He nodded, agreeing with his own statement. "This is really bad for you."

Dave seemed to wish to express more, but was torn from his thoughts when Carl reentered the room and shouted.

"What are you doing, man?! You are right in view of the cameras!"

Carl reached out a hand to Troy, which Troy refused to take. He looked away.

"Dammit Carl, the old man called me a candyass. I can't let that kinda slander slide," Troy defended. He sighed and looked back to Carl. It took further hesitation for him to scoot in a way that he could offer a hand back to Carl. With a sharp heave, Carl pulled his coworker upright.

"He probably meant candy-striper," Dave interjected. It was a feeble attempt to smooth over the situation and he seemed to realize it, but doubled down regardless. "Are you sure he didn't say 'candy-striper?'"

"What the hell's that mean, Dave?" Troy's speech slurred while the taste of blood intensified, but he was unwilling to swallow the slurry that accumulated in his mouth.

"That's probably a worse insult to Troy," Carl added.

"Yeah. True," Dave acknowledged, letting a loose chuckle slip from his lips.

"What the hell does it mean?" Troy repeated with frustrated emphasis.

"Candy-striper is an old-timey name for a teenage girl who volunteers as a nurse's aid," Dave revealed. He took a step back, probably worried that Troy's temperament was about to reach a fever pitch.

Troy remained calm for the moment and leered at the stark white metal door that the old man had exited. His temperature rose and the flame to fight reignited in his heart.

"I'll kill the bastard," he tried to shout, but spit and blood gurgled in his mouth and droplets sputtered on his lips. He ignored this and thrust towards the door. After a few short steps, he was stopped by Carl, who grabbed him by the shoulders.

"Calm down, Troy. You don't need to dig your hole no deeper," Carl assured in a calming yet patronizing tone. "Nature has done most of the job for you already, buddy. It wouldn't be fair to rob it of the finale."

Troy paused. The fire of anger coursing through his body subsided a bit and he was finally able to gain control of it, extinguishing it after a few deep breaths. He then locked eyes on a white towel slung over Carl's shoulder.

Troy tugged on the cloth. "This got any bodily fluids on it?"

Carl shook his head, which prompted Troy to jerk it away. He dabbed his lips and expelled the slosh in his mouth into the deep fabric, which stained the bright white cloth with splotches of red and pink. As he did this, Troy continued to glare at the door.

"Stupid nature," he finally muttered with an empty mouth.

Dave smiled and nodded. "There you go," he started to

say more but was interrupted when Troy jerked away and slinked towards the opposite door from where the old man had left, tossing the soiled towel in the middle of the floor.

"I'll be in the break room if anyone wants to laugh at the guy who got owned by geriatric Rocky."

An hour passed and Troy remained in the break room. His thoughts whirled with an assortment of emotions. Like berries in a blender, they swirled and churned as the downward torrent funneled them into the tearing blades of regret, whirring them into a smooth mixture of nothing. Through the numbness, he began to cycle wildly through the five stages of grief, though he had nothing to mourn. Perhaps the future, or perhaps the past that led him to the present were good candidates to lament. Either way, he was rendered nearly catatonic with emotions when the Director of Nursing, Jill, found him and ushered him to the staffing office.

It was a room he had been in before, and for more reasons than just his initial interview. He had a long history of shenanigans at the nursing home. Deeds that he thought could be tucked away in the corners of the sprawling building. But there were cameras everywhere. Every corner of the nursing home that would not be deemed an invasion of privacy was recorded.   Elder abuse became nonexistent as a result, but Troy's misdeeds were easily exposed. He felt now that his days may be as over as his gurney-surfing days had been just months earlier.

Another hour inched by and Troy was still seated in the empty human resource director's office. He had been led to the small room by Jill and abandoned. Left to suffer in the silence of the world once again. It was in the silence that his thoughts most screamed, bellowing aching words that his physical body could not answer. His right leg bounced nervously as a result, and his eyes took turns staring at the floor and darting around the empty room.

It was after normal work hours and that meant the director had already left for the day. For all his run-ins with management, he still managed to get along with her better than most. Being called back to work would likely negate any goodwill the director had previously harbored for Troy.

A large desk separated him from the director's workspace and his eyes eventually landed on the far wall. He gazed blankly until his vision focused on all the notes and restaurant coupons posted on a cork bulletin board on the opposite wall. Dueling flyers for York Café, Seneca Sandwich Company, and The 33 Restaurant – fierce competitors for the community lunch dollar – hung by one another and boasted near-identical specials, though the 33's bore the more professional design of the trio.

Other notes were scrawled and pinned to the board, but in too tiny a script to be read without squinting. Troy attempted anyway, to no avail. Moving on, Troy scanned further and was able to hone in on a crudely drawn letter from one of the director's nephews. He leaned forward out of the chair as he read the waxy, colored letters that simply spelled out "TO ANT ADRI, FROM COLE." The "E" in the name was written backwards and several stick figures of different colors were sketched on the lower half of the paper. Troy leaned in and inspected the kid's handwriting for a moment, like it was a fine art piece hung in a museum.

Troy grimaced and slumped to a hunched position, then plopped backwards into the metal chair, the force pushing the seat on two legs before settling into place. He brushed his fingers through his short, wool-like hair, eyes fixated on a large picture frame on the opposite wall.

It was a round metal frame with six individual photo compartments housed within it. In each of the slots was a different picture of the same woman. She was an older woman with shoulder-length gray hair, sunken eyes, but a youthful face. Only one picture contained another person, and that was of the director. Her arms wrapped around the woman from behind and she smiled as if things could never be better than they were in that snapshot of time.

The office door swung open as Troy spotted one final detail. Wording at the top of the large frame simply read "Mother."

"Hello Troy," a short, slender woman greeted coldly as she walked past him and rounded the corner of her desk to seat herself on the opposite side. Jill had entered with her but remained near the door after it eased to a close.

"Miss Knotts," Troy replied pensively, leg still bobbing.

Miss Knotts scolded. "I don't appreciate coming in here after hours to address a situation so ridiculous." She produced a key, unlocked a desk drawer, and pulled a manila file from an envelope that was labeled with Troy's name. "Why were you fighting with Mr. Harry?"

"He called me a stripper," Troy replied. Whether he misspoke or attempted to lie had not yet been decided in his mind, but he decided to run with it regardless.

"And I don't take my clothes off for no one."

Miss Knotts shot a confused stare that chilled Troy to the core and he panicked, wondering whether he should correct himself or think of a new lie.

"He called me a candyass."

"I don't care if he called you a candy cane, you don't fight with the residents," Miss Knotts snapped back. "There is no instance where this is appropriate."

"For what it's worth, he won," Troy conceded, placing a hand gently to his bruised jaw.

Miss Knotts shook her head in disbelief. She said nothing for a moment, which let the room fall into an uncomfortable silence.

"I'm going to have to let you go," Miss Knotts stated softly before the tone intensified. "This is just too unacceptable. I know you've been through a lot and came a long way since your overdose, but we just can't support these antics."

Troy leapt out of his seat. "This is not fair!"

"It's plenty damn fair, Mr. Mason! We could have gotten the sheriff involved. Be thankful for what you're getting. This isn't surfing a gurney. This is a human in our care that you were fighting with. This is serious stuff! If you really can't understand the fairness in this decision then you need to take some time to soul search about what exactly fairness means. You've acted unprofessionally for too long and this is the last straw. You have endangered a resident and I can't let that slide."

Troy locked eyes with Miss Knotts for a moment. He tried to hold the gaze, but her piercing brown eyes stabbed deep and he broke contact. His eyes gravitated back to the pictures in the frame, back to the one of her embracing "Mother."

"Good luck, Mr. Mason," Miss Knotts finished, motioning for him to leave. Jill pulled the door open and stood aside, waiting to escort the disgruntled man from the building.

"Adriane," Troy replied disrespectfully. He made one final attempt to glare into her eyes, but found reestablishing contact was just as difficult as maintaining it. He broke gaze immediately and started out of the room.

Adriane Knotts sighed as she sat back down. Troy saw this over his shoulder while Jill pushed him onward. She stopped and left him standing in the center of the hallway.

"Don't move."

Troy remained facing away from door, but turned his head so he could view as much as possible in his periphery. He watched the director spin her office chair towards the photo wall and stare longingly at the same pictures Troy had just been scrutinizing.

"How did I do?" Miss Knotts asked Jill without turning from the photo.

Jill answered. "That sounded fair to me."

Miss Knotts cupped her hands and placed them over her face. Troy made out one last phrase as Jill's hand returned to the small of his back.

"Oh Mom," he could barely make out. "That was a tough one."

* * *

An hour after Cabel had called Miranda, the two were enjoying drinks at Robinson's Tavern, the only legitimate bar in Chancy. There were dives, some with beer and wine licenses, and some just operated on a word of mouth basis.

Chancy was the only incorporated town in O'Brien County, but calling it a town was questionable to the city folk who regularly day-tripped to more desirable places in The Mountain State. Chancy had once been a place of pristine beauty. It had a historic district once lined with Victorian style houses that towered over the river valley. Pictures from the early twentieth century painted a portrait of a quaint country town steeped in the essences of Americana.

Like all things touched by time, that portrait had changed to a place that was weathered and eroded. Some of the homes fell into ruin and had been razed, some burnt to the ground in unfortunate fires decades before anyone alive remembers. The rest were reduced to aging timbers that were becoming unstable under coats of chipping white paint.

Those portraits. Those black and white snapshots taken what felt like an epoch ago were all residents and historians had left to remember that pristine town. Some of the structures still remained and served as a reminder to how things used to be. It couldn't be fixed now, save some rich savior buying up the town and restoring it to its former glory. But doing so would give the town away to someone who couldn't appreciate it for its heritage. That was a bridge too far. So it continued to fall into obscurity, and all the inheritors could do was whine and lament how they didn't know that all things ultimately crash into an inevitable wall of change.

"Okay, so tell me about your name," a punch-drunk Miranda Murray prodded mischievously at Cabel.

Cabel smiled sheepishly at her. To his relief, Miranda had not over-dressed for their date. She wore a modest grey dress that had most likely been her outfit worn to her teaching job earlier in the day. "That was the first thing you said to me when I called earlier, but it took twenty minutes for you to get to it now. What gives? Are you less interested?"

"Was desperate to get a drink in me first," Miranda coolly responded. "But really, tell me what kind of name is Cabel? Kah Bell? Cat bell, but without the T?"

"Cat bell without the T does seem like the simplest way to explain it," Cabel reluctantly agreed. "I've tried to explain it other ways, but most people take to saying it wrong. It's pronounced the same as Cabell County, but only West Virginians get it then."

As a Marylander, Miranda ignored the slight. "Is it a family name?" she pressed.

"No. I was meant to be named Caleb, but my mom was dyslexic," he responded with playfulness, swirling a glass of neat bourbon.

Miranda's eye widened for a moment as she attempted to

withhold a giggle, but was unable to do so.

"That's... ridiculous," she choked, spritzing a small amount of drink through her painted lips beforehand.

Cabel quickly gulped down another sip of his drink before he replied, "Ridiculous? You should try introducing yourself with that name."

Miranda laughed politely as she looked away for a moment and brushed long, copper hair from her face. Her glass had been empty for some time now without Cabel realizing it. She took small sips from the glass, getting drips of the melting ice with each pass until he noticed and motioned the barkeeper for another.

"I have an idea," Miranda transitioned after receiving a full glass. "Why don't we say one thing about us that's super awkward and that we normally wouldn't tell anyone else."

Cabel looked to the floor. He quickly scanned his memory for something that he could disclose with minimal embarrassment. "Okay, but you go first," he eventually complied.

Miranda rolled her eyes. "I like to watch people squirm by asking them random, super uncomfortable questions," she admitted. "Religious questions are the most fun."

"What?" Cabel chortled. "So to clarify, your awkward quirk is making people feel awkward? That feels redundant."

"What can I say, I'm an enigma," Miranda replied with a confident shrug. She took one more sip of the fresh drink and sat the glass on the bar. "Now it's your turn."

"My parents named me Cabel," he answered wryly.

"Come on, be serious," Miranda insisted and kicked his leg lightly.

"Okay, okay," Cabel relented. "I... like to shower in the dark."

"What?" Miranda exclaimed. "Do you not like seeing yourself naked?"

Cabel shook his head. "No, no, nothing like that. It's just relaxing. I akin it to being in the womb — warm, wet, naked, and in the dark."

"And weird," Miranda added. "I guess you won that round." She caught an eye on something on the television across the bar and turned to watch, mesmerized by a Virginia Lottery commercial that was playing.

Cabel took notice of her distraction and it took little effort in finding the reasoning. "We're a border county, so most of our TV stations come from Virginia. They're sadly more relevant than the few we get out of central West Virginia."

"I wondered," Miranda confirmed. "I never bothered to get cable here since there's only about 50 channels offered."

"Please," Cabel scoffed. "Growing up in Tipperton, we only had thirteen, and two or three of those were PBS channels."

Miranda giggled and leaned over Cabel briefly. "Maybe you weren't meant to be named Caleb," she said softly. "Maybe your parents enjoyed their thirteen channels so much that they meant to name you Cable."

Cabel put his hands on her shoulders and helped her upright, both laughing as he did so.

"Seems like you've had enough," he commented before Miranda shifted in her chair to lean over the polished bar.

Cabel turned towards the bar as well and took a long sip of booze. He gazed behind the bar at the mirrored wall that was mostly obscured by neon signs for various brands of beer and liquor. He took in the atmosphere of the room and tried to eavesdrop on several conversations happening around him, but was unable to hone in on any particular exchange. Though smoking had been banned in the bar some years ago, the latent fragrance of spent cigarettes could still be detected in ghostly whiffs.

"So you live in Chancy, but work in Huntsville?" Miranda asked after a few beats. She had gotten control of herself and the levity had dissipated enough to ask a more serious question. "That's a bit of a drive, isn't it?"

"Yep. Two counties over," Cabel mumbled, his tone turning serious as well.

"Why there and not here?" she inquired. "What does that newspaper have that the local one doesn't?"

Cabel didn't answer right away. He remained facing towards the bar and slowly set his glass down. Miranda, even in her half-inebriated state, caught on quickly that this was a sensitive topic and cautiously leaned in to gauge his reaction.

"Respect," he finally mustered.

"You've worked there before?" Miranda asked instinctively, sitting back in her stool.

Cabel pursed his lips but found the strength to force a polite smile. "Three years ago. I had worked there since I was in high school and really thought I was going to go places with a career there."

"What happened? If you don't mind me asking," Miranda inquired more guardedly.

Cabel turned back to the bar for his drink. "Creative differences."

"What creative differences?"

"I was creative, they were not," Cabel replied with a facetious smirk.

Miranda smiled back and playfully tapped his shoulder. "Oh, you," she squealed with vested bemusement.

"I hope to come back to it someday," Cabel remarked without prompting. "Perhaps when the family sells it or puts someone else in charge who has the taste for a guy like me. But for now, I'll remain in exile."

Miranda stared into his eyes again and her existing smile widened a little more. "It's good to have ambitions, especially while we're still in our twenties."

Cabel smiled back and winked. "Indeed."

JOB

Another hour passed before Miranda decided to retire for the night. They shared a hug that was awkward enough to indicate more than going through the motions.

"So what is this now, a third date?" Cabel questioned with a facetious glean after separating.

Miranda leaned back and feigned disbelief. She placed a dramatic hand to her chest. "You aren't keeping count? How would I expect you to remember a potential anniversary down the road?"

Cabel placed a hand in his pocket and cocked his head

confidently in the middle of the bar. "Oh, if there's an anniversary down the road, I'll be sure to remember it."

He let the moment linger a beat more. "And this is our third date. I knew, I just wanted to see if you did."

Miranda rubbed her hands together and joked. "Are there presents to celebrate a third date?"

Cabel saw an opportunity and leaned in close to her face. "I think you've celebrated my presence just fine." He then gave her a peck on the cheek and strutted backwards to his bar stool.

Miranda gave him a cockeyed look. Whether it was for the kiss or the bad joke, he didn't know, but she blew him a kiss from the center of the room before moving to the exit.

Cabel remained at the bar for a final drink to celebrate a pretty good night. As the bartender delivered the last glass, his eyes surveyed the room once more. It was the usual Friday night crowd. The young blue collars were in the corner booths, bragging about past conquests and conquests still to come. They were not ones to plant their feet under a table for very long. Phone calls and friends took them through the exits often, and in higher frequency depending upon tobacco preferences.

There were also the old pros who were at the bar every Friday, sitting at the same stool. They were the ones who acted almost mechanical, entering and leaving the building in exactly the same pattern from week to week. One could even predict exactly how many drinks they'd consume before calling it a night.

Cabel could not call himself a regular, but he'd been there enough to see the social clockwork tick away, beating in time with the loud country music playing on the modernized jukebox. LED-emblazoned words flashed along the music box's outer casing, long eschewing the days of the pale neon glow.

Cabel felt pride in his small town, but disappointed that sucking down cheap alcohol and paying property tax was all he had to contribute to the community. He had thought about leaving, but the warmth of love on the top layer of this small community made him feel too at home to ever seek another.

One thing that did not feel at home to him was his actual hometown of Tipperton, in the northern part of the county. In childhood, Cabel had been relentlessly bullied and beaten by other kids on the playground. By the end of his elementary days, he'd stopped speaking to anyone, distrustful of his peers at a tender age. But it was prodding and encouragement from an English teacher his freshman year that had set him on a path to social resurrection.

He had mostly put those days at Tipperton Elementary School out of his mind, but his subconscious held on to the resentment like a loaded weapon in search of a trigger. That hidden resentment manifested itself as distrust in humanity and made him an ideal reporter. He could always see through a dishonest source, but it was those same misgivings that made interviewing the least favorite part of his career.

Cabel's deep thoughts were interrupted by the clank of bottles from across the room and he glanced over to locate the source of the noise. He noticed someone sitting at the nearest booth to the jukebox who had just knocked over a couple empty bottles on the table. He adjusted his eyes and realized it was someone who he had not seen in some time. And in just a blink, a friend from his deep past, seated last in his thoughts, suddenly returned to the forefront.

Troy Mason sat alone at the booth closest to the music. His head was slumped, eyes locked on a tinted bottle that he was twisting with both hands. He made no attempt to recover the fallen bottles and watched them slowly spin in small circles on the edge of the table.

Curious, Cabel stood to walk over to him, but immediately realized he had too much to drink when a lightheaded feeling came over him. He paused and squared up the ability to walk in a straight line before proceeding.

"Troy? How have you been?" Cabel greeted when he reached the booth.

Troy raised his head with a bobble and furrowed his brow as he squinted. Cabel could tell right away that Troy was much worse off than he.

"Cabel?" Troy finally responded with some uncertainty. "I didn't realize that was you over there."

"Yeah, it's me," Cabel replied happily as he sat down across from Troy. "I just finished up a date with this school teacher."

"A date!" Troy exclaimed, taken aback by the news. "What happened to Terri?"

"Terri?" Cabel answered with surprise, having not heard that name in a while. "We haven't been together in almost a decade."

Troy pushed his bottle to the side and stared at Cabel, still trying to straighten out his vision with a few hard blinks.

"But you loved that girl!" Troy finally exclaimed with a dramatic flair.

"In high school," Cabel shot back sternly before fading into sullenness. "College wasn't good to us, though. She's working in Texas now at some research laboratory. Particle physics or some shit like that."

Troy nodded his head. "Well, I hope she has an accident and turns into some type of super villain."

Cabel nodded back. "Harsh, but I won't disagree."

Troy nodded solemnly and shook one of his bottles to detect if it still contained booze. Cabel watched and decided to continue with the pleasantries.

"What about you? Any luck with the ladies?"

Troy pursed his lips as if he were uncomfortable with the questions. "A couple. I had one long-term relationship that went sideways because of the drugs. After that, she took off and hasn't spoken a word to me since. I went away for a while, too, though. Reckon I should've looked to reconcile in the meantime."

"Ah gee, I'm sorry to hear that," Cabel attempted to console. "Sounds like it has been a rough time for you."

"You don't know the half of it," Troy remarked and returned to his beer. There was a lull and Cabel looked around the bar, noticing that the regular folks were shuffling out for the night. Pulling out his phone, he checked the time to make sure the place wasn't about to close.

"I lost my job today," Troy finally admitted after polishing off the bottle. He sat the dark bottle down but picked it up again a moment later. He repeated the motion a few more times and Cabel absently observed the rings of condensation made on the table's surface with each pass.

Troy finally continued, "I should be angry, but it was a shit job anyways."

"Where did you work?" Cabel asked, realizing he had no clue.

"CNA at the old folks home," Troy answered.

Cabel raised an eyebrow. "Wow. Literally a shit job then."

Troy sighed. He had said he wasn't angry, but it was clear to Cabel that the undisclosed amount of alcohol consumed couldn't drown out the consternation Troy was feeling towards his sudden loss of employment.

"It's hard to find a job in this town when you've been known to have drug problems," Troy lamented. "The overdose I had a few years back really did a number on my cred in this place. I've jumped from job to job in this town and I'm damn near out of options."

Cabel nodded. "You could have just said 'it's hard to find a job in this town' and left it at that. I can't get one either. The important thing is that you're alive. That's something."

"Don't you work at the newspaper?" Troy asked, seeming to know a touch more about Cabel's life than he did Troy's.

"I haven't been there for three years," Cabel admitted, speaking more candid about it than he had earlier in the night. "We had a pretty public falling out. You know, it was embarrassing and I have regrets. There for a while, I was working night shift at the gas station because I didn't want to have to interact with people who knew my situation and were quick to judge."

"What did you do to get canned?" Troy inquired, his speech sounding a little more sober.

Cabel paused like he had with Miranda, but gave a different answer. "Insubordination."

He broke again and felt an instant déjà vu before a sigh prompted him to continue.

"I wrote a story that the publisher didn't want running. It was an investigative piece that I didn't have all the facts confirmed for, and they could have been sued for if it turned out not to be accurate. The publisher wasn't in the office the day the paper went to press, so I snuck the story in there. He didn't realize it until he saw it in print."

Troy questioned, "They get sued?"

Cabel shrugged. "Nah. I don't think so. It was a pretty solid tip. But I didn't get to stick around long enough to find out. I wrote a letter afterwards telling him about how incompetent the paper was under his leadership, and how senile he had become. I mean the dude was like eighty."

"Don't get me started on old bastards," Troy grumbled angrily while poking at his jaw.

Cabel continued, "I mean, don't get me wrong. What I wrote in that letter was heartfelt and was meant to inspire a dialogue that could have led to some constructive changes. Like people of that era though, he'd rather just kill the problem than make any meaningful attempt to fix things for the better."

Troy nodded and attempted to understand what Cabel was saying, but only twisted his lip slightly in response.

"Anyways, I'm working at the Huntsville Herald two counties over," Cabel finished. He sighed in conclusion just the same as when he'd started and leaned back in the booth.

"Two counties over!" Troy exclaimed a little louder. "That's a damn shame. I know I ain't gonna be working two counties over. Don't think my old truck would make it there and back for too long."

"You sound like you have a plan," Cabel stated. "I'd like to hear it since we've established each other's job predicament. Maybe I'll take a cue from you."

Troy stared off in the middle distance for a moment, as if a plan he had been formulating was suddenly coming together. He shakily looked back to Cabel.

"I do have a job I want to check about tomorrow. Would you mind coming with me? This fella is back up the holler a ways and I could use a spotter in case I get lost. Those backroads can be unforgiving."

"On a Saturday? What kind of job is it?" Cabel wondered.

"An odd job," Troy answered without a passing beat. He started to get out of the booth but stumbled a bit. Cabel jumped up to help balance him, but lost his balance as well and the two slammed into one another.

"I suppose I can do that," Cabel replied after the two got steady on their feet. "Let me get you out of the building for now."

"Goodnight!" The bartender yelled as the two hobbled to the tinted doors. Both Cabel and Troy flung a hand in farewell as they exited.

The two stumbled into the parking lot, but both realized that they didn't know what the other's vehicle looked like.

"You're probably in no shape to drive," Cabel told Troy as they staggered along.

Troy laughed. "I could say the same for you."

"I'm only a mile from here," Cabel answered defensively. "I got a house up on the knob."

"Well la-de-da," Troy mocked. "Look at you being all high and mighty. I live down at Dusty Hollow. You know, the trailer park by the creek?" Cabel nodded and Troy quipped, "If poverty doesn't cause me to lose my home, the next bout of high water ought to do it."

Despite the duo's state of inebriation, the concern of drunk driving never came up again. The two remained silent until they arrived at Cabel's vehicle – a newer model sports utility vehicle that Troy awed audibly at even though no actual words were mentioned about it.

"It's weird that we're both living in Chancy, but haven't really seen each other until now," Troy noted with a slurred inflection.

"I don't do much in the community anymore," Cabel clarified with an air of defeat. "I work two counties over, so I figure I may as well shop and do my socializing two counties over. There isn't much I do outside my home these days. If Chancy really needs me, I figure it'll send for me."

Troy made a garbled sound that was in between a groan and a chuckle. "Hope you're not expectin' to hear anytime soon. Chancy don't call too often."

"I'm aware," Cabel admitted. "But if it calls, I'll be ready."

Despite the gracelessness of their interactions, Cabel was pleased to have spoken with his friend again. The two had first met when they were four-years-old at a church Halloween party. From there, they were best friends through much of elementary school, but less so as they climbed in years. During adolescence, the two developed differing outlooks on life and gravitated to other cliques, speaking little through middle school, high school, and beyond graduation.

"Did you kill that dog?" Cabel asked suddenly.

Troy appeared confused. "What dog?"

Cabel sighed. "You know the one. I never told anyone about it, but you also never told me for sure if you ever went through with it."

Troy grinned as the recollection seemed to appear in his mind. "Oh yeah. I don't want to talk about that. Got anything else – anything more positive? I reckon I could use some good stories."

"Laser tag in the woods?" Cabel suggested as a question to see if it sparked a memory.

Troy perked. "The pew-pew game? I beat you in that every time. I never told you how I did that either."

Cabel placed a hand to his hip. "How did you always beat me?"

Troy shook his head. "Again, I ain't telling you. I did tell our teacher at the time, though. I forget her name. Miss Olly?"

"Miss Olin?" Cabel also guessed.

Troy wagged a finger. "Yeah, that sounds right. That secret stays with me and her, if she's still alive."

"I doubt she would be," Cabel guessed. "Her hair was bright white more than twenty years ago."

Troy shrugged. "Guess I get to take that secret to my grave then. I'll even write it on a piece of paper and stick it in my coffin just to rub it in your face."

Cabel sighed and shrugged off the comment to go in search for the next pleasant memory that stood most vivid in his mind.

"You remember when we broke into that old opera house?"

"Oh gee, what were we, like eight or nine?" Troy replied, seeming to remember the time quickly.

"Something like that. I remember you scared the crap out of me because you told me the place was haunted," Cabel reminisced. "And when I wasn't looking, you threw one of the drum cymbals out into the auditorium."

Troy laughed sincerely. "You hit the ceiling with how high you jumped."

"I got the hell out of there, that was for sure," Cabel concurred while he struggled to unlock his SUV door.

Finally conquering the lock, Cabel sat down in his driver's seat, leaving Troy to slump over the truck parked in the next stall. The two nodded almost simultaneously.

"What time tomorrow?" Cabel asked, implying he had decided to go.

Troy looked up to the dark sky. "Let's say 'round noon."

"Meet you back here?"

Troy nodded.

Cabel smiled. "It was good to see you again."

"You too. I reckon I'll see you again soon."

"Yep," Cabel replied, pulling his door closed.

Cabel lived on one of the hilltop communities that blanketed the surrounding hills of Chancy. This was where most folks resided in the area, with the immediate miles around the town containing more residents than inside the town limits. It was a short drive from the small-town lights to the dark countryside, and in less than five minutes he was back in his driveway. He sat for a moment, too tired and too out of sorts to attempt immediate movement. He decided to take a respite there and reclined his driver's seat, a sigh turning to a groan as he leaned back with it.

His thoughts were at first of only Miranda, if not for a moment, before flickering back to Troy. Cabel quickly merged the two encounters into a narrative and found it interesting that the first person he'd formed a social bond with reentered his life the same night he'd felt an even stronger bond developing with someone else.

Cabel formed a smile that no one else would see and glanced at his neighbor, Jimmy's house. He was sitting on a folding chair on his porch, having a drink like he did most Friday nights when the temperature wasn't below freezing.

Cabel liked to razz him about various social and political issues, just to raise his blood pressure. But there was a strange feeling of tranquility in Cabel's heart at the moment that informed him, at least for the night, that everyone would have peace.

3

DEATHTRAP

Troy's truck rattled loudly as it lumbered up Cucumber Hollow Road, a poorly maintained mountain path a dozen miles north of Chancy. Once paved, the forest thoroughfare had thoroughly eroded away and was now a mishmash of washed-out gravel and crumbling asphalt.

Troy's rig was an early 1980s Ford Custom pickup that looked as old as the path it beat, but shook like it was slightly less held together. Cabel clamped down on any handle he could find and struggled to cover his nervousness as the antique vehicle chugged along.

"They say that the settlers named this area Cucumber

Hollow because of the large number of copperheads found in this area about that time," Troy casually dispensed while he swung the oversized steering wheel from side to side, whichever way the hairpin turns dictated.

"Copperheads smell like cucumbers, you see," he added after a beat of awkward silence. "If you're up in the woods and smell cucumber, you best be cautious."

Cabel, disaffected, feigned a smile. "I've had the good fortune not to meet one face to face."

Troy nodded. "Wouldn't be a big deal if you did. Copperheads are poisonous, but there's never been a recorded instance of someone dying from one in West Virginia."

"But copperheads can kill you," Cabel countered.

"They can. I reckon." Troy agreed thoughtfully. "I reckon us mountaineers are just better about handling our poison."

At the end of Cucumber Hollow the road forked. The southernmost path led into Virginia, to a small town called Whitman. Troy instead chose the left prong, which took them deeper into the O'Brien County woods, eventually landing on Turkish Knob Road, a narrower road that was still paved despite its lonely position in the backcountry.

Troy finally took notice of Cabel's growing discomfort and slapped the dashboard near him.

"Relax, we're almost there," Troy assured. He then leaned over and haphazardly patted Cabel's shoulder, never hitting the same spot twice as he jostled to and fro with the truck's motion.

Cabel pursed his lips as he shook his head. "It's just that this thing you're driving is a deathtrap."

Troy raised a brow in surprise. "Deathtrap?! I love these old Customs. They break and you can fix them with some baling wire and a few turns of the screwdriver. You buy this new computerized garbage and you can't fix it without a PhD in Internet or whatever. You have to take it to a specialist the second something goes wacky and they charge you bookoos of bucks just to smack a few buttons. Such a racket!"

"I don't dispute your point," Cabel admitted. "But there's some degree of safety in the new ones – some piece of mind. For example, you generally don't get the smell of gasoline in the cab while you're driving them."

"Oh that," Troy shrugged. "That's one I'm still working on."

"What?" Cabel asked with a nervous squeak. "What are you still working on?"

"The gas system is leaking somewhere," Troy revealed nonchalantly. "Probably the fuel line. I haven't quite gotten around to figuring it out."

"Or even looking at it," he added after a pause.

Cabel was dumbfounded and at a momentary loss for words.

"What happens if we run out of gas?" he asked finally, avoiding the obvious question of whether the truck would catch fire.

"I gotta couple of milk jugs of gasoline in the bed," Troy answered as calm as ever.

"What the hell?!" Cabel exclaimed loudly with suspended politeness. "Do you have any idea how dangerous that is?"

Troy gave Cabel a side-eyed look. "I don't expect it's any more dangerous than running out of gas in this area. Buncha cutthroats live back in these here woods."

"And that's the other thing," Cabel continued and tamped down the urge to gesture his arms in frustration. "You still haven't told me what this job is yet. You drug me all this way in your deathtrap of a pickup under what I'm beginning to feel are false pretenses. There can't be a job this far back worth doing."

"I swear to you it's a job," Troy defended with some underlying irritation in his voice.

Cabel barked back. "It better be a damn good job because it's starting to take a dump on my day." He then crossed his arms and slumped in the bench seat before staring out into the endless crowd of passing trees.

The autumn sun at midday still hung at a low angle and sent slivers of light through the trees, settling in long lines across the roadway. The truck passed over the lines that flickered light to dark, feeling like a filmstrip that animated nothing – nothing but a dusty path that led Cabel towards the question mark of the day.

The two said no more as they concluded their trek through the hollow. Part way up one of the many hills they came across

an old white campaign sign stuck in the bank along the road –
the wording was long gone, bleached white from years of
sunlight and mountain weather. The sign was apparently their
cue to stop. Troy immediately slowed and began to look for a
pull-off area further uphill.

Stopping the truck, Cabel observed a path-like drive almost
hidden by the fresh foliage. It dipped steeply down the hillside,
which forced Troy to almost stand up in the cabin to see the
bottom of the grade. The pathway dropped far enough below
the bank that vehicles parked there were invisible from the
road. At the bottom of the parking location was a small, flat area
just large enough for a vehicle to turn around. The thick trees
masked the steep grade of the hillside, which made the parking
area the perfect hiding place from the road. Gingerly, Troy
guided the old truck down to the bottom where he parked and
shut the engine off.

"There's nothing here," a perplexed Cabel noted.

The Ford's sputter dissipated, which was followed by the
hinges to Troy's door groaning as he pushed the rusty door
open, leaving his keys in the ignition. He stepped onto the leaf-
carpeted ground and took a long stretch, lifting his arms
overhead as he bent backwards to get his back to crack, which it
did with a muted pop.

"They told me to park here," he explained and looked to
Cabel, who had already exited and circled the truck. He then
turned back to the road, now high above them, and pointed to a
place even higher above the road. "I need to go up the hill a
ways."

Cabel glared sternly at his old friend. "Dammit dude, that's
a heck of a climb," he expressed with soft frustration. He shook
his head a few times before finally complying. "Okay, okay. I'm
only still doing this because I'm curious."

"Oh no, you need to stay here," Troy insisted and
motioned for Cabel to get back in the pickup. "When you're
seeing someone about this kind a job, you don't bring a friend
with you."

Cabel thought for a second and finally bobbed his head in
agreement. "I'm not sure I want to know what kind a job this is.
But what's the purpose of me coming with you?"

"I'll tell you about it when I get back," Troy responded. He turned to the hillside, but broke his stride almost immediately before he pivoted back to Cabel.

"Oh, also, if I'm not back in a half hour, something went wrong and you should take the truck back to town," Troy suggested as he walked to Cabel. Cabel watched as Troy passed him and returned to his truck. He creaked open the rusty door and pulled a lever on the side of the seat, causing the entire bench to swing forward and downward.

Cabel continued to watch and tried to process what Troy's last remark meant. He observed Troy pull a thick window envelope from behind the seat and tuck it in his flannel pocket. Cabel noticed the paper in the window of the envelope was tinted a faded green – like money.

Troy flipped the seat back into position and slammed the door. He then turned to Cabel and paused for a moment before giving him a grim smile.

"I'll try not to be long," he declared facetiously. "Oh, and when you get back to town, you better tell Sheriff Diggle where to look for me."

Cabel's jaw was unhinged as Troy departed quickly.

* * *

Troy huffed uphill back to the main road. The leaves crunched under his boots as he labored upward, thankful he had skipped his morning cigarette, but also lamenting that he ever picked up the habit. Once he reached pavement, Troy relocated the old sign and walked down the road to meet it.

Orienting himself, he peered up the steep hillside and eventually located a structure near the top. Hopping across the drainage ditch along the road, he started begrudgingly up the steeper slope. Thick brush and briar patches blanketed the hillside and erased the path briefly in spots, but there were enough offshoots where worn places gave way to past travelers. Places where the sod was worn to exposed root gave Troy an idea of where to advance upward.

Further along the path, the trees and brown brush gave way enough to show Troy a better glimpse of the structure he was approaching: a small hunting cabin. It was decidedly derelict on the exterior with weathered gray wood wrapping around a slanted frame. The roof tiles were not visible because of the amount of moss, fallen leaves, and miscellaneous vegetation that blanketed them. It was so unkempt that a nursery of saplings was beginning to sprout from the drooping gutters.

Troy stopped for a moment to wipe the sweat off his brow. Despite the cool autumn air, he grew heated in his actions and unbuttoned the flannel outerwear that was required when he left the trailer that morning.

He was just a few feet away now. A small porch reached out from the doorway and appeared to be a newer construction than the rest of the building. It rose a foot from the forest floor and felt sturdy as he stepped onto the surface.

His boots thudding on the floor must have alerted those inside because the door opened unexpectedly. Troy was taken aback by the action until he noticed someone holding it open from the other side. He cooled his demeanor and strutted inside casually.

The bearded man holding the door was tall with a slender build. He wore a long black coat over what appeared to be a finely tailored suit. A black tie completed the dark look and matched everything he wore, including his black hair, cropped short on both his head and face.

Deeper in, Troy caught a full view of the place. The cabin interior was surprising in its upkeep compared to its outward, decrepit appearance. It was a single room with a rustic, open-plan layout. To the right side was a kitchen, complete with stove and refrigerator. There were a few boxes of cereal on the counter and a pot of coffee brewing near the sink, but looked otherwise untouched.

The left side of the room was a different story in terms of cleanliness. A long dresser sat along the wall with the drawer bursting with clothes. The top seemed to once have a vanity mirror, but it was completely missing, leaving only the cardboard backing. The surface was covered with bottles and boxes of various medicines and toiletries. Next to that was a roll-top desk, which had stacks of papers and newspaper clippings lying in disheveled piles so tall that it was hard to make out the style of desk at first glance.

A bathroom stall was tucked away in the back corner with both a toilet and a shower installed within the walls. Dirty clothes and towels littered the area in jumbled piles.

To the center was a large bed, and this was where Troy caught sight of two more men. To the left was a man dressed similarly to the one holding the door. He was of similar height to the other man, but had a more rotund waistline and scruffier, angular face. He was not as neatly groomed as the other and had a light beard with longer, brown hair.

"Welcome," greeted the third person. An older man, he sat on the foot of the bed, wrapped in a gray, shag blanket. It was hard to tell from thickness of the blanket, but he appeared to be a stocky man. A thick, white beard covered his face with equally long hair on his head, making very little of his appearance recognizable. When he spoke, it was in a gravely, labored voice and Troy noticed that his lower jaw pivoted off center anytime it moved.

"Wasn't expecting you this early," the old man barked. "It's laundry day and I'm working to get my unmentionables loaded up for the wash."

"I understood it that you were to receive word that I was coming," Troy defended. "Janice was supposed to make a call last evening."

"Yeah, I got the call," the old man ceded. "Was asleep at the time so I didn't appreciate it, but I'm not one to turn away business. Still, I don't let just anyone see my dirty laundry."

The old man pressed along with the business. "You come alone?"

Troy hesitated before stating, "Yup."

"Good. Don't need unknowns traipsing up here," the old man grunted before being joined by the dark-haired man, who closed the door and stood to the right of the bed.

Troy just nodded, still trying to adjust to the idea that this old man was the one he was here to see. They stared at each other for a moment, the grizzly old coot appearing to size him up. Troy returned the glance, but quickly became distracted as he caught sight of the fact the man was lacking feet at the end of his legs. His face must have had a reaction because the man was quick to notice.

"Diabetes!" the man snarled. "Was betrayed by the only sweet thing in my life. Moral of the story: don't trust anything sweet. Food, women, opportunities... they'll all reduce you to nothing in the end."

The old man shuffled in place and shifted topics once again.

"Who's your daddy?"

"Mitch Mason, sir," Troy swiftly replied and straightened his posture as he did so.

"Mason," the old man parroted as he leaned back slightly and crossed his arms. "There are a few Mason's down Tipperton way, but I never knew any of them. Most of them came here after the Civil War."

"My dad ain't that old," Troy remarked, half joking.

The aged man let out a gravely chuckle and leaned forward again. "Genealogy, my boy! I've read every book on the subject that this county has ever published. I can tell you, from memory, every family name that took up land in this area before George Washington knew how to wipe his own butt."

"Never was much into history," Troy dismissed. "Nothing but dead people."

The old man tittered and slumped. "I tell you this only to demonstrate that I've deduced that you are Troy Mason of 212 Dolly Drive in Chancy. Your parents live at 1832 Edmund Road in Tipperton. The power of genealogy has helped me figure out who you are, which led me to where you live."

"Just my dad lives there," Troy corrected. "Mom moved back to Pennsylvania to take care of my aging grandparents. They had been divorced for decades anyways."

The old man snorted. "It's not an exact science, but I've found with locals that I'm given the information I don't have freely. You just proved that."

Troy grew bored of the exercise and became increasingly pensive about getting down to business.

"Can you tell me who you are?" he asked in order to end the topic

The old man's bloomed smile receded and he began to chew his lip as he decided whether to answer.

"I don't do real names. Can you accept that?" he quizzed.

"I don't care," Troy admitted.

The old man nodded. "In this world, they call me El Oscuro."

"El Oscuro?" Troy repeated. "Is that Spanish?"

"Spanish for The Recluse," Oscuro responded threateningly and flicked his tongue dramatically when he hit the right syllables for it.

"The Recluse? I guess you're in the right place for being a recluse, that's for sure," Troy noted and tried to finally steer the conversation to its nexus. "Can we get down to business?"

There was a long pause before Oscuro questioned quietly, "Gettin' tired of me?"

As Troy decided how to answer, Oscuro honored his request, glaring at Troy while he spoke. "Let me introduce you to my associates."

He pointed to the man on his left and then to the one on the right.

"This is Len VanHoven, and this is Frank Bombardi. They are my fixers of this terribly broken world."

Troy nodded at them before looking back at Oscuro expectedly, who questioned, "Who is the mark?"

"Her name is Mary Knotts. She's the mother of the retirement home HR manager, Adriane," Troy stated.

"Knotts," Oscuro restated and seemed to scan his internal bank of local names for the historic details. He finally came back with, "Whelp, there's not too many of them left around here."

"Tell me about it," Troy remarked sarcastically.

"Any particular way you want it done?" Oscuro further questioned.

Troy thought for a second. "Don't care really. I mean I don't want it to look like an accident. I want it to be clear that her life was cut short."

"Do you have a time frame?" Frank interjected.

"Not really," Troy replied coldly. "Just do it when you can."

"We'll do it for $10,000 with 10% down today," Oscuro stated. "The rest of the payment is due the day we confirm to you that the mark is deceased."

Troy reached into his flannel pocket and pulled out the envelope he had retrieved from behind his truck seat. He carefully opened it and removed a wad of $100 bills as the entire room looked on. He licked his finger before counting ten bills off the roll. When he finished, Len stepped forward to immediately take the cash from Troy. Once he had the money, Len stepped back in line with the other shady men and counted the money a second time to confirm it was correct.

"Consider it done," Len confirmed, before he handed the money to Oscuro.

Oscuro tucked the bills into a shirt pocket. "Thank you, sir. We will be in contact with you when our part is completed." He then motioned for Frank to get the door.

* * *

Cabel had grown restless waiting and exited the pickup. He couldn't quite piece together what Troy was up to, but he knew from their personal history and current settings that it couldn't be good. He knew that no one goes job hunting in an area that should only be reserved for actual hunting.

Lost in his thoughts, Cabel paced about the area, eventually finding himself back at the main road. The wind blew through the trees and contained the crispness of impending cold weather ready to take its turn on the calendar. There were still warm days ahead, but fewer and scattered across the forecast.

Shoving his hands in his jacket pockets and hunching slightly against the cool wind, Cabel relocated the bleached white yard sign and meandered down to it, curious of what it had once displayed. He immediately recognized it as a political sign. The word "VOTE" was extremely faded in the top left corner of the sign, but the who and what office was unreadable. He could barely identify a giant R on the left side of the sign, but the rest had been flushed out by years of unrelenting ultraviolet.

A rustle of leaves crackled from above and Cabel peered uphill to see Troy returning. As he descended, Cabel caught sight of the weathered cabin within the mess of trees and began to notice other interesting items within the brush. Small devices were attached to a number of trees along the way. Cabel recognized one near the base of the hillside as a trail camera. He had priced them in the past at his father's request and recognized this as a fancier model capable of producing live feeds – if the signal was good enough. The other, smaller devices were a mystery, but Cabel made the guess that they were some type of motion sensors.

When Troy reached the opposite side of the ditch, Cabel pointed at the cabin near the crest of the hillside.

"Speaking of deathtraps."

Troy looked confused. "What?"

"That cabin looks like the building version of your truck. It's an accident waiting to happen. Sneezing could bring that thing down."

Troy turned and took a long gaze at where he had just been.

"You want to go to the uphill deathtrap or the downhill deathtrap?" he questioned, pointing to the cabin then to his truck.

"Neither," Cabel replied bluntly.

"Well I'm choosing the deathtrap downhill," Troy decided. "That cabin was actually kinda nice on the inside."

"Was it?!" Cabel asked, glaring once more into the forest.

"You'd be surprised by the things you might find hidden in the dark corners of nowhere," he finally replied.

"Did you get the job?" Cabel changed subjects, with the intent of ferreting out the actual purpose of his visit.

"I gotta wait to hear," Troy replied vaguely.

Cabel sighed because he knew he needed to dig deeper. "Great. What kind of job is it?"

"I told you, it's an odd job," Troy reiterated.

Cabel shook his head in confusion. "Sure, but an odd job is usually spoken in the plural as odd jobs. You can't have just one odd job because then you would know specifically what that job is."

Troy appeared to be shuffling thoughts around his head and Cabel stared, trying his best to understand what was so hard to admit.

"It's clean-up work," Troy finally relinquished. "And the money is under the table, so I didn't really want you to know that, being a journalist and all."

Cabel furrowed a brow. "Money under the table is not that unusual. Besides, we're two counties over from where I do my reporting, so this is all off the record anyway."

Cabel paused for a second, wondering why he felt that he should dig deeper. It was often an internal sign that his investigative instincts had been triggered, but he decided to tamp down on those in this instance.

He finally added, "Besides, why would I do that to you? You're my oldest friend."

A moment passed without either speaking until Troy chuckled under his breath.

"Do you remember the time we got into the fist fight?" he recalled. "We were at some Halloween event at the grade school and you were so scared going through the haunted house in the school basement."

Cabel shuffled his feet around in the dirt and leaves. "You're remembering it wrong," he retorted. "You were the one who was scared, but you pinned it on me so that the other people in our group wouldn't rag on you about it."

"Exactly, and that's when we got into the fight," Troy added.

Troy had given Cabel a new irritation. What he was forgetting was that this was the divisive moment that severed their youthful friendship at Tipperton Elementary. Beyond that point, they spoke little as middle school gave way to high school, and then the oblivion of adulthood.

In the silence, Troy looked to Cabel to see him fuming again and quickly scrambled to find out the reason why.

"What's your problem?"

"That was a pretty terrible moment in our history," Cabel admitted. "Why did you bring that up?"

"Because you won," Troy answered simply. "You're a fighter, but you don't let that be known until you're boxed into a corner. Helluva left hook, as I recall."

Cabel thought more on it for a moment and ultimately cracked a smile. "Yeah, I guess I did win."

4

LEMON

The pair returned to town and decided to have a late lunch at The 33 Restaurant, named so for the route number of the U.S. highway that ran through the town. The food establishment often saw a crowd on the weekends, especially in the prime of leaf peeper season when tourists would daytrip to gawk at the colorful hues of the countryside.

It was now late in the afternoon and that crowd had all but disappeared. The few souls that remained occupied the wide booths along the wall and were mostly there for an early dinner. Most of them were elderly gentlemen beyond the prime of their lives with no better way to pass the time.

The latter fact visibly disturbed Troy, who seemed to react by making a point to take the booth furthest away from the old diners. He stiffened his posture and focused on a booth in the back corner while he marched beyond the patrons, almost goose-stepping as he went.

"Hate these old folks," Troy uttered while shuffling into the booth. "They come into places like this to drink their coffee, then never leave. They may as well rename this the senior center and be done with it."

"I can't imagine why you weren't retirement home employee material," Cabel sarcastically responded as he slid in across from Troy.

The waitress promptly arrived and handed them their menus – an oversized laminated sheet with food items listed in large print. Both men feigned smiles and nodded after they accepted the listing, each giving their drink orders, water.

"Seriously, what did you do to get fired?" Cabel pressed once the waitress left. "Based on your earlier reaction, it has to be something worse than bed surfing."

Troy turned his head away in displeasure. It was clear he considered giving an honest answer, but began to shake his head before any words could precede it.

"Come on," Cabel continued to pry. "I told you what happened to me at The O'Brien Times and I've never been honest about that to anyone."

By the time the waitress returned with the drinks, Troy still hadn't given an answer. Cabel thanked the woman, but Troy continued to gaze at the table in consideration. A straw landed in Troy's line of sight and he immediately retrieved it, tearing off one end of the paper wrapping. He carefully removed the straw from the sheathing without further damage to the paper. Almost subconsciously, he began to fidget with what remained – wrapping it around his finger, unwrapping it. The process repeated incessantly. The straw was never placed into the glass.

"I got punched by an old man," Troy finally mumbled, almost unintelligible.

"You punched an old man?" Cabel repeated, unsure if that's what Troy had said.

"No!" Troy corrected. "I was punched by an old guy. I didn't even land a blow."

Cabel was confused and took a slow sip of his water before removing a lemon wedge placed on the side of the glass. "Were you fighting with this guy? It sounds more like you were assaulted."

Troy sighed. "No. We were fighting. Old jerk was calling me names, so I challenged him to fisting cuffs."

"Fisticuffs?" Cabel corrected, a word he was surprised to hear in casual conversation.

"Yeah, fisting cuffs. Ass whooping didn't sound too refined in the moment," Troy clarified, though his quirk of mispronouncing words shined. "Anyways, he did whoop my ass, and I lost my job and the fight."

"Well yeah, you're lucky they didn't get the law involved," Cabel noted. "I think that's general protocol for that situation. I think your boss was actually going soft on you."

"I tend to agree," Troy acknowledged before changing the subject. "Are you going to use your lemon?"

"Wait," Cabel stammered as he handed Troy the lemon that he had discarded on a napkin. "You agree that this lady went soft on you? So, you're well aware that your actions have consequences, you just don't care."

"I think it's something to do with my addictive personality," Troy mused and waved his hand around that was grasping the lemon. "Actions are the drug and the consequences are the drug's effect. But you never know what the consequences are going to be, and it packs a hell of an adrenaline rush. But like all addictions, there are negative effects."

"They're all negative effects," Cabel scolded. "The feeling surely can't be worth it."

"You don't like lemons? Why don't you like lemons?" Troy brought up in an accelerated voice, blatantly trying to change the subject. While he was doing so, he took the lemon he'd been waving around and squeezed the juice from it into his water before following with the rind and remaining pulp.

Cabel didn't want to take the bait, but felt his position on lemons demanded clarification. "Every time I've had any liquid with a lemon wedge on the side, I've ended up swallowing a lemon seed. Every frickin' time! I've probably got a damn lemon forest growing in my gut."

"When life gives you lemons, you make a lemon forest in your gut," Troy replied smugly, satisfied that Cabel had taken the diversion. "That just doesn't have the same ring to it."

"I hate that phrase," Cabel sputtered. "The real one I mean."

"Come to think of it, so do I," Troy added with a groan when his straw wrapper suddenly snapped in two. He discarded the smaller piece and continued with the motions. "When life gives you lemons, make lemonade. What they don't tell you is ninety percent of the time is that lemonade still manages to taste like sour piss."

Cabel was taking a sip from his cup and choked as laughter and water traded places in his throat. He coughed violently while trying to set his cup down without tipping it over from the convulsions.

"Lemon seed?" Troy asked wittily, though Cabel paid no mind.

"So what's your point?" Cabel asked after finally clearing his throat.

Troy thought for a minute as he considered the meaning behind the metaphor he had put forth. As he did so, the waitress returned with their lunches.

"Grilled cheese, small fry," she stated to Troy while handing him a plate with a golden-brown sandwich sliced in two and placed on opposite ends of the plate with French fries piled in between. Troy nodded in appreciation.

"Ribeye sandwich with cheese sticks," the waitress repeated to Cabel as she placed his meal on the table.

"Thank you," Cabel acknowledged before the young lady turned to leave.

"Ok," Troy started as he stared hungrily at his lunch. "I guess what I'm trying to say is that we can try to put a sugar coating on every damn thing, but it means nothing. It all goes sour in the end. It's like polishing a turd."

"You're mixing your metaphors," Cabel criticized before taking a bite of his sandwich, pulling out a fatty piece after he ripped into it.

"Alright then, let's throw all that aside," Troy conceded. "I'm thinking more about skeletons in the closest."

Cabel squinted as he chewed on the overcooked meat. "Now we're in the closet?"

"Skeleton! The skeletons are in the closet," Troy repeated, irked. "We all have skeletons in our closets. I don't think we seek to do that; it's one of those life things that just happens while we age. The problem with skeletons is that 'em bones were bodies once. And if they were bodies, that means they once had souls. You can't trap a spirit in a closet, Cabel. They will haunt you. And haunt you they do!"

With that, Troy aggressively gripped one of the cheese-filled triangles from his plate and took an exaggerated bite. Cabel stared at him cockeyed as he swallowed and took a drink. Troy was all over the place in his analogies, but in all the sputtering managed to home in on an idea in which Cabel could respond.

"I understand spirits," he admitted, thinking about his rift with The O'Brien Times. "The ghosts of our past won't die. We can wish them away or whatever, but that can never change the fact that the past happened. That the skeleton was once a body. Make no mistake, I do have skeletons, and I am haunted just the same."

"You're talking about the newspaper again, aren't you?" Troy asked with a mouthful.

"Is it that obvious that this is something I obsess over," Cabel answered curtly.

Troy nodded just after he stuffed a handful of fries in his mouth.

Cabel continued. "It's just that a newspaper is the historical record of the county. It's the thing we'll look at a hundred years from now to know who we were. The Internet or TV or radio doesn't really possess staying power like the printed word does. Secondly, a newspaper should always be an advocate for the community it serves. The publisher has a responsibility to empower readership into action, and into bringing about new and great changes. We don't have any of that here. Honestly, I'm partly glad I don't work in this community anymore. I could feel the crushing weight of the resistance to change – both at the paper and in the community after we wrote story after story of beneficial proposals being defeated by a county that wanted jobs, but not the will to allow them to be."

There was silence as Cabel took another bite of his sandwich and chewed intently as he stared into the distance. Troy did not interrupt, as if he could sense more was coming.

"An editor or a publisher could change that with a few well-written editorials. Such great power they can wield and they aren't even aware of it here."

Even though Troy had obviously been shoveling food faster than should be healthy, he had been listening as he cleared his plate. After emptying most of his glass, he finally responded as Cabel took his turn eating.

"Man, what's happened to us? We were kids just days ago and now we belong in here with these geezers. We're old enough to have skeletons, or sour lemons, or whatever. I've lost track of what object you want to relate that to. Time passing is something I've thought about a lot lately. It all started with my fingernails."

"Huh?" Cabel hummed through a full mouth.

Troy looked to the back of his hands. "I noticed I trim my fingernails a lot anymore. Seems like every time I turn around, I need to give them a cutting. I don't remember ever having to do it that much when I was younger. Recently it hit me what that was all about. I wasn't cutting them more often. Time feels like it's moving so much faster now that it just seems like I'm cutting them more often."

Cabel had finished half his sandwich and picked up one of the four fried cheese sticks on his plate, pointing it at Troy as he spoke. "I would subscribe to that theory except that I feel like I hardly ever get my hair cut. It's all keratin, you know."

"Please," Troy snapped back, "we're twenty-seven-year-old men. Our hair growth is slowing down for a reason."

"Sure," Cabel replied haughtily before taking a bite of the cheese stick, "but that keratin has to go somewhere – so if one is slowing down, it would make sense that the other would speed up."

"Ok, never mind," Troy relented, frustrated that his theory had holes in it.

Troy was about to say more when Cabel noticed him looking at something behind him. He wasn't sure who or what it was, but he could see Troy's eyes widen as the sound of heels clacked to a stop next to their table.

"Troy, it's good to see you out and about," a lady commented, her full focus on Troy. Curious as to whom she was, Cabel took in the red dress suit she was wearing and the long blonde hair hanging loose against her shoulders as he continued to quietly eat his lunch.

"Tamera," Troy greeted through his teeth.

"Get'n into trouble?" she chatted carelessly. Cabel recognized that as a phrase used a lot in these parts, usually jokingly, but there was a serious undertone to the way it was asked.

"You know it," Troy answered flatly, finally making eye contact with the woman.

Tamera huffed dramatically. "Well, I just hope you're staying off the drugs."

Cabel suddenly felt appalled by this interaction. "Hey now, why is that any of your business anyways?"

Tamera's shoulders lifted, almost surprised that there was someone else sitting at the booth. She slowly panned so both men were in view.

"And you are?"

"Listening," Cabel shot back, assuming this was someone that had worked with Troy during his past recovery. "I'm not sure who you are, but what you're doing is very unprofessional."

Tamera snorted and smiled condescendingly at Cabel. "I don't know who you are, but would you mind staying in your lane?"

Cabel leaned back in his seat and stared sternly at the woman. "Not always lanes on these country roads."

The two locked eyes in dead silence for a moment, and as uncomfortable as it made Cabel, he held her gaze steadily until Tamera became the one to break away.

"Well, I need to get back to work," Tamera stated abruptly before beginning to walk away.

"Where you working now?" Troy hollered. "Reckon it's another place you're going to put out of business!"

Tamera paid no attention and kept a hurried stride until she had fled through the exit.

"Mmm," Troy scoffed. "That lady's a hot mess."

"An old friend?" Cabel joked.

"Far from it," Troy commented. "She was a drug prevention and recovery specialist. Started her own nonprofit outfit to help those in need, of which I was one at the time. With an attitude like that, you can imagine how long it was before she stopped receiving any funding for the operation."

"And now someone else has employed her, attitude and all," Cabel remarked with disgust.

"Couldn't imagine that she's in the same line of work," Troy speculated. "But some folks are much better at gettin' second chances."

"You don't have to be so grim about it," Cabel tried to reassure. "If someone like that can find work here, I'm sure you can."

Troy pushed his plate to the side and leaned in, resting both elbows on the table. "You know, maybe she's terrible, and maybe I'm terrible too. But I reckon we're terrible in different ways. She's an irritation in a way that locusts are. She swoops into a position, gobbles up all the resources, and flutters into another place to do the same. I'm an irritation in a way that roaches are. No one wants me around and I have to skitter around in the dark looking for scraps to cobble together a life."

Cabel continued to press for a solution. "I could give you a ride to Huntsville every day if you were willing to get a job there. It's hard to make a living off just odd jobs."

Troy leaned back in the booth and looked to the ceiling uncomfortably. "That's no life."

Cabel scoffed. "It's my life."

Troy writhed uncomfortably. "What would it take for you to understand what living is like as a cockroach in the darkness? My darkness? What would it take to crack that upstanding citizen facade that you so masterfully portray to let you see things from my perspective?"

"I get it. You've had it with life mistreating you," Cabel deflected, raising his palms to calm Troy. "Life has mistreated me, too. I bit that bullet and work two counties over. You gotta just keep your head down and move on."

"I'm not talking about me now," Troy replied with a quieter tone. "I want to know what it would take to get you to the beaten-down level that I am currently at."

Cabel considered it and remembered the other thing that haunted him. "You know how much I was bullied as a kid. It would have to be that. If I were pushed around or bullied now, or perhaps I witnessed someone I cared about being pushed around or bullied. That would be just the thing to bring out that rage."

Troy smiled widely and slapped the table. "Now we're talking."

Cabel thought about it a little more before continuing. "I was never good at fighting bullies directly, but I suppose if I saw an advantage, I would destroy them. I would not hesitate to burn everything about them to the ground."

"Light the world on fire!" Troy whooped, responding to the energy he could hear rushing into Cabel voice as he finished.

"I'd light the world on fire!" Cabel repeated, pumping a fist as he did so.

As they settled down a bit, the waitress appeared with their check.

"Is there anything else I can get ya?" the lady asked.

Troy got an idea and his eyes lit up, of which Cabel immediately took note.

"Ah, yes. Can I get a job application?" Troy requested.

"Certainly," the waitress replied before disappearing back to the front of the restaurant.

Cabel gave Troy a pleasing nod. "See, now you've got the right idea."

Troy simply grunted and crossed his arms to wait for the woman to return, which she did after a brief moment.

Troy took the application and a pen from the waitress and eyed the single sheet while he waited for her to disappear out of sight. Once she did, he started to scrawl vigorously on the form.

"This is what I want you to do," Troy stated while he filled boxes. "When the waitress comes back, I want you get up and go to the front - pretend like you're looking at their pies or something. When they bring my application back to the front, take a gander at what they do with it."

A few minutes later, the waitress came back to take their money and collected the application. Cabel followed Troy's suggestion and excused himself and went to the front area of the restaurant, where a row of pies inside a refrigerated case tempted patrons as they entered. Cabel took a quick look over the assortment, but also kept his eyes to the front counter, where a man he recognized as the manager stood wiping the surface with a steaming washrag.

Cabel observed as the waitress handed the form to her boss. He took it with a smile, but when he read over it, the smile rapidly melted away. The man lowered the hand holding the document and when he raised it again, it was no longer there. He then turned and disappeared through the swinging doors of the kitchen.

Curious, Cabel started back towards Troy, trying to get a better angle to see what was behind the counter. As he was just about to round the corner, he finally caught sight of a trashcan that sat just below where the manager had stood.

Cabel returned to Troy, disappointed about what had happened. Troy sat complacently with both hands tucked behind his head, leaning back against the bench.

"Threw it away, didn't they?" he predicted conceitedly.

Cabel returned a defeated nod.

"And that's where I'm at," Troy stated as he stood. "It's not bullying, but it may as well be. People know something about me from the past and I can't change that. I can't time travel back there and tell myself not to pop pills or inject dope into my veins. It's always going to be hanging over me. I'm always going to be that guy who had the overdose and that's why I'm in the darkness."

"I get the darkness, but I don't get the method," Cabel admitted when they passed through the exit. "You've traded actual drugs for your substitute drug of actions and consequences. You have to quit both if you want to stop being a pariah. More darkness doesn't create light."

"But actions create sparks," Troy countered passionately, taking a step into the late afternoon air. "And the consequences of sparks are fire. You have to find those frayed edges, no matter where they are, and apply fire to that. That's the only way it can spread. With luck, we'll find ourselves with the world on fire."

Cabel didn't say anymore as the two walked back to Troy's truck. Troy, however, was still considering the imagery and eventually summarized by shouting to the sky, arms dramatically flung open in defiance to the heavens.

"With the world on fire, there can be no darkness!"

5

OBIT

Cabel was two counties over from any news relevant to Chancy, but there had been a flurry of activity in Huntsville to keep his mind off O'Brien County events. A string of robberies that had taken place in the previous weekend dominated the newsroom chatter of the weekly paper and the editor had sent a small team of reporters out on the hunt for information.

The newspaper had a small staff. Not as small as the O'Brien paper, but nowhere near the workforce of a midsized daily. Their editor, Chris, investigative reporter, Kelly, and eager stringer, Wes, were all in the field to cover various aspects of the story, which left Cabel to hold down the copy editor's desk while he waited for other stories to emerge. He sat at his station, an old metal desk that had seen many occupants, and pecked on his keyboard. Cabel was sure that the desk was first used to hold a typewriter, and evolved from there to the high tech instrument he used to process words today. There was gracelessness in the task today. He tapped in cumbersome fashion on the keys while staring at a handwritten note on his lap.

Country letters were a huge staple of small-town papers. Designated writers from different necks of each county would record their observations and accounts of who was sick, who had a new grandchild, or who paid a visit to whom in the previous weeks. Often times, in lieu of any of these topics, the writer would resort to talking about their own problems or add a favorite recipe to best fill the page.

The country letter resting on his thighs was written in what he called "old folk's language." The bright yellow notepad paper had handwritten words scrawled on it in blue ink and was noticeably written from a shaky hand. Cabel studied each word carefully, typing one out when it was deciphered. Occasionally he'd have to seek a coworker out to help translate. After an indiscernible amount of time, Cabel finally wrapped up that letter, which was from a community known as Cat Bottom. It was a hamlet stuck somewhere in the folds of the fat mountainous region to the north of Huntsville.

Satisfied, Cabel stretched out the kink in his neck and placed the yellow sheet aside before smacking the Command and P keys simultaneous on his keyboard. He heard the desktop printer roar to life in the next room and took a breath to savor the moment. That moment of being furthest away from a tedious weekly task made the air smell sweeter and Cabel took some time to revel in it before he had to focus his attention on the bowling news.

Before he could switch to the task, a mechanical sound clicked over his computer speaker. The sound was the digitalized reproduction of a slideshow projector changing pictures, but the origin of the noise was increasingly unknown, becoming endangered in a world that no longer supported the technology. Cabel recognized this as his email tone and straightened from his slumped position in order to slide closer to the desk.

There was a single email, a message from Yockim Funeral Home, one of the local mortuaries, submitting a listing for their latest deceased. Cabel made a low groan, an almost inaudible tone that blended with the low hum of the furnace.

He clicked on the message and his tone grew higher when the body of the email caught Cabel by surprise. It was a name he recognized. Names he knew upon sight were names that caught him off guard when they were spotted in some out-of-character place. Like seeing your childhood teacher in the grocery store, it was a denial that someone could exist outside the parameters of where they were commonly known to be.

FLOYD WILLIAM ALAN.

The big, bold name seared into Cabel's retinas enough that even when he closed his eyes, he could still see the hazy letters on his eyelids.

Cabel leaned back in his chair and wondered what had happened to the esteemed drug store owner. He wasn't very old to Cabel's knowledge. A quick scan of the death notice revealed he had been 61. He further reviewed the obit for the rare possibility that a cause of death was listed, but found no luck in the attempt.

Typically, the death notices submitted by the funeral homes are minimally edited to fit the newspaper's style; however, Cabel knew the importance of this individual required more volume than what most mortuaries provide. The front page sometimes gave a home to such dignitary deaths, but only the most upper of the upper crust made the cut.

It was not an assignment Cabel relished, but he put his head down and slogged through the keyboard strokes while eyes periodically darted to the clock, hoping for it to hop ahead despite constant notice. It was nearing the end of the workday when he approached the final paragraph and his cell phone chirping startled him.

"Hello," he answered enthusiastically, glad to get away from the screen for a moment.

"Cabel?" a distorted voice questioned on the other end.

"Troy?" Cabel guessed. The man's voice sounded much deeper than Troy's, which was made more unrecognizable by the poor reception quality.

"What's going on?" Troy asked in a hushed tone. "Working?"

"That is a thing I do Monday through Friday," he replied condescendingly, keeping most of his attention glued to the obituary. He proofread a sentence before shifting attention back to Troy.

"Did you get the odd job?"

"That's actually why I'm calling," Troy pensively replied. "I have a final meeting with them tonight and I was wondering if you could come with me again."

"So I can get the sheriff if you don't come back again?" Cabel snapped in reply. "I'm gonna start charging you if I have to keep being your bodyguard up the holler."

Troy paused long enough that Cabel wondered if they'd been disconnected.

He finally continued, "It's at a different location from before. This place is a lot easier to get to."

"It'll be dark when I get back to town," Cabel noted, cradling the phone between his ear and shoulder before taking an editing touch to the final sentence.

"That's okay. It won't be until after dark anyways," Troy assured. "Also, this poultry farm is in Tipperton."

"Tipperton?" Cabel mimicked. The location piqued his interest. "Which one? There's several back near my family's farm."

"Not sure," Troy admitted. "The road is off Barnswallow Drive, so I don't think it's back your way. There are a few other chicken houses off the main drag past the general store. I think it's one of those roads."

Cabel nodded silently, agreeing to go even though it was impossible for Troy to see his body language. "I have to come through that way to get to town. How about I just meet you at Victor's General Store down there? That way I don't have to backtrack."

"Fine by me," Troy replied with a poorly hidden tone of appeasement.

Cabel saved his text file and glanced at the time. "Did you know Floyd Alan died?"

"Who?" Troy shot back quickly.

"Mr. Alan of Alan's Pharmacy. He owned the drug store down here and bought the Right Pill Pharmacy in Chancy a few years ago."

"Oh, Right Pill," Troy realized. "No one calls it Alan's Pharmacy."

Cabel laughed. "It's like the grocery store. We still call it Grocery Giant, even though Super Foods bought it like twenty years ago. Change is hard for us fatalists."

Troy didn't respond.

"Hello?" Cabel checked.

Troy returned, suddenly disinterested. "Anyways, I'll see you at Victor's."

"Sure," Cabel answered just as he heard a click. He grew concerned momentarily but dismissed it as his mind drifted back to the story on the screen.

* * *

Twilight was at day's doorstep when Cabel and Troy pulled onto a gravel road in the heart of the small agricultural community of Tipperton. Cabel had made good time getting to the general store, but then he had not taken into account that it was fifteen minutes shorter than the full distance to Chancy. Meeting up with Troy, he joined him in his old truck for the drive to the chicken house.

The darkness had yet to consume the sky when they started up an unpaved road, passing two long, metal buildings that each could house thousands of chickens. The orange sunlight reflected off the shiny building surface and illuminated the edges of the forest around them.

As they passed, Cabel made out a sign posted at one of the entrances.

MAYFLOWER CHICKEN CORP. FACILITY
OPERATED BY BRIAN & MIUCCIA RANDOLPH
AUTHORIZED ACCESS ONLY

Cabel also noticed through the dying light that the grounds

of the two poultry houses were pristine in their upkeep and landscaping. Though the road was coarse gravel, there were few divots or thinned-out places in the rock layer. It looked as if it was the first time a vehicle had touched its surface. Around the chicken houses were plump evergreen bushes neatly trimmed of any overgrowth. The rest of the vegetation was also well-maintained, but slowly turning brown and thin only because the season dictated it.

They passed by it all as the road continued. The two remained in stilted silence for a quarter of a mile further with nothing but the sounds of the engine and the pop of rubber against stubborn gravel.

"Were those not the ones we're supposed to stop at?" Cabel questioned, pointing back at the chicken houses. "I'd prefer to meet the owner of those."

"I think the one we're going to is the same owner," Troy stated and Cabel could detect a tinge of apprehension in his voice.

"Everything alright?" Cabel wondered.

Troy shrugged. "Just don't want to be late."

Cabel glanced at his phone and saw the time as 7:17 p.m. Plenty of time to be anywhere nearby by 7:30 or even 8:00.

Eventually the secluded road led to a sharp bend that started up a steep hillside. It was at the base of the slope that a dark car sat parked with the front end pointed uphill. Standing at the trunk of the car was a large man in a suit.

Troy braked suddenly.

"Crap! I didn't know he was going to be down here."

Cabel looked to Troy and back to the man, who had now caught sight of the stopped truck and waved them forward.

"That guy is Len. It's probably not good that he sees you with me," Troy sighed in resignation.

Cabel's eyes widened as Troy began to creep the truck forward. "There's not really much that can be done about that now, is there?"

The husky man walked across the graveled road and waited for them to pull up even with him. Troy came to a stop, put the truck in park, and lowered the window.

Len was slow to acknowledge them. He seemed only

interested in the final drag of the cigarette he was nursing. Finished, he dropped the butt to the ground and extinguished it with his foot. To Cabel's surprise, Len then picked up the yellowed nub and placed it in a metal case he had removed from a jacket pocket.

Finally, Len approached the truck, casually leaned against the vehicle, and peered into the cabin.

"Who the hell's this guy?" Len asked Troy, pointing to Cabel.

"He's a friend I brought along for protection," Troy blurted thoughtlessly.

"Was he with you the last time?" Len proceeded to press. "We thought we saw someone on the cameras near the road while we were talking to you."

Troy looked away from Len and placed both hands on the steering wheel. "He's the same guy."

Troy remained frozen and stared forward through the windshield while Len pulled an LED flashlight out of his pocket and shined it on Cabel.

"If it makes any difference, I have no clue what's going on," Cabel reassured Len.

"It doesn't," Len answered flatly before he stepped from the window.

He then rounded the pickup and shined the flashlight into every dark crack and corner of the vehicle that he could find. He finished the sweep and returned to the front of the truck before lowering the light. He nodded at the men, not saying a word, before he returned to his car. With a roar of the engine his dark sedan began to chug uphill.

Troy silently put the truck in gear and followed the other car uphill.

Cabel grew anxious as they tailed. "What was that? What is this?"

"I made a mistake bringing you," Troy lamented. "You're about to find out how deep the darkness goes."

"Troy, what kind of job is this?" Cabel asked once more. And when Troy did not respond, Cabel demanded again in a louder voice.

"What kinda job is this?!"

"Hit job, Cabel," Troy finally revealed with an undertone of condescension. "I hired these folks to whack my boss' mother."

"Holy shit, Troy!" Cabel exclaimed, shocked and appalled by the revelation. "Why are you even telling me this?"

"You're going to find out in a few minutes anyways," Troy speculated, his resolve somewhat returning. "The truth may as well come out now."

"Seriously?!" Cabel spit. "You're seriously going after your old boss's mom? For firing you? Literally, for doing her job. You even admitted that you deserved what you got"

"There's more to it than that," Troy struggled to admit. "More that I can't tell you."

"Worse than what you're doing now?" Cabel fired back. "Something worse than having someone murdered?"

"No." Troy droned flatly.

"So what then?" Cabel asked, his levels of anger fluctuating wildly. "What great injustice did this woman inflict on you to make you want to take a life of one of her loved ones?"

"I can't get by!" Troy shouted back, finally breaking his composure. "Every damn place I work in town eventually gives up on me. I mean, you saw it for yourself! I know Jesus says to turn the other cheek, but I'm outta goddamn cheeks. This time somebody's gotta pay for it."

"I'd say you're the one paying," Cabel remarked. He found enough peace in the quip to give him calm, enough to consider better questions. "What are you paying them for this?"

"Ten grand," Troy answered with a muted tone.

"Damn. Where did you even get that much money from?"

"Borrowed from my mom," Troy reluctantly admitted. "She gave it to me when my wife left."

"Wait. You were married?" Cabel squeaked in reply, barely able to keep up with all the shocking revelations.

"A few years," he replied solemnly. "She left after she got pregnant. Went out west... maybe east. I don't know."

"You have a kid somewhere?!" Cabel shrieked again, even more staggered than before.

"Yeah. I mean, maybe," Troy wavered. "She said she was

leaving because she didn't believe I would be a good father. I don't know. It's possible the kid wasn't mine to begin with."

"Why didn't you tell me that part days ago?"

Troy made an exaggerated shrug. "They're not really a part of my life. My wife barely was and my son never was. Why would it be worth mentioning?"

Cabel was exhausted by all the sudden revelations and flung back in the bench seat. "I want to go on record as saying that it will be a miracle if either of us survives this."

"Ah, it's fine," Troy dismissed, his mood already returning to the typical. "I've got the $9,000 I still owe them behind the seat. As long as they did their part, I will do mine. Everything is square. No worries, man."

"Except someone who didn't deserve it is dead," Cabel reminded him as he felt a pain ping in his now nervous stomach.

The vehicles rounded another hairpin turn to a level area on top of the hill. In the clearing was another chicken house, identical to the ones at the entrance. The night had arrived, but Cabel could make out the same exterior landscaping as the other lot.

"They do quite an upkeep on these buildings," he commented aloud, attempting to take his mind off what could be waiting for them.

Troy grunted in reply as he pulled his pickup next to Len's car near the entrance of the long building.

Len exited his car and approached Troy's side of the truck.

"Alright, gentlemen, I need you both to exit the vehicle to check for weapons and recording devices."

Len backed up and motioned for the two to exit the truck. Troy complied immediately and assumed the frisk position against the bed of the truck. Len pulled black latex gloves over his hands and looked to Cabel to do the same.

Cabel removed his phone and immediately turned it off. "My phone is all I have, and I have just turned it off and sat it on the floor of the cab," he narrated to Len and then mimicked Troy's position after Len finished his first check.

Cabel had never been frisked before and felt slightly emasculated at the feeling of another person patting him down.

It was over soon and Len stepped back.

"This way gentlemen," Len allowed before removing his gloves.

Len pulled the thick metal door of the chicken house open and gestured for the pair to enter. Inside the door was a smaller room that had no finished walls. The wood skeleton of the room only consisted of a small empty desk and a pair of weathered rubber boots. Clipboards of handwritten charts hung from nails in some of the wood studs, the brightness of the paper appearing as if they were updated on a regular basis.

Len stepped inside and pulled the door closed behind him. He made sure it was locked before moving to a door on the opposite side of the petite room. This door had two deadbolts on it but, in contrast to the outside door, was made of wood. Len inserted a key in the uppermost lock and pounded on the door three times before turning it. The second bolt was apparently already unlocked as this was all it took to get the door open.

"I'm going to need a minute," Len stated to the men after he cracked the inside door slightly. He then pointed to Cabel again.

"Tell me your name."

"Cabel Walsh."

"Oscuro will want to know that for his records," Len commented before squeezing through the crack and pulling the door shut behind him.

Cabel turned to Troy. "Oscuro? What kind of name is that?"

Troy laughed, "I know, right? It's his alley list."

"Alias," Cabel corrected.

Troy continued, "He told me the other day it was Spanish for 'The Recluse'."

"Oscuro. The Recluse," Cabel continued to mock. "What a bullshit alias."

"Yeah. It's like it's from some poor translation program," Troy added.

After a few minutes, Len returned and motioned for the men to enter the main building.

"Holy shit," Cabel exclaimed under his breath as the three

stepped into the cavernous room, which ran as long as the building.

"Those ain't no chickens," Troy added while the two gawked slack-jawed at the endless rows of marijuana plants that lined the center of the room. About twenty rows of the tall green plants ran the length of the building and appeared to be in various stages of germination. Every hundred feet or so, the crop varied from a pitiful sprig to a fully budded shrub ready for harvest.

"That is pretty damn brilliant," Cabel hated to admit, but couldn't help himself in doing so. He placed hands on his hips and gawked around as he momentarily forgot the danger he was in. His gaze eventually noticed another man, similarly dressed as Len, pushing a wheelchair-bound man between the rows of the illicit crop.

"What do you think of my cannabis operation?" the old man beamed with pride as he asked the question.

"That's Oscuro," Troy quickly explained to Cabel.

Cabel nodded in acknowledgment and quickly answered, "It's pretty amazing, actually. How long have you had this operation?"

"I'd have answers, except you weren't exactly invited to this party," Oscuro huffed. "What are we going to do about that?"

"I can tell you for sure that all of this will be off the record," Cabel assured.

Oscuro squinted. "Off the record? You're saying that like some type of reporter."

"He is a reporter," Troy stupidly interjected.

The old man straightened his posture and the two suited men quickly assumed a defensive posture, each placing a hand inside their jackets. "Reporter! Geez! Why would you bring us a reporter, Troy?"

"No! He's not a reporter in these parts," Troy assured while he made a pushing down motion with his hands. "He writes for a newspaper two counties over."

"This community is in no way in my editorial jurisdiction," Cabel reassured. "Anything that happens here is strictly off the record."

"Well la-dee-frickin-da," the old man mocked. "I trust

journalists about as much as I expect you to trust me at this juncture. Ain't all that much, is it?"

"I trust you just fine," Cabel fibbed with nervous undertones. "With reporters, our words are our lives. I'm fine with you keeping your words off record as long as we can keep our lives on record."

The man behind the wheelchair removed his hand from the jacket and started for the door, as if to show Troy and Cabel out. He paused when the old man stopped him by raising his arm.

"I will give him the benefit of the doubt for now," Oscuro conceded as he cocked his head to one side.

The suited man nodded once, moved back behind the wheelchair, and placed both hands back on the wheelchair handles.

The old man continued, barking his question at Cabel, "Son, tell me your name again. I heard it, but it didn't make no damn sense." While he waited for a response, he raised his chin and bobbed his jaw as he looked him over.

"Cabel, sir."

"Cabel?" the old man snorted. "Kah-Bell? Not Cable? What kind of fancy boy name is that?"

"It should have been Caleb, but my mother was dyslexic," he recited reluctantly, but pressed forward with his standard joke answer.

"If it were dyslexia, wouldn't that be Calbe?" the man on the left asked.

"Both my parents were dyslexic," Cabel replied calmly and offered a slight smile in hopes that the man would get the joke.

"Your parents sound like idiots," the old man coldly remarked.

Cabel didn't have interest in being offended because he had just caught sight of the man's absence of feet and quickly glanced away.

Oscuro continued to grill, "Who is your daddy?"

"Tom Walsh," Cabel answered without hesitation.

"Another Tipperton boy," Oscuro guessed. "I'm glad we can all get together in your hometown for this."

Cabel nodded silently.

"Is your grandpappy Earlie Walsh?" he correctly guessed.

Cabel was silent for a moment. "Afraid so."

"Your family has a rich history in this county," Oscuro remarked and shuffled his posture on the chair so he could place a free hand on his stomach. "Y'all have been here a while."

"It's true," Cabel admitted, almost proudly. "Pretty much all of my direct lines lived in this county before West Virginia was a state."

"Does that make you purebred or inbred?" Oscuro jibed.

Cabel stammered, "Um... I ahh... don't see why they are mutually exclusive."

Oscuro chuckled. It was a low bellow that started deep in his lungs and transitioned to a cough by the time it was ready to emerge.

"I'm joshing ya, boy. Ole Earlie is a good fella."

Cabel wasn't shocked by Oscuro's knowledge of his family. Anyone who had spent any time in O'Brien County was aware of the family lines that rooted deep into the country ground. It was somewhat of a final exam for outsiders to know these families before they could be accepted in the community with proper credentials.

Oscuro added unprompted, "Plus your lineage is pure Irish as far as I can tell. I don't let no one into my life with direct Italian descent. My brother was killed in Italy during WWII, so I don't let anyone in my sight who could potentially be related to his killer."

"Not a trace of that in Grandpa Earlie," Cabel answered apprehensively.

The man chuckled. "I went to school with ole Earlie. We did some running around back in those days. He liked to chase the skirts. Had a place up the holler down that way he liked to take the ladies so they could do some neckin'."

"That wasn't something I needed to know," Cabel stated candidly.

"Ahh," the old man tittered. "Nothing wrong with that. After all, your pappy wouldn't have came to be, and neither would you, if he hadn't done some neckin' in those woods."

The old man shuffled in place and shifted his attention to

Troy.

"I'm guessing you fellas attended Tipperton Elementary?"

"Yup," Troy replied proudly.

"Unfortunately," Cabel answered almost simultaneously, but it was his answer that the elderly gentleman latched onto.

"Unfortunately?" the man gasped. "Tipperton Elementary was a fine educational institution. The teachers were top-notch and the class sizes were small enough that students could get one-on-one time with fabulous educational professionals."

"Were you a student there, sir?" Cabel snapped, Oscuro's prodding finally causing him to fail in tamping down his offense to the running commentary.

The man was clearly surprised by the query. "Don't get to be interviewing me, reporter," he blustered.

Cabel interrupted, "Because I was a student, and I can wholeheartedly disagree."

The old man paused and a corner of his lip curled slightly. "I sense you wish to file a complaint. Perhaps you were a bullied one. That plays well with me."

"I want to know about your operation," Cabel returned curtly. He felt the overwhelming need to steer the conversation back to where it had begun.

"Off the record questions?" Oscuro growled hoarsely and weakly lifted an accusing finger.

"Yes, off the record." Cabel replied indignantly. "This is purely for my curiosity."

Oscuro grunted reluctance but nodded in approval. "Frank." He then motioned for the man behind him to push him closer to better hear the query.

"How do you get these plants the proper light and water? I mean, obviously you're doing something right."

"There are heat lamps on the ceiling that run the length of the building," Oscuro answered and pointed a walking stick towards the roof. "They simulate sunlight for chickens in normal houses. In fact, when you turn them off in a regular house, the chickens go right to sleep."

"Huh, emulating the sun," Cabel replied, deeply awed. "And the water?"

"There's piping that runs the length of the building too,"

Oscuro answered freely and with an unapologetic smile. "The chicks would drink off nipples on the underside, but we've refitted them to drip out onto the soil around the plants."

Cabel was about to ask about the soil too, but before he could, Oscuro continued unprompted.

"We dug the concrete floor out of here years ago, so these beauties had room to stretch their roots. The first couple batches didn't grow too well, but we began supplementing with the composted chicken shit from the other houses and boy those suckers took off then."

"Wow," Cabel uttered, otherwise speechless.

Oscuro continued, "We've been experimenting with poppies too down on the further end, but they're a little finicky to grow in a similar environment."

Troy had wandered off while Cabel grilled the crime boss about his operation. He appeared to make an attempt to walk the length of the building, but returned quickly once he seemed to realize how far the building stretched.

"How do you not get caught?" Troy wondered after he returned. "Doesn't the chicken company notice they're not servicing one of the buildings?"

Oscuro's smile turned wider. "This building was built in error. By which I mean I created the error intentionally. Basically, the chicken company comes out and builds these buildings for us, but then they stick us with the bill while we make back the money by raising their chickens for them. It takes more than a decade to turn a profit on these, typically. I had this one built, knowing full and well that the chicken and feed trucks were too large to make the turns to get up this hill. Soon after it was finished, the company considered the building decommissioned and abandoned it, leaving us free to use it without suspicion."

"And because you keep it up, anyone in the public who wanders near it just thinks it's another one of your operational houses," Cabel deduced.

"You are correct," Oscuro acknowledged. He then motioned for Frank to push him along the rows. Troy and Cabel followed to his left side as Len walked behind them.

"Down to business then," Oscuro shifted subjects and

made a finger pinching gesture to Frank. This signaled his associate to pull some papers out of a bag that hung over the back of the wheelchair. Frank then passed the papers on to Len, who passed them to Troy.

"Mary May Knotts," Oscuro trumpeted loudly as Troy riffled through the papers. "Born in August of 1951. We tracked her to her last known residence, but did not find her there. With some digging in the public archives, we found her current home."

Cabel peered over Troy's shoulder as he flipped to the second page of the documents. On that sheet they found a copier-duplicated newspaper clipping. The picture had been darkened harshly because of the toner quality, but the words were still legible.

> *Mary May Knotts, 64, of Deer Heights, Va., passed away on Nov. 3, 2014. She was born August 16, 1951 and was the daughter of the late Fred and Elma Suzette. She is survived by three daughters, Adriane Knotts of Chancy, Katy Dresden and husband Scott of Fort Smith, AR and Ginger Knotts of Dover, DE...*

"What is this?" Troy questioned in befuddlement.

"Don't you read a newspaper, son," Oscuro scolded. "It's a death notice. Mary Knotts died just over two years ago."

A sudden jitter came over Troy and his hands started involuntarily crumpling the papers.

"What does that mean for us?" he rattled with an unstable voice.

Oscuro groaned facetiously. "Well, we did our part. Our job was to make sure someone was dead, and we did just that."

The group had stopped their stroll through the building and all eyes turned to Troy, whose face was becoming a beet shade of red.

"You expect me to pay you for this?" he snarled in restrained anger.

"I do," Oscuro replied, disaffected by Troy's boiling rage.

"We took the time to do the research – track down leads, crack open musty books and whatnot. Normally, I'd give a discount for such simple work, but you lied to me about Mr. Walsh. You even lied to me about him last time at the cabin when you said you didn't bring anyone with you. I don't give discounts to liars."

Troy clinched his jaw and lowered his head towards the ground. His thumbs gyrated in and out of clinched fists while the whole of his body began to tremble.

Oscuro reiterated, "We did our job, as I said. It's not our problem that you failed to complete basic due diligence to make sure the person you wanted dead is not presently in that state."

"You bastards!" Troy roared with a little more heft, still yet to reach critical mass.

Cabel could sense what was about to happen and attempted to take a few steps back. Len placed a palm in the center of his back to stop the movement.

"What if I refuse to pay?" Troy asked through gritted teeth.

Oscuro snorted derisively. "I think we could convince you one way or the other. That is the sorta thing that's directly in our wheelhouse, son."

Oscuro paused and it was becoming apparent that anger was starting to build in him also.

"We could do it the quick and painless way."

The old crime boss snapped a finger and Frank pulled a handgun from a shoulder holster and pointed it at Troy's head. Troy remained undeterred while Cabel instinctively put his hands in the air.

"Or we could do it the elaborate, painful way," Oscuro continued, pivoting his head back and forth to eye both men. "The choice is yours, fellas."

Troy was still red, but he unclenched his fists and eased his posture. "Given the current prospects, I'm going to have to go with slow and elaborate, though a bullet to the head will get you as much as you gave me just now."

"We can collect one way or the other, so that's still not my problem," Oscuro answered uncaringly. He then nodded to Frank to holster his gun. "I can tell your life is just a constant stream of poor decisions. You've built an existence for yourself that's about as meaningful as seat warmers in South Florida."

Oscuro raised an arm and made a circular motion with his fingers. Frank, knowing the sign, turned the wheelchair around and started back to the door. Everyone followed except Troy, who walked slightly ahead of the pack, his posture straightened a tautly is it could elevate.

"So I'll tell you what I'm going to do," Oscuro dictated. "I will give you a day to change your mind. I really want you to think about it too. Because if you haven't given me an answer by the time your eyes close tomorrow night, I will make sure they do not open the morning after. I will render upon you the full consequence of your default."

"You don't know me," Troy snapped back, expelling the pent-up fury. "You can come at me all you want, but you don't know shit about anything I do!"

Oscuro closed his eyes and sighed. "It's a small town. You can find out everything you need to know in five minutes of conversation with any waitress or a ten-minute dive into the newspaper archives."

"Try me," Troy dared as he wagged a stern finger.

"Spoken like the packaging of a baby doll," Oscuro quipped as he wrinkled his nose in fleeting disgust. "I'll pull your string more later. Show them the door."

Len placed a hand on the backs of both Troy and Cabel, but Troy shrugged it off and stormed ahead of the two,

"One more thing, Mr. Walsh," Oscuro requested, prompting Len to release Cabel from his grasp.

"Yes?"

"People who come to see me about these matters are generally not smart people," Oscuro posited. "In fact, the lot of them are god-dang morons. Now you are an outlier that I never would have let in my sights. You aren't desperate and you have a good job that requires you to be educated on past and current events. That means you are by no instance someone I would do business with. Most are dumb enough to keep quiet, but you're smart enough to do the common sense thing and go to the police. I know it seems like I let you off easy, especially given your friend's reluctance to pay for services rendered, but make no mistake that this is very serious. Now as much I like your grandpappy, I would not hesitate for a second to rain fire down on your entire family if you so much as utter a word of the things you saw or heard here today."

"Off the record means off the record," Cabel reassured firmly. "I take it as seriously as you do, rest assured."

"My eyes will be on you," Oscuro concluded, pointing two fingers towards his eyes and back to Cabel. Len then resumed his escorting duty and pushed Cabel fully out the door.

Troy was already sitting in the idling truck by the time Cabel emerged from the chicken house. Cabel walked to the truck but looked back to the door to see Len standing guard to make certain that the two exited the property. Stunned by what just happened, Cabel quietly got into the truck and closed the rusty door.

Troy put the truck into drive and coasted back down the steep road while Cabel silently retrieved and reactivated his cell phone.

"Hey Troy," Cabel finally spoke evenly when the two reached the main road.

"Yeah," Troy answered in a matched, lax tone. The shades of anger he displayed before dissipated.

"I don't think I'm coming with you on job leads anymore."

6

GHOST

From the chicken houses, Troy took a different route to return Cabel to his vehicle. Still angered from the confrontation, Cabel only absently noticed this. He was too frazzled by what had just unfolded and didn't feel up to asking why when he finally noticed. Still, since he had grown up in the area, he wasn't too bothered by the alternate route. It was a way he was familiar with and knew it would take him to his destination – if only taking a few minutes longer.

Much like Cabel's nerves, the truck rattled as it barreled down the dark thoroughfare, along the path beaten by cars,

trucks, buses, and tractors in equal measure. The dim
headlights cast shadows upon the passing trees and projected
eerie apparitions that signaled something more could be lurking
in the darkness.

Troy followed the solid yellow line a few miles more until
it came to a familiar clearing on a balding hilltop. A trio of unlit
buildings sat shadowed in the night. The first was a shuttered
Methodist church, which sat on a grassy slope in a yard with no
discernable area to park a car. The structure had a classic white-
paneled exterior with a bell tower rising above the tin roof of the
modest frame. Mighty oak trees surrounded it and masked
much of its quaint appearance.

The second building was also abandoned and aging. In a
time of necessity in a small hamlet like Tipperton, several
general stores thrived along the roads of the farm community.
Travel and technological advancements rendered many of these
country shops unnecessary and the number of these trading
posts dwindled to just Victor's General Store. The name of the
particular store in front of them had been lost to most. Neither
Cabel nor Troy knew, though they had spent time near it their
entire lives. The rusted gas pumps adorned with faded Esso
logos still gave recognition to what it once was. In the decades
that passed, the building was used for nothing more than storage
for the final proprietor, and later his family, who came to forget
the property – storage contents and all.

The third structure was much larger than the others and
boasted a huge paved parking lot that still had relatively upkept
maintenance, though hoopless basketball poles spaced around
the lot still gave a clue to the property's former life.

This was Tipperton Elementary School.

Even though the school had been long closed, the building
had been sold to the county to be used as a recreation center by
the communities of the northern county. To Cabel's surprise,
Troy abruptly steered the truck into this lot, pulling midway
between the road and the building before shutting off the
engine.

"The girl's thirsty," he stated and patted the steering wheel.
"Gonna give her a sip of momma's milk."

Cabel nodded, not taking his eyes away from the brick

façade of the building. After Troy exited the truck to retrieve one of his gasoline jugs, Cabel instinctively exited the truck too and continued to stare pensively at the school.

"Why did you stop here, Troy?" Cabel asked woefully. "Of all the places in the world you could have stopped."

Troy was busy holding the short lip of the milk jug against his gas tank, trying not to spill the fuel as it emptied into his truck with a gurgle.

"Girl was thirsty," he repeated. "Plus I knew this lot would be empty. The firemen do a haunted house fall festival type thing here at the end of October and basically shut it down until spring. They used to do hunter's dinners here the weekend before buck season, but it was taking revenue from the churches that sorta do the same thing."

Cabel nodded, though it was too dark for Troy to see it. Despite Cabel's upstanding nature, terrible thoughts were running through his mind.

"Our fifth-grade teacher, Mr. Geisterkoch. Do you remember him?" Cabel inquired unprompted.

"Uh-huh," Troy replied after the milk jug gurgled empty. "Terrible name for a ten-year-old to try to spell. Big ole jerk, too."

"He was a jerk," Cabel agreed with a tone of aggression. "He didn't like me. When I went through the worst of being bullied, he helped punish some of the worst of the kids. But I guess because I wasn't the best student, he felt betrayed that I wasn't better because of his help. He then became a bully, too. He was the worst kind of bully, though – the kind with authority. He would routinely give me bad reports at parent/teacher conferences despite not doing too terribly bad. Because of that, I spent a lot of time grounded at home for things beyond my control. It created as much of a hell in my home life as it was at school."

"What an ass," Troy simply responded.

"What an ass!" Cabel mimicked, failing to control his antipathy. "I sat in the class... ten-years-old... I sat in the class and tried to figure out a way I could murder that bastard. Who thinks about those kinds of things at that age?"

"Boys from the nineties thought about those kinda things

all the time," Troy assured, though Cabel acted as if he didn't hear it and continued.

"And then they closed this school. They killed it! I was so happy that they killed it, but they didn't go far enough. They should have torn the shithole down. All the way down!"

Troy reached into the bed of his truck and tied the empty jug to a strand of bailer twine. His hand moved to another part of the bed and Cabel heard the clank of thick metal. Troy removed his hands from the bed to reveal a long crowbar.

"Sounds like you could use some therapy on this matter," Troy declared casually. "Could I interest you in some light misdemeanors?"

Cabel understood the theme Troy was suggesting. Of all the slights and setbacks Troy had encountered over the years, it boiled his desire down to only vengeance. It was enough to seek revenge for himself, but he now seemed to wish for Cabel to experience the taste of doling out retribution. Though conscious to this notion, Cabel was now in the frame of mind to allow himself the satisfaction. The ease of agreeing to such a deed made Cabel wonder if it was a blatant maneuver on Troy's part.

"You got me in deep tonight," Cabel scolded Troy. "I guess if I'm trapped in a life of crime now, I might as well find some satisfaction in it."

The two walked briskly across the long lot and crossed into a grassy area along the brick wall. Near the back of the building, they located a weathered side door that looked promising. Troy wedged his crowbar into a thick gap and it took little effort to jimmy it open. The weakened wood cracked easily as it popped and separated from the locking mechanism. Troy pulled it open enough for the grown men to squeeze through.

Removing a small flashlight from his keychain, Troy shined it around the musky room.

"This must have been the boiler room."

In the center of the room was a large cylindrical tub, an ancient contraption of heating technology's past. Its best days were long gone, the metal patched over with duct taped metal scraps and held together by rust and a prayer. Dozens of pipes of different thicknesses extruded from it, bending in a variety of angles before exiting the room through designated holes near the top of the wall.

Cabel stepped cautiously and could hear and feel the crunch of dirt and glass on the grimy floor. Troy moved ahead of him, using the crowbar to unlock the inner door that led up a short flight of stairs to the main hallway.

The two entered the dark corridor, which ran the length of the building. Its painted tan cinderblock confines felt much larger as a child. To Cabel, it now felt as if the walls were shrinking around him.

"They didn't take the decorations down," Troy stated after he shined a light to the wall, which revealed a number of laminated cutouts of Halloween monsters taped in a row. The spook of each of the creatures was dulled by their cartoon representation, but the light shining on them suddenly sparked a jolt in Cabel.

"They tried, but nothing was going to make this place any creepier," he remarked.

"I'm detecting some negative feelings with you," Troy observed with thick sarcasm.

"I..." The words weren't there, so Cabel left the syllable lonely in the air.

Troy didn't comment and continued down the hallway, flicking the light beam across each darkened door before moving on to the next.

"There it is," Troy announced finally, flashing a light to a small hardwood door with clouded glass panes divided into four panels on the upper half. A sticker on the door had long been peeled away, but Cabel knew that at one time it had displayed the name of his despised teacher.

"Look, it's not even locked," Troy proudly revealed after he turned the loose knob.

With a yank, the door flew open and a light breeze followed its path. Just being at the door made Cabel angry and he clinched both hands into a fist as he forced himself to move inside.

"I thought this was a community center," Cabel stated, seeing stacks of boxes and artifacts from the building's education days.

"When the school board sold it, there was a bunch of stuff

they left behind. The new building managers just stuffed it all into boxes and threw it in this room," Troy informed. He shined the light to each of the boxes, but few had visible labels.

"How do you know this?" Cabel questioned flatly while he surveyed the few boxes that were labeled.

"I worked their haunted house a couple years ago," Troy revealed. "We kept a lot of the decorations in the back corner of this room."

"Did you get into a fight at that job, too?" Cabel snipped.

"Hey now," Troy shot back in an offended tone. "Not everything ends with me getting into a fistfight."

Troy held the light to the back of the room and Cabel could spot more Halloween decorations tucked away in the corner. That was the spot in the room where kids were sent when the teacher felt they were acting badly. Cabel spent a lot of time in the sea foam green desk chair that was once there. It faced the corner as the student occupant was also forced, depriving them of the connection with the rest of the class. The corner was now full of cobwebs, as many real as decorative.

Cabel turned towards the front of the room and something caught his eye in the dimness. "Wait, shine the light back over there."

Troy repositioned the light to reveal the teacher's desk still in place.

Cabel walked to it and stared grimly. It was the same battered oak desk that had sat there when he was a student eighteen years earlier. Even in the dim light, he could remember every contour and every scratch and groove the desk had worn into it.

The sight of the desk enraged Cabel and he shoved the storage boxes off its surface with a fierce grunt.

"Where is the firemen's storage?" Cabel aggressively requested.

"Next door down in the fourth-grade class," Troy replied anxiously.

Cabel disappeared for a moment and returned with a fire axe. He clasped it with both hands and turned to a position in which he could heave it over his shoulder.

With a shriek, Cabel swung the blade downward and

plunged it into the desk with all his strength. The axe split deep into the grain and stuck there for a moment. Cabel grunted as he struggled to wiggle it free. The blade finally gave and he continued to strike the surface several more times as he cursed and spit at the unfortunate icon of his childhood.

"Bunch of bullies ruined my life!" Cabel commented breathlessly before chucking the axe to the floor. He turned away from the desk and slid down alongside it to sit on the floor – back propped against the side. He slouched into an exhausted pose before Troy joined him on the floor.

"You became a bully eventually too, you know?" Cabel noted mournfully after catching his breath. "Peer pressure and all, I can't blame you. We all feared Lucas, and it would have only been a matter of time before he turned his sights on you, and you could have either joined the crowd or sank to the bottom with me. Isn't that why we stopped being good friends?"

Troy fell silent for a moment, ultimately letting out a long sigh. He placed the flashlight on the edge of the splintered desk and began a surprisingly thoughtful answer.

"That could be true," he responded softly in a deeper register. "I can't speak for what I did as a kid, but I can speak for who I am now. I was abandoned by my friends as well. I didn't overdose alone, you know. They knew it was happening and left. I only made it because someone called an ambulance on their way out the door."

"I'm sorry," Cabel stated solemnly.

"Don't apologize. I don't. That's just a hard and fast rule that I've maintained throughout my adulthood. Sure, I've done a ton of shit wrong and it shows, but as sorry as I've ever felt about anything, I've never said it... not aloud at least."

Troy leaned in a little closer so that Cabel could look him in the face.

"I tell you that because I want you know that it means something when I say to you that I'm sorry. We can either call it even, or those things are just gonna have to haunt us."

Cabel maintained eye contact for a moment before looking away again, compiling the swirling of thoughts in his head. He finally bobbed his head in agreement as he continued to process.

Then the two grinned simultaneously and burst into inappropriate laughter.

"I'm twenty-seven years old. It doesn't make sense that I should be tormented by the past any longer. Mr. Geisterkoch is probably long dead, and most of our classmates have moved onto other parts of the world. I should have moved on, too."

Troy exhaled deeply as they both got back to their feet. "After my overdose and the wife leaving, I went out west for a year or so. Thought I could get away from it all. What I found was you can't get away from it all. You can move physically, but the stuff in your head don't move. You can alter it with drugs, you can alter it with alcohol, you can try to rehab it with therapy, but all it does is welcome more of the same into an already crowded space."

"So, what do you think the answer is?" Cabel asked with genuine interest, impressed by his friend's sudden insightfulness.

Troy arched his head towards the desk. "Destroy shit that reminds you of how awful it was." He looked to Cabel and smacked proudly his back. "You're off to a good start."

Cabel let out a long sigh before finally turning to Troy with a smile. "I will admit, this was cathartic; but let's get out of here before I change my mind."

PAGE

Cabel took Tuesday off work – nerves still rattled by the previous day's unpleasant events. He and Troy had parted ways late the previous evening without having any more meaningful conversation, but agreed to meet for lunch.

It was a quarter past noon and Cabel had already been seated at a booth at the York Cafe for nearly an hour. About thirty minutes in, he had finally ordered lunch, not willing to wait any longer for Troy. While he ate, he watched as the crowd filed in and shuffled across the black and white checkered tiles to the orange booths that lined the long walls of the narrow storefront. Normally, he didn't enjoy the social norms of small-town public life, but Cabel felt the irresistible urge to be around people that day.

Having finished the majority of his meal, he was listlessly poking at the unwanted parts of a seasonal fruit salad and regretting an earlier consideration that lead him to not bring his laptop along. The idea of lugging a messenger bag around town was unappealing at the time. Now there was nothing to do but people-watch.

His back was to the door, but his position near the front of the shop gave him a birds-eye view of the other patrons. Most of them he knew by name. Many of them he had interacted with during his employment at The O'Brien Times and a few had even been the subject of published articles.

Just across the street from the Times, the York restaurant was a popular spot for O'Brien employees to eat. Cabel knew this, but hadn't considered the possibility of running into any of his former colleagues while he sat and waited.

The bell to the front door pinged as a new customer entered the building and Cabel turned his head slightly to the sound, but not enough to see who was there. He thought briefly that it could be Troy, but whoever it was went directly to the front register to place a to-go order.

"Cabel?" the man at the counter inquired. Cabel arched his head around to see who was speaking.

"How are you?" the man asked, stepping closer to Cabel's table.

It took Cabel a moment to recognize who was asking. His realization was met with a brief horror, but quickly faded to cautious optimism. The man was Corey Paxton, son of the newspaper's publisher.

"I'm doing well," Cabel finally responded.

Corey smiled and shoved both hands in his pants pockets. "Good. Good."

Cabel didn't know what else to say. He still felt a lot of anger towards his final treatment at the paper, though much of it was the work of the father. Resentment aside, his time at the paper was some of the more fulfilling times he had experienced in his young life.

Cabel forced a smile back, but said nothing.

"I saw your lifestyle piece in the Huntsville Herald about the old man that lives off the grid," Corey stated. "It was a really fun to read article. It was laid out on the page in a very eye-catching way as well. It was all very impressive. Very creative."

"I did the layout, too," Cabel shared, biting on the compliment. "The paper there has a staff slightly larger than yours, but we generally do the page design along with the writing."

"Hmm," Corey purred gutturally. "Well, you did a great job."

The waitress returned to the counter with a brown bag containing Corey's order and he returned to the counter to take it. After a brief chat with the waitress, Corey went back to Cabel as he headed for the door.

"Come see me sometime and we'll catch up," Corey offered as he passed.

Cabel smiled involuntarily. "Will do," he replied before Corey hurried away.

It was nearing 12:30 and Troy had still not shown up. Cabel had begun to worry that something happened to him during the night. Finally, he paid the check and exited the café. He paused and pulled out his cell phone before looking to the bustling street. Cabel wasn't used to the buzz of activity. His time in town now was only on weekends when the residents retreated to their homes or left the county altogether in search of retail therapy in the cities beyond the mountains. In the lull of an already sleepy town, the REM cycle happens on those days.

Now in the thick of small-town foot traffic, Cabel started to look up Troy's number. As he scrolled, the phone began to ring of its own accord. Alarmed, his thumb jerked up slightly, pausing in its scrolling efforts. Thinking he had done something to set off the sound, he soon realized from the displayed number that it was the Huntsville Herald calling him.

"Hello," Cabel answered as he searched for a quieter area on the sidewalk.

"Cabel? It's Chris. Do you have a minute?" his editor inquired.

"Sure," Cabel replied, sitting down on the stoop to the building next to the York.

"Read your piece on Mr. Alan. Good stuff!" the woman complimented.

"You mean the obituary?" Cabel clarified passively.

"Yeah," Chris stated. "Anyways, it turns out there's more to the story than that. We got some new information today that makes it a little more interesting."

"Really?" Cabel replied in interest.

"His autopsy came back with a potent mix of heroin and opioids."

Cabel shook his head. "Drug overdose? That's not typically a part of the person's life that makes the obit."

"True," Chris admitted. "That's not the point, though. When his body was found, there was no trace of paraphernalia or syringes that would have been used with these drugs. Additionally, they went back over his body and found the injection site in the back of his thigh."

"Foul play then?" Cabel deduced as he caught sight of Troy approaching.

"It would seem that way," Chris responded. "Anyways, along with the arson last weekend, this next edition just got overloaded."

"If it bleeds, it leads, as the old news expression goes," Cabel commented.

"This is a hemorrhage then," Chris added with a chuckle.

"Sorry I'm late," Troy interrupted, standing over Cabel.

Cabel looked to Troy and tried to wave him off so he could hear the editor, but Troy continued.

"The clock I was looking at wasn't changed for daylight savings," he persisted and ignored Cabel's motions for silence.

"Is there a way you can get down here today?" Chris asked.

"I wasn't expecting to sleep that long," Troy mumbled.

Cabel stood. "Yeah. I actually have a chance to head that way now. See you in an hour."

"See you in an hour," Chris replied.

The two said goodbye and disconnected.

"Dammit Troy, I was on the phone," Cabel scolded.

Troy, dejected, slumped his shoulders and replied, "It didn't seem that important."

"It was pretty damn important," he angrily stated. "And now I've got to go in to work."

"What about our meeting?" Troy whined.

"Meeting was an hour ago. You missed it," Cabel answered in irritation, starting down the sidewalk. "Change your dang clocks!"

"I got some pretty serious stuff going on, too," Troy protested as he followed behind. "We got one day to figure this out."

"Pay them!" Cabel responded loud enough that Troy could hear without him turning around. "You owe it to me to do that so I'm no longer involved in your crap."

"Shh, not in public," Troy hushed as he hustled along.

Cabel stopped for a second to face Troy. "Come with me then. It's not like you have anything else going on today."

"Fine then," Troy agreed in a huff as the two went back into motion. "We're not taking my truck, though."

The idea actually eliminated some of his annoyance with Troy and Cabel snickered. "I don't ever want to be in that piece of garbage again," he declared while the two crossed the street to the town parking lot. Unlocking his vehicle, he settled in behind the wheel and waited for Troy to join him.

"This is a pretty sweet ride," Troy conceded, looking over the touch screen panels of Cabel's newer SUV. "I can see why you hate mine so much."

"This ain't no deathtrap," Cabel proudly declared, his temperament having returned to normal. "And all my gasoline resides inside the tank."

"Well yeah, when you can make it where you're going with what's in your tank," Troy retorted as Cabel pulled out of the lot.

The two were passing through Tipperton on their way to Huntsville when Cabel decided to take a rarely used shortcut. The route involved some backroads, but shaved a few minutes off the trip. It also had the benefit of passing Oscuro's chicken houses.

As they went by, Troy peered up at the two buildings that contained actual poultry and were easily seen, but the illicit house was buried too far into the woods to spot.

"What keeps the law from finding out about the weed house?" Troy wondered aloud, his gaze returning to the road.

"There's something to be said about hiding in plain sight," Cabel replied after some silence. "If he had barbwire fences and pit bulls guarding the place, it would easily tip someone off."

"But we know," Troy observed. "And we're in their debt. What's to stop us from going up there and torching the place in retaliation?"

"They're monitoring the place," Cabel answered quickly.

"How do you know?"

Cabel smiled as he revealed his cleverness. "I watched the trees as we went down the hill last night. In at least three spots I saw motion sensors, with another device that looked like possibly a trail camera, or some type of wireless enabled camera, though I didn't have my phone on when I thought to check for Wi-Fi service."

"That's pretty damn observant of you," an unimpressed Troy commented. "I noticed a few up on Turkish Knob on the way up to the cabin," Troy revealed.

"I saw one by the road up that way," Cabel added. "It was a camera. I expect they use that one like a camera on a rich person's front gate. You know, to vet people before they're allowed inside."

"That makes sense," Troy admitted before a pause of reflection. "Though I didn't get stopped by it. If you remember from when we were kids though, I'm pretty good at sneaking around a forest. Those sensors would be no match for me."

"Sensors are a little more observant than a six-year-old trying to find you in a pew-pew game with nothing at stake," Cabel mocked. "This is serious stuff. If they didn't see you coming, they would have acted hostile. Did they act hostile?"

Troy cocked his head like he was thinking of a reply, but when he finally spoke the subject had entirely vanished.

"You think Oscuro employs a bunch of people to tend to his weed house? I mean, it's just the three men and he don't got feet."

"It's probably too late to ask for an application if you're interested," Cabel noted dryly. "I doubt he'll let you work off the debt."

Troy shook his head. "No. I mean he's got to have folks already doing it for him. That was a lot of pot, and I doubt they're doing the cutting, drying, and distribution themselves."

"Hadn't thought of that," Cabel admitted and his mind seemed to retreat inward to find an answer.

"Don't have any good reasoning for that one?" Troy continued with a smirk. "I think I've got this one."

"Enlighten me," Cabel requested and tapped a drum roll on his steering wheel.

"See, these grower chicken houses run on six-week cycles. They drop the baby chicks off and six weeks later pick them up as full-grown chickens and take them to the slaughterhouse or whatever," Troy explained. "The chickens are picked up by folks called catchers, which is a pretty horrible job. I've never done it, but I had some buddies who did – and it's purely a crap position to be in."

"So?" Cabel egged on, eager for the point.

"So, because Americans aren't about crap jobs, they bring in Hispanics or other immigrants on work visas to do the part – sometimes illegals, but always folks desperate for work. It's entirely possible that Oscuro has coerced them into moonlighting for him at his special chicken house for extra money."

"Huh," Cabel uttered, impressed. "That actually makes perfect sense, since they would risk deportation if they were discovered to be involved in illegal activity."

"Also, they would be less likely to speak about it to the local gossip circles, keeping rumors out of circulation," Troy added, smiling hugely – obviously feeling proud of himself for coming up with such a theory.

The subject changed a few times after that, focusing more on old acquaintances and classic video games before returning to the tasks at hand. It was an uncommonly clear day for mid-November, a time when gray clouds usually formed the backdrop against the hills of disrobing trees and yellow ragweed that ran alongside the roadside, intercut between the long lines of wire fencing that divided the farmland. When they crossed into the next county over, Cabel decided to address the situation once again.

"You're really not going to pay them?" he inquired.

"I'm not," Troy answered tonelessly, his chipper expression wiped away instantly.

"What's your endgame then? What's at the end of your path?" Cabel pried, sensing what the core of the issue was. "You're not one to think things completely through, and I'm not sure you've arrived at the conclusion I have."

"They'll probably kill me," Troy replied, his demeanor still disaffected.

"And you're fine with death?"

"All paths lead to death," Troy replied sternly and drew a deep breath. "Most folks find a longer way around, but the destination is always the same."

"Most folks aren't looking for a shortcut, either," Cabel argued.

Troy audibly inhaled again. "I've made peace with it, but that doesn't mean I'm not going to fight like hell."

Cabel grew frustrated and withdrew for a moment, unsure of whether there was a point to regroup. Since there was nothing more to do during the journey, he pressed onward. "What's this money mean to you if you'd rather die than give it up?"

"Principle!" Troy shouted, holding both his hands outward and shaking them wildly. "They screwed me over, and the satisfaction of my demise can no way be as valuable to them as the money they want."

"It's $9,000. It's not even that much money in the grand scheme of things," Cabel attempted to reason. "My car was more than twice that."

"Mine was less than half that," Troy shot back. "The point is, it doesn't matter. They will never get that money. And by the time they put me in the ground, they'll discover it wasn't worth the effort anyway."

"How about me? Do you not care about me at all?" Cabel asked, making the final appeal to reason. "Have you even taken the notion that what you're doing is inconsiderate to me?"

Troy had a harder time answering that question and sat silent while he pondered and fumed. He locked his jaw and stared longingly through the side window. He took all the time within reasonable comfort before he gave an answer.

"You're the last good thing about my childhood," his voice broke briefly and he swallowed hard to dispel the welling emotion.

"My parents separated after grade school and I spent a lot of time between the two of them. I got into drugs, I got my heart broken, and everything since those days has been a shit show. Before all that bad, there was you. Those memories of hide and seek in the woods and monster hunting are good, and that's the only good I've had to hold onto all this time."

The rustling of wind around the moving car was all that could be heard for a time.

Cabel finally broke the silence. "It makes sense, I guess, that we've spent this time together the last few days. I've been running from my childhood and you've been longing for yours. If you strip away those bad things and overlay the good, we've collectively led a pretty good life."

"I don't get that, but okay," Troy responded. "Sounds like you had the better length of the good times."

"Time feels longer when you're a kid. Remember what you said about the fingernails?"

Troy held his hands up and briefly stared at the backs. "I could use a trim now."

"I've got some clippers at the office," Cabel answered mindlessly. "I feel like I have to trim mine all the time."

The two arrived at the Huntsville Herald and Cabel parked in a gravel lot in the back of the building. He led Troy to the back door and through a narrow hallway into the production room. The building was old with aging wood panels covering the ancient timbers that bore the load of the once-proud building.

"My office is over there, if you want to hop in there until I get briefed." Cabel pointed to a windowless room in the middle of the building.

Troy entered the small office and sat in an old chair just inside the door. The burgundy walls were covered with clipboards of notes and technical paperwork about advertising rates, sizes, and technical specs of the newspaper. There were no pictures of family, or anything that tied Cabel back to home. Only work-related items adorned the walls. The desk was equally cluttered, with stacks of paperwork, consisting of notes and Xeroxed pictures that hid the desktop surface.

Troy would have dozed off in the quiet room if not for the uncomfortable chair. The padding had long worn off the seat, and the metal frame underneath made its presence known to Troy's lower region.

After about ten minutes, Cabel finally entered the room. He burst in with a bolt of energy and said nothing as he closed the door behind him and sat behind the desk. Despite the silence, it was clear that something had jolted him.

"Remember Floyd Alan?" Cabel finally asked, turning to Troy.

"Who?"

"The pharmacy guy," Cabel answered excitably. "I literally just told you this yesterday."

"Oh. The one that died," Troy recalled.

"Yes. It turns out he died of a drug overdose."

Troy seemed offended. "Are you telling me this because I'm the foremost expert on overdoses?"

"Not at all," Cabel replied, struggling to get to the point. "He didn't do drugs and there was no evidence that he ever had. So the police are investigating his death as a homicide."

"Wow, kind of ironic for a pharmacy owner," Troy commented. "What did he take?"

"Mixture of OxyContin and heroin," Cabel answered.

Troy sat in a stunned silence for a moment. Cabel shot him a perplexed look before continuing.

"Word I just received is that he had some dealings with some bad people. Rumor has it that he siphoned off much of his opioids to a drug gang that distributed them to a local network of dealers. It'll be hard to get confirmation on a lot of this, but..."

"You said this guy owned Right Pill?" Troy interrupted.

"Yeah, Alan's Pharmacy now."

Troy sighed and stood. He ran his index finger across the

grooves in the wall and walked to the other side of the room.

"I can vouch for the dealer end," Troy admitted.

"What? Why?" Cabel questioned.

"My overdose was Heroin and Percocet," he answered in a soft-spoken voice. "And my supplier was the pharmacist at Right Pill."

"Alan's Pharmacy," Cabel corrected.

"No, no. It was Right Pill at the time. The pharmacist who sold me the pills still works there. Name's Gordon McCann."

Cabel began breaking down this new information. "So if the pharmacist is still there, then that means the illegal operations likely continued."

"Mr. Alan did get into trouble," Troy concluded, which mirrored Cabel's thoughts as well. "The question is, who did he get in trouble with? I would guess that Mr. Alan wasn't the one doing the siphoning if it was going on long before he bought Right Pill"

"Well the answer as to who killed him feels more obvious by the minute," Cabel replied.

Troy grinned gleefully and slapped Cabel's desktop. "This is what you do for a living? It's like police work, but without all the confrontation!"

"Oh, there's confrontation," Cabel admitted after he turned to his computer screen. "It's more like police work, but without the firearm to defend oneself."

"Just to make sure I'm following you, you're saying that Oscuro whacked Alan?" Troy inquired.

"It had to be," Cabel insisted, swinging his office chair around. "How many crime bosses could be in these parts?"

"We could be safe then," Troy noted with a glimmer of hope. "If he's already knocked off one person this week, what are the odds of him coming after us this soon?"

Cabel nodded in agreement, but didn't speak as he swiveled to his keyboard. A notion was taking hold, centering around the fact that he had someone with inside knowledge of how all this drug-dealing business worked sitting right in his office, but he needed to put his thoughts in order first.

"What are you doing now?" Troy questioned.

"Notes," he answered while plastic taps of the keys

sounded. "This story is getting blown wide open and I need to make a list of what is and isn't off the record."

BRUSH

Night came and Cabel feared that Oscuro's fixers would as well. In the apprehension, he did all he could to avoid going home. After he turned Troy loose in town, Cabel phoned Miranda to ask her out that night for a drink at the tavern. He didn't expect her to agree, and she was reluctant at first since it was a school night. However, his desperate undertones must have rung apparent because she eventually agreed.

"I don't think I'll drink tonight," she told Cabel outside the bar. The November weather was indecisive with warmer days still on the forecast. The wind, however, had made its choice and blew through with enough frigidness to remind them of the winter yet to come.

"That's probably a good choice," Cabel admitted and shuffled his feet. He regained eye contact with her and revealed a genuine smile. "I just felt like spending some more time with you."

"I see," she smiled back a bit flirtatiously. "That's why I'm here, too."

Cabel pulled open the door. "I really appreciate it," he poured on the sincerity and then wondered if it was perhaps too much. "I won't keep you long."

The two sat at their familiar place at the bar and Cabel ordered a mixed drink for him and a soda for Miranda. After receiving their drinks, they sipped silently while looking around in different directions. Hair metal cranked loudly over the LED jukebox, dispensing rock ballads to an inattentive room. It was an hour before closing and the weekday crowd was much lighter than the previous Friday night when they had met for drinks.

"So, what have you been up to?" Miranda asked with an interested inflection as she nudged his forearm. "It's been a long time since... last Friday."

"Uhh, you couldn't have said it better," Cabel groaned. "It's been a rough couple of days. That's mainly why I needed to get out. To be here with you."

"What's the matter?" she asked, her hesitant smile retreating to concern.

"I've got a friend who is in trouble," Cabel answered and took a hard swig. "He's probably not got much longer to live."

"Oh dear," Miranda sympathized, but her tone quickly shot back to the positive as she followed with cautious optimism. "But maybe it's not that bad. Is there anything I can do? Should I pray?"

"Prayer would be helpful," he returned warmly, a smile flashed across his face. "Are you very religious?"

Miranda was surprised by the question. Before she could answer, Cabel let out a cackle.

"Caught you at your own game, didn't I?" he teased. "You're right, religious questions are the most fun."

She slapped at his arm playfully and laughed before taking

another sip of her soda. Cabel was about to continue when he noticed that Troy was sitting in the same booth he was last week. He wondered if he had been there all the time or just slipped in unnoticed.

"How does he keep doing that?" he pondered under his breath.

"What?" Miranda asked, catching only a few of the words.

Cabel finished off his drink and slapped the glass down on the bar. "That's the friend over there. I totally didn't see him there until now."

Miranda turned to study Troy carefully, and then suddenly whipped her head back to Cabel, her lengthy hair spinning outward with centrifugal force. Her eyes were narrowed in slight suspicion.

"He doesn't look like he's dying."

Cabel didn't have a great response for that and offered, "I suppose not," in lieu of an adequate answer.

"Well. Let's go talk to him," Miranda insisted, leaping from her bar stool.

"Wait!" Cabel objected, taken aback by her enthusiasm towards the subject of Troy's demise. He was too late to stop her. Miranda had already scurried to Troy's booth and stood above him.

"Cabel says you're dying," she stated frankly and without introducing herself.

Troy's eyes widened, momentarily thinking that she was one of Oscuro's assassins. "I don't know you?" he replied with confusion, his pitch trending higher as he said it.

"Troy, this is Miranda Murray," Cabel interjected, catching up with her. He placed a hand on Miranda's shoulder to balance himself as he sat down. Once in place, he scooted to the inside so she could take a seat next to him.

"Good to meet you," Troy answered cautiously, speaking at a slower pace than normal.

"Have you accepted Jesus Christ as your Lord and Savior?" Miranda asked abruptly, breaking the ice in her trademark fashion.

"Whoa!" Troy and Cabel both exclaimed in unison. Even Cabel was caught off guard by the question.

Miranda looked to Cabel confidently and wiggled her shoulders. "That's how you do it."

"So are you like one of those nutty church types?" Troy shot back just as bluntly. His speech was slurred and listless. Along with his reddish glazed eyes, it became clear he had been drinking for a long time.

Miranda was about to answer when Cabel spoke over her.

"How long have you been here? And how do I keep missing you when I come in?"

"Few hours," Troy replied, pulling a beer bottle up from the seat and polishing it off. He exhaled contently as he placed the bottle near the edge of the table. "If you scoot all the way in, the jukebox blocks you from view from the bar area."

"Ah," Cabel acknowledged.

"Back to my question," Troy began, turning his attention back to Miranda. "Are you some kinda Jesus freak?"

"Depends on my mood," Miranda replied, careful with how to word her answer. "On good days, when things are normal and the sun is shining, Jesus is in fact my homeboy; however, in the darker times – the times when I feel a sense of hopelessness, the times when I just want to punch stupid walls – well my outlook could go full non-believer."

Cabel nodded and commented coolly. "I'm digging this latest date. Drinks on one date, theological discussions on the next."

"Right?" she chuckled and raised her hand for a high five, which Cabel obliged.

This irritated Troy, who in his drunken haze, was genuinely interested in a biblical discussion.

"So do you believe that Adam and Eve rode on the back of dinosaurs and when it came time for the flood, Noah was like, 'screw you, T-rex, no room on the boat'?" Troy pressed as he pantomimed dinosaurs with his hands.

Miranda laughed at the question and the associated gestures. There was a playfulness in Troy's eyes that signaled to them the need for the kind of intellectual conversation that could only be enjoyed while inebriated.

To Cabel's bemusement, Miranda seemed to have decided not to let the moment slip away.

"Well, for one thing, I think Creationism is a load of crap."

"Ooh, now we're gettin' down to business," Troy verbalized giddily as he shimmied and leaned forward in his seat – the most physical movement he'd attempted so far. "Tell me why. Doesn't that conflict with Bible teachings then?"

"I follow the logic," she retorted and matched his excitement. She answered as if there had been a longing to make a case for her own beliefs. "The dates in the Old Testament don't line up with what we know today in the science world. The days of creation and the begat this–begat that which followed only add up to something like 5,000 years. It's rubbish – to borrow a British term."

"So you're a Christian, but believe that science is right?" Troy questioned for clarification.

"Well science is a law of God, and God has to obey his own laws."

Troy cocked his head in confusion and surprise, and Cabel more or less did the same.

"God obeys his own laws?" Troy finally asked.

"Absolutely," Miranda replied, pleased with how hooked she had the men. "I usually make a flow chart for this kind of thing, but there is neither napkin nor pen in front of me. Look at it this way: Does God obey his own laws? Yes. If the answer were no, then what was the point of Christ dying for our sins? He did so to break the laws of death – the law God made stating we cannot get into heaven if we are not perfect. If God could break his own laws, he would have done just that instead of initiating the divine loophole that is his son."

Both men were stunned by the soundness of the answer and Cabel knew his mouth was gaping as he stared at his lady friend with new appreciation.

"That's also why most miracles can be explained by science one way or the other," she added.

"God doesn't break his own laws?" Troy mumbled to himself, impressed by the idea. "That's too damn bad because I am in need of a miracle."

"So what do you actually believe?" Miranda pressed. "If you are truly about to die, the parameters of your faith need to be defined pronto."

Troy sighed. "I'm lost. I think there is something out there, er, up there. But, if God exists, I can't feel him."

"But you still believe it?" Miranda asked, leaning forward.

"I still believe it," Troy confirmed after a break.

"A dying man would much prefer the idea of staring at his creator as opposed to staring into the black abyss," Cabel added.

"Yeah," Troy nodded thoughtfully. "I can't picture nothing. I can't picture an abscess."

"Abyss," Cabel corrected.

"Then I'd say that's worth something," Miranda replied with a smile. "I'll pray for you. Maybe you can beat this thing. Either way, I think there's something waiting for you in the beyond."

Troy chortled at the offer. "Lady, I'm going to need all the help I can get."

Satisfied, Miranda leaned back in the seat as Troy turned to Cabel.

"You've been mostly silent about the God talk," he noted. "Tell me Cabel, what do you believe?"

Cabel straightened up in his seat. He had thought about his answer, but never put it to words.

"My parents were pretty religious, and because of that I found Jesus at a young age. I have always kept that core value locked in my heart, but over time it has been blanketed with heavy layers of cynicism."

There was a break in the monologue as Cabel decided if he wanted to continue.

"You know, my family spent a lot of time railing against church versus state. They wanted so badly for politics to rule them the same way God could, so they eventually hitched their wagon to a party to fill that need. They thought that their faith would inform their politics; but the more time passes, the more I came to believe it was the other way around. When you mix religion and politics, what you end up with is politics. The last time I talked with my parents, we got into an argument about this point, which culminated in me telling my mom to be careful who she worshiped. We didn't talk for a year after that. In that time, I clocked out from Christianity. Jesus is still in my heart, but the religion that claims him has no clue they left him in the dust."

Miranda's eyes widened at his confession. "Oy, now we're into politics. I think I may go ahead and have a drink now."

* * *

After the bar closed, it was apparent that Troy was in no shape to drive home. So Cabel drove Troy's deathtrap truck to the trailer park while Troy slouched over in the passenger seat. Miranda followed closely behind so that she could give Cabel a ride back to his vehicle at the tavern. Cabel thought this was the perfect plan, since Miranda sitting with a running car in the driveway would keep any potential attackers at bay.

As Cabel drove in silence, he thought about the discussion over drinks tonight and slowly came to the realization that he was exhausted with trying to help Troy. He was a great friend in their childhood, but his actions over the last week had cast them both in peril. Troy's stubbornness in the face of certain doom was the final nail in the coffin and delivering Troy to his fate was the only way he knew to stay out of a coffin himself.

Pulling into the driveway, he shut off the ignition and worked on getting Troy out of the truck. Cabel kept Troy propped up on one of his shoulders as they struggled up the steps to the weather-beaten trailer. The door was locked, which gave Cabel some peace of mind about threats waiting within. He shuffled Troy's deadweight, kneeling as if he were going to throw Troy over his shoulder. Cabel used his body and right hand to keep Troy upright while he used the other to remove the keys from Troy's pants pocket.

Shifting his stance again, Cabel inched to the door and cumbersomely placed the key in the lock. It turned with ease, but the door fought against the forces and took a shove to push open. Cabel felt around for a light switch but couldn't find one by the door. He abandoned the search when he realized he could make out the furniture shapes now illuminated by the headlights of Miranda's car.

The silhouette of the couch appeared in the center of the room and Cabel's feet sunk into the carpet as they stumbled closer. The room smelled of new carpet, which prompted a feeling of guilt from Cabel that he had not removed his shoes when they entered.

The guilt soon retreated in favor of fear, delivered by the dark room and the terrible thoughts of what could be. Was someone else lurking in the shadows? Cabel quickly plopped Troy on the sofa and received a mumbled swear, almost immediately followed by a loud snore. Not even bothering to take the time to make his inebriated friend more comfortable, Cabel fled back to the door. He did pause long enough to lock it from the inside and pull it tightly closed, double-checking with a few jiggles to make sure it was secure. Then he raced to Miranda's car and plopped into the passenger seat. Thankfully, she wasted no time putting the car in reverse, seeming to sense his need to be far away from Troy.

"Who is he in trouble with?" she asked with a stone-cold expression.

Cabel pressed his lips together and his eyes widened. "Wow, you are on point with the frankness tonight."

"Men in their twenties aren't dying unless they have cancer or a debt with dangerous people. And I can't help but notice he has a full head of hair."

"Well, you're right," Cabel admitted, throwing his hands outward. "He has the money and he has until tonight to pay up. But he won't do it."

"Well, that's dumb," she commented. "You can't take it with you."

"Right?" Cabel agreed rhetorically. "But he doesn't think they deserve it. He's going to die for what he believes in; I'll give him that."

"But what he's dying for is dumb," Miranda reiterated. "You should probably not be friends with him anymore. Well, assuming he makes it through tonight."

"I'm not sure I'm friends with him now," Cabel answered introspectively after a lull. "He's a ghost of my childhood. My best friend in those days, but if I had met him brand new yesterday, he would be someone who I wouldn't care for – possibly couldn't stand at all."

"Feelings of the past have a way of nullifying feelings in the present," Miranda philosophized as she turned into the parking lot of the now closed tavern. "Nostalgia is a hell of a drug. It can be as dangerous as hired goons, if you let it. Love makes us do dumb things. Love of what you once had is no different. Don't do dumb things out of love."

Miranda stopped and Cabel immediately got out of the car. He walked around the car and bent down to speak with her through her open window.

"You're saying I should never do dumb things for you."

"Is that a backdoor way of admitting your feelings for me?"

"It's a trial balloon to gauge your reaction."

Miranda placed a hand near her mouth and mimed an expression of surprise. "Good golly, I am flattered."

"So you won't do anything dumb for me either, right?" Cabel pressed.

Miranda brushed her hair back and her expression returned to a happy normal. "I hope to see you again soon."

Cabel smiled at her. "Yeah. Soon," he replied simply.

She smiled back and they shared a quiet moment in awe of one another.

"I do have a request," Cabel stated as he bent down further. "If you're doing some praying tonight."

"Yes?" she replied.

"Pray for me, too," he entreated quietly. "I got into this situation accidentally. I don't think I'm deep into it like he is, but I'm in danger of being drug down with him. Sometimes you can't tell how far into the darkness you've gone until you can't see to get out, and I'm not sure where I'm at now."

Miranda's smile gave way to a steely look of determination. "I will pray for you, too."

Awkwardly, Cabel kissed her offered cheek before she drove off into the night. He thoughtfully got into his vehicle and drove home.

* * *

The closing of the front door startled Troy just enough to bring him to consciousness momentarily. He managed to get his shoes off and shuffle into a more comfortable position on the couch. Once that position was achieved, he was out cold for the night. Neither the neighbor's barking dogs nor the siren from firehouse down in the valley could rouse him. Neither could Frank, Oscuro's right-hand man.

Frank had arrived an hour earlier. He jimmied open a window in the back of the trailer at a part of the structure not in view of neighbors. Once inside, he found a semi-comfortable spot in one of the neglected back rooms to wait. In the silent darkness, Frank eventually heard the commotion of Troy's arrival, but did not act since the clamor masked the number of people entering the trailer.

Now that it had been quiet for some time, Frank was ready to move. He slowly pulled the door open of the room he'd been waiting in, unavoidably making noise as the door rubbed tightly against the carpet. Frank stopped after a few inches to see if there was any reaction from the front of the trailer.

It was dead quiet.

Frank pushed the door a little further, enough for his thin frame to squeeze through the gap. He kept his focus to the front of the trailer and crept forward. He knew no one had passed the door while he waited, so there was no reason to keep his guard up for a potential attack from the rear.

At the end of the hallway, Frank's eyes were adjusted enough to the darkness that he could see the living room and kitchen area well. He could also see the shadowy outline of Troy sprawled out on the couch.

Having cleared the area with his thorough gaze, Frank approached Troy and stood over him. He examined the unconscious man and knew from the smell and deep snore that he was passed out drunk. In addition, the sound of someone leaving told him that he was dropped off by a designated driver, and the fact he afterwards heard no further stir – other than the plop of two shoes – told Frank that Troy was most likely too intoxicated to be aware of his surroundings.

To confirm this, Frank grabbed Troy by the shirt collar and pulled him up enough to slap him lightly across the face. Troy's snoring stopped momentarily, but he otherwise did not react.

Frank let go of the collar and erected himself once again.

He scanned the dark room for different items in which to stage an accident and discovered a few objects on the lamp stand next to the sofa.

Troy started to snore again.

In the black, Frank could make out an empty glass, an ashtray, a lighter, and a hairbrush laying on top of a stack of old newspapers. Frank thought carefully for a minute before selecting his weapon of choice.

* * *

Cabel woke up in the corner of his laundry room. He had barred himself in the small area and slept under a pile of dirty clothes and towels. Upon seeing morning light glimmering through the window, he scrambled out from under the laundry and checked the time.

"Crap," he groaned, realizing he would be late for work. He quickly pulled down his makeshift barricade and did a cursory inspection of the house while making movements towards the bathroom. Nothing appeared different from the night before.

In the shower, he began to wonder about Troy. Wondered if he was alive, and what the ramifications would be if he were.

Would I have to spend every night in the laundry room? he thought as well.

Once out of the shower, he picked up his phone off the bedroom dresser and rang Troy. The ring tone chirped and ultimately went to voice mail. Cabel continued to dress and attempted to call Troy again before he finished. He engaged the speakerphone option this time and tossed the phone on the bed while he put on socks.

The same result.

Cabel waited until he was completely dressed before he tried a final time, his anxiety level increasing as his friend's fate became more apparent.

One chirp... two chirps... three chirps...

"Hello," a groggy Troy answered.

"Hey!" Cabel replied, surprised to get an answer. "You made it through the night."

"You brought me home?" Troy asked in a groan. "Where's my truck?"

"Yeah, your truck's out there in the driveway," Cabel answered as he exited his house, jacket in hand. "You were pretty far gone last night."

"Thanks... for everything," Troy said slowly.

"No problem," Cabel replied. "Are you up for interviewing your pharmacist friend tonight?"

There was a hesitation on Troy's end.

"Oh yeah, about the Alan guy's death. Sorry, my mind ain't too good yet. Yeah, we can do that. I think he works on Wednesdays until six."

"Great," Cabel answered as he leapt into his vehicle. "I'm heading to work and I hope to be back by dark. I'll swing by around five-thirty. See you then?"

"Sure, that works," Troy agreed around a yawn.

Cabel disconnected and breathed a sigh of relief. Troy survived the night. He felt some guilt in his choice to leave Troy to his fate. Even more guilt filled him though in the realization that Troy was still a useful partner in helping him understand the criminal underworld he had lived around unknowingly for some time.

* * *

Cabel had a great day at work despite the negative thoughts swirling in the peripheral of his mind. His story on the suspicious death of the pharmacy owner came together nicely, with the local police force being surprisingly helpful with answering his questions. Knowing about Oscuro's possible involvement helped matters as well and he was able to mentally fill in gaps as he told the verified parts of the story.

Finishing what he could at the office, Cabel told his boss he was heading out to interview a pharmacist before driving straight to Troy's. Cabel pulled into the driveway while a muted orange twilight colored the sky.

Something felt amiss when he noticed Troy sitting in the bed of his truck, smoking a cigarette.

"You're like right next to your gas jugs," Cabel cautioned

after he got out of his vehicle.

"It's over," Troy declared in a sullen voice, flicking the butt of the cigarette into the dusty yard. "Oscuro has us outplayed. He is not just a criminal boss, he's a criminal mastermind."

Confused, Cabel walked up to the truck as Troy jumped from the bed.

"I was just interviewed by the sheriff," Troy revealed as he looked around the neighborhood to make sure no one else was within earshot.

"Why?" Cabel asked, his confusion growing.

"They killed Adriane Knotts," he revealed and lowered his head in unspoken shame.

"Your boss?" Cabel asked in shock, his eyes darting around the residential area now, too. "What happened?"

"Strangled," he answered, thinking back to the unpleasantness of the interview. "They didn't exactly tell me that, but I called a few friends that are good with rumors. Thankfully, I could act genuinely surprised when the cops told me what happened."

Cabel winced. "In a roundabout way, this is what you wanted," he pointed out, but not really wanting to do so. "You wanted to inflict pain on her. You got your wish."

"Emotional pain, though," Troy corrected unsympathetically. "Physical pain is a little much."

"I just don't get you, man," Cabel resigned. He started to say more when Troy's phone rang.

"Don't know the number," Troy noted before answering with the speakerphone option.

"Hello?" he answered, sounding more alert in the answer than what Cabel heard that morning.

"What did you think of our handiwork?" Oscuro barked over the line.

Troy recoiled in surprise but quickly regrouped to mock back. "Close, but no cigar. Still not what I hired you for."

"You're in some deep shit, so let me lay it out for you," Oscuro growled. "I'm sure you've been interviewed by the police by now. Being a disgruntled former employee, your name registers pretty high on their suspects list, but won't be enough to garner an arrest. We nudged that along by extracting some hair from a hairbrush one of my associates found in your trailer last night. Those hairs, for whatever reason, ended up on Miss Knotts' lifeless body. My estimate gives you about a week for the authorities to match those hairs to you."

Troy said nothing, but gave Cabel a jolted expression as the color left his face.

SON

The duo postponed their interview with Gordon until the next day. Thursday morning found the town rocked to the core by the news of Miss Knott's murder. Because heinous crimes were so rare in this area, news of the act spread like wildfire and found itself on everyone's lips.

It was hard for Cabel to know the truth about what really happened and not to use it to dispel all the rumors that were spreading. Even though a huge part of his job as a journalist was rumor control, the fact he would have to always withhold this truth made him uncomfortable. Therefore, he made every attempt to shy away from direct social interaction for most of the day's early hours.

It was late afternoon now and the pharmacist, Gordon McCann, would be getting off work soon as he had worked the morning shift at the drug store. Cabel and Troy had spent the past twenty minutes on stakeout duty in Cabel's vehicle, waiting for him to emerge from the store. They watched as the elderly and a few sickly younger adults filed in and out of the business, most leaving with white paper bags filled with a remedy for their ailments.

"Waitress at the York was telling folks it was a scorned lover," Troy noted as he clutched an empty Styrofoam coffee cup with the York Café logo printed on the side. "Jeff... something. If the cops take her lead, it could buy me some time."

"I think you have more time than you think," Cabel reassured. "Evidence like that goes to the state lab in Charleston. That's the only lab in the state and they tend to have a backlog. You have weeks, maybe a solid month until they get something back."

"I gave them my DNA when they interviewed me," Troy revealed, while the two continued to sit in Cabel's SUV. "I wouldn't have done that if I knew I had something to be guilty about."

"Not doing so would have suggested guilt," Cabel rebutted. "You did the best possible thing you could with the information you had at the time."

Troy scoffed. "That's easy for you to say when it's not your ass on the line."

Irritated by the comment, Cabel turned his head away from Troy and looked out the driver window, canvassing the cars in the half-full parking lot.

"I wouldn't have taken another day off if I didn't think my ass was on the line too," he admitted finally. "Your antics are also going to cost me my job, if nothing else."

Troy was irritated now as well and fidgeted in his seat. "Well la-de-da, you rich bastard. Does my life look like the Taj Mahal to you? I'm not like you, where I can drive around in this fancy robo car and dine on whore's ovaries and filly ming non every night."

Cabel furrowed his brow. "Hors d'oeuvres, and I think that second one was filet mignon. Neither are things I eat, by the way."

"Whatever," Troy dismissed.

"Also, the Taj Mahal is a giant tomb, so that's an analogy I would like to stray away from," Cabel added.

Troy sighed in dismissal.

"Besides," Cabel continued, "I've worked hard for the things I own. I saved up for a down payment on this car and make payments every month. I try to use my money wisely and not for idiotic things, like killing people."

"Screw you, dude," Troy shot back passively as he returned his gaze to the storefront of Alan's Pharmacy.

The sound of breathing was all that could be heard for a few beats until Troy began tapping nervously on the cup he was holding. He then turned to Cabel and changed the subject completely.

"That girl the other night. Terri?"

"Miranda," Cabel corrected curtly.

"Miranda, Miranda," Troy repeated as if he were trying to commit the name to memory. "I like her."

"So do I."

"That conversation with her the other night was weird, right?" Troy inquired, his voice raised in pitch. He was curious.

Cabel chuckled under his breath. "Yeah, she does that. It's a quirk of hers. That's the first time I've seen it deployed though."

Troy hummed from deep in his throat and looked away from Cabel. "It got me thinking about this community and the way they look at me. The way they judge. I'm not sure I fear God's judgment, but I damn sure fear theirs."

"Christian love can be a potent hate if utilized improperly," Cabel lamented. "It's hard to convince someone they're doing wrong when they're so sure they're doing the opposite. Maybe that's why they fear God's judgment. It means they can no longer act as the judge."

Troy turned back to Cabel. "Right? Give the judge mallet back to who it belongs. Just leave me alone."

There was silence for the moment as the topic dissipated into the stale air.

"Maybe we're no different," Cabel started, but was cut off by Troy.

"Here comes a special customer." Troy pointed to a younger man walking down the sidewalk.

The slender man wore a baggy red shirt and an equally loose pair of jeans. He had long black hair pulled into a ponytail with thick black stubble covering the sides of his face. He casually walked up to a newspaper box next to the door of a pharmacy. The box contained a stack of newspapers from a daily publication out of Virginia. Despite not being a great seller in the area, this particular box was always stocked full of the current edition.

The slender man put three quarters in the box, carefully pulled open the spring-loaded door, and bent down towards the stacks. He only had his hand in for a moment before he pulled back and let the door slam. From there, he vanished down the street just as casually as he had arrived.

"He didn't take a newspaper," Cabel noted.

Troy smiled and nodded. "That's how you can tell he's been in the game a while. He's gotten sloppy."

"What did he do?" Cabel asked, feeling the same sense of intrigue as he did at the chicken houses.

"Money drop," Troy replied matter-of-factly as he pointed to Gordon exiting the pharmacy. "Here comes McCann. He'll get into the box now to exchange the money for a bottle of pills."

"I've dealt with those machines before," Cabel added, filling in the blanks he knew. "There's a compartment underneath where the newspapers sit inside the machine. It's not easily visible and you could fit a lot of items under there. We used to put bricks inside ours to weigh it down."

"That's correct," Troy confirmed. "Different kinda bricks go in these."

"The hard stuff too?" Cabel checked.

Troy nodded. "Sometimes."

"More questions on that later. For now, how does McCann obtain extra pills without getting caught?" Cabel inquired as they watched Gordon round a corner into an alley.

Troy popped the passenger door open. "Let's find out."

The alley led to another alley that was directly behind the pharmacy. It was wide enough to fit five diagonally-parked cars, which was enough for all the employees the store had at any given moment. It was convenient parking for the employees, in that they could avoid parking on the street and paying the meter. The only downside was that the dead-end passage was difficult to back out of, which Troy and Cabel used to their advantage.

"Mr. McCann," Troy shouted from the mouth of the alley.

A startled Gordon looked up to see both men standing at the exit in a defensive stance. "Can I help you?" he asked guardedly.

"Come on, man, you know me," Troy announced loudly.

Gordon squinted. "Troy!" he realized before adjusting his voice to speak more softly. "There's cameras back here. I can't offer you anything."

"I'm only looking for words," Troy replied as he began walking closer. "Do those cameras have sound?"

"They do not," Gordon replied. "Is this about your overdose?"

"No, no. That's water over the bridge," Troy answered. "I'm more interested in the death of Mr. Alan."

Gordon began to look tenser as the other two approached. "I think my deeds are catching up with me," he admitted nervously. "I've got a go-bag ready and an exit strategy in place. Are you telling me it's time to flee?"

"We're not police," Cabel assured. "We've run into trouble with the same group of thugs and wanted to compare notes."

Gordon suddenly appeared a little more relieved. "Ok. I've got time. They're looking more into Mr. Alan's death in the Huntsville area rather than here. It's unlikely anything they find will point them in this direction, but you gave me pause for a moment."

"How do you get the pills out of the pharmacy without anyone noticing?" Cabel asked quickly before they got too far away from the topic to broach again. "They keep thorough logs on what comes in and out of drug stores. How do you keep from getting caught?"

Gordon's eyes abruptly darted to the camera, as if he momentarily doubted whether it had sound recording capabilities. The alleyway was otherwise sealed off from sounds other than loud echoes it had the potential to create. The back wall of the pharmacy was windowless, with white cinderblocks making up the long wall. Only a metal deadbolt door and electric meter broke up the monotony.

"I produce my own placebos that look identical to the painkillers we dispense," Gordon revealed in a whisper. "I then intersperse them with the actual painkillers at a ratio of one to ten so that every ten bottles of painkillers we sell gets me one that I can sell at a black-market price."

"Wow," Cabel sighed without bewilderment. "That would really add up over time."

Gordon beamed with pride in his expression. "I can usually fill a couple bottles in a day."

"Did Mr. Alan know this was going on?" Cabel pressed.

Gordon looked solemnly to the ground. "He was about to, hence me having the go-bag ready. I expect his death wasn't an accident. Someone else knew he was about to discover this operation."

"You think you know your community," Cabel groaned, feeling a mix of awe over the illicit enterprise and sadness in the existence of an underground economy that could support such a trade.

"Rural living seems like such a sunny disposition on the surface," Gordon commented, almost mockingly. "Just because the sun is shining doesn't mean the darkness isn't still there in the shadows, waiting. All it needs is a moment for the sun to go away. When it does, it pours over all."

The comment rubbed Cabel the wrong way, but he could not address it because Troy was feeling neglected.

"Back to my thing," he interjected. "Did El Oscuro take out Mr. Alan?"

Gordon quickly scanned the alley again. The very mention of Oscuro's name brought him back to an edgy state.

"He is that darkness."

"What do you know of him?" Cabel pressed. "We need more details about him or his associates."

"I'll give you his real name," Gordon offered, starting towards his car. "That should be lead enough for you."

"We'll take it," Cabel replied without hesitation.

"Chester Randolph."

Cabel's brows wrinkled. "Really?"

"Please go now," Gordon insisted and opened his car door. "I only offered you this information because I almost killed your friend here, and for that I hope this conversation serves as a suitable apology."

Troy shot a forgiving nod to Gordon. "Close enough."

Gordon gave a hasty nod and settled into his car, the slam of the door signaling the end of the interview. Troy and Cabel exchanged glances and headed back to Cabel's vehicle, contemplative silence trailing them.

"Why does Chester Randolph sound familiar?" Troy asked when the two were back in the SUV, driving down Main Street Chancy.

"He's a former mayor," Cabel revealed, keeping his eyes on the road. "Probably when we were in junior high, fifteen years or so ago."

"You would think people would have caught wind of him by now," Troy commented.

Cabel shook his head. "When I worked for the O'Brien Times, I spent a lot of time on slow days going through the archives and reading old editions of the paper. I saw a few pictures of Randolph back in those days, and I can tell you he is unrecognizable today. Aside from being in the wheelchair, he's put on quite a bit of weight, not to mention a hefty amount of facial hair."

"Probably helps that he lives in isolation, too," Troy added.

"Wish I had read more into the articles to find out what had happened to him," Cabel lamented. "I don't recall reading about the beginning and end of his time in office. I just remember the name and picture."

"Do we have to go back to the newspaper office to do research? Would you even want to go?" Troy asked before he noticed Cabel's mouth drop in revelation.

"When we went to the chicken house, there was a name on the sign when we went onto the property. Brian Randolph. The name looked familiar, but it just hit me. Wasn't he a couple years ahead of us in school?"

"Oh yeah! I know Brian," Troy replied excitably. "Remember Janice Fisher? It was his ex-girlfriend from way back. She's big into drugs and junk now. And she was the one I was talking to at the tavern that recommended hiring Oscuro for the hit!"

"Well, there we go," Cabel commented, thrilled at how good a lead they had. "Now where can we find her?"

"The tavern – no doubt," he confidently answered. "She basically lives there."

They were passing the funeral home at the edge of town when something in the parking lot caught Troy's eye.

"Pull over. Pull over now!" Troy shouted as he banged on the window.

"What?" Cabel yelled in reply as he swerved into an empty space on the main drag.

Troy did not answer, and before the vehicle could come to a complete stop, had leapt out and rushed to the funeral home parking lot.

Cabel put the vehicle in park and craned his head to where he could see what was happening. In the lot was a young woman holding the hand of a small child. The woman wore a sundress, which seemed like an odd choice for November – even though it had been unseasonably warm of late. She was fair-complected and had a full head of auburn hair. They were walking towards the funeral home's entrance before being intercepted by Troy, who stood a good ten feet apart from them.

Cabel continued to watch as all three stood completely still, staring down one another, not knowing if any words were being exchanged. Suddenly, the woman broke free from the child and rushed Troy. A purse the woman had draped over the other arm suddenly came into play as a weapon, which she used to strike Troy across the chest. Troy hunkered down as another strike came in, this time with the addition of an open hand, to slap him in the exposed areas of his shielded face.

Cabel was not surprised, given the week's events; however, he was confused as to what prompted Troy to engage the woman. Once she finished her assault, the woman regained her composure and returned to the child. Taking the boy by the hand, the two walked in agitation past Troy into the funeral parlor.

A crestfallen Troy returned to the car, his face red in the places the woman managed to land a blow.

"What the hell were you doing?" Cabel asked. "Isn't this the funeral home where your ex-boss is? Was it not enough to destroy her that you have to harass her family now, too?"

Troy put his hands on his face and slumped down on his seat.

"I haven't been entirely honest with you," Troy started. "Me and Adriane's history goes a little deeper than the standard employer/employee relationship that I have with normal bosses. It wasn't so much that I wanted to inflict pain on her as it was to inflict pain on her sister."

"Katy or Ginger?" Cabel asked, remembering the names from her mother's obituary.

Troy nodded. "Ginger. My wife."

Cabel had just put the car in motion, but pumped the brake in reaction to the revelation. "What?"

"See, the hit on her mother was to be three-fold. For one, it would have evened the score with Adriane, who was a horrible boss and even more horrible sister-in-law. Two, it would have caused Ginger to come out of her hiding place and, if nothing else, I could at least find out if I had a son or daughter."

Cabel was conflicted about this revelation and tried hard to cast the news in a positive light. "Well. I guess that's a bit more noble than killing someone for vengeance. Still, you could have just told me that."

"And three, I just really didn't like their mom," Troy concluded. "The feeling was mutual too."

Cabel shook his head and became more critical as he spoke, "How did you not know your mother-in-law passed away? We live in the age of information, and besides that, small towns like this pass on that kind of information rapidly. Further evidenced by the fact that I've heard twelve different rumors to Adriane's death just this morning, and that's with trying to avoid people."

"It was when I was away," Troy explained while he continued to stare back in the direction of the funeral home. "I knew she had been in poor health for a while, which is why her death shouldn't have been a surprise to anyone."

"Instead it was a surprise to you," Cabel noted and bit his lip at the thought of the irony.

Troy remained distracted.

"Search engine results probably would have given you the answer more quickly," Cabel continued. "Even then, you could have hired a private investigator. That probably would have cost you less that ten grand."

"It was a son, by the way," Troy revealed dourly, ignoring everything else. "I have a son."

"And the obituary from two years ago said they live in Delaware," Cabel stated, having noticed earlier.

"I hope she named him Dixon," Troy added, ignoring what Cabel just said. "I told her early on that if we ever had kids, I wanted a boy named Dixon. You know, like Mason Dixon but backwards." He sighed in amusement thinking about the cleverness of the name. "I told her it would mean a lot to me. I hope she did it."

Cabel decided not to say any more as they headed to the tavern. In the aftermath of a pocketbook beat down, Troy had won a small victory, and since winning was a feeling Troy knew little of, Cabel decided to let him have it. Instead he turned his focus on what sort of information he might be able to glean from Janice.

When he pulled into the parking lot, Cabel decided to remain in the car, skeptical that Janice would be at Robinson's Tavern. He did, however, instruct Troy to bring her outside if she was, in fact, there.

While he waited, Cabel contemplated their situation and considered the various outcomes. The specter of death loomed large in all the scenarios he worked through and he slowly arrived at the conclusion that they may have to be the ones to summon death to suit their own needs.

But getting away with it? There was little Cabel could recall getting away with when he chose to create low-level chaos in the past. But the ineptitude of the dwindling local law enforcement would help. The sheriff was finishing his final term and had retirement in sight. Though he had done a fine job in the past, he treated the position like a senior in the last days of high school.

School? It was that word that took Cabel back to a specific memory of grade school. Of the bullies of his youth, there was no greater than Lucas. The chief bully was reprimanded one day for throwing rocks near the teacher's parking lot, which ran parallel to the playground.

The teacher, Mr. Giesterkoch, had been heavy in his verbal abuses of students that day. An unpleasant man who employed the punishments of days past didn't judge based on behavior, but whom he preferred among the children.

This was not Cabel, and the amount of poor reports sent home reflected that. Sometimes erroneous, sometimes fair, but always scathing and resulting in some form of punishment.

Lucas was not one the teacher favored either, but the chief bully had a particular knack for getting himself out of trouble. Whether it be sweet talking or outright threats of violence against other students in exchange for their silence, he rarely ever saw the punishment he really deserved.

On that particular day, Cabel saw an opportunity to even a score. Near the end of recess, he asked to go to the bathroom, but slinked off to the teacher's parking lot when no one was looking. Because it was a small school, there were no hall monitors, or even any personnel not on the playground, with the exception of the cafeteria staff. There would be no one to verify his whereabouts.

At the edge of the lot, Cabel located a rock that fit firmly in the palm of his small hand. He grasped it tightly as he located the Wagoneer of the despised teacher. He hunkered down next to the opposite vehicle and waited for the bell. It rang minutes later, a shrill cacophony of clanging metal, which prompted Cabel to begin counting. He knew from other kid's observations that there was exactly two minutes until a second bell sounded, and his destination number was 120.

At the two-minute mark, Cabel flung the rock as hard as he could at the passenger window, breaking it just as the clamor of the bell drowned out all other sounds. Cabel quickly leapt to his feet and slid along the brick wall to the front door of the school, slipping in just as the crowd of students was sorting into their respective classrooms.

Lucas was blamed for the damage and his parents were called in for a conference that resulted in them having to pay for a replacement window. He was also suspended for two days, which left Cabel with a twisted satisfaction of knowing he had struck back in a way no one expected.

Cabel had all but forgotten the incident and felt it had returned to him at the time he most needed it. He would have to strike back again in a way no one would suspect.

His thoughts were interrupted by the thunk of the vehicle's back door swinging open. It seemed that Troy had been right about Janice's whereabouts and had brought her back to the SUV for interrogation.

If it had not already been mentioned, it would otherwise be apparent from Janice's appearance that she had a drug problem. Her frail frame left few bones in her body to the imagination and the sleeveless shirt she was wearing exposed a good number of them. Sunken eyes were nearly covered by her dirty blonde bangs that reeked of cigarette smoke. Cabel, one to keep his vehicle as clean as possible, immediately regretted the decision to invite her inside.

"We need to find Brian Randolph," Troy demanded as soon as he closed his passenger door.

"Got yourself in trouble, didja?" Janice replied, her Appalachian accent thicker than most.

"That was crappy advice you gave me, Janice. It's been a shit show ever since," Troy replied in irritation.

Janice gave an unconcerned cackle. "Well, ya didn't have to take my advice. I was jest throwin' out some options. I noticed yer boss turned up dead. Do ya not have the money to pay 'em?"

"I didn't have her killed, for the record," Troy clarified and aggressively tugged her arm. "Don't you go telling anyone that I did that, or that I was even involved in that!"

"Calm yerself down," Janice attempted to soothe, making a pushing down motion with her free hand. "I ain't gonna tell nothing to nobody. Papa Randolph pays me on the side to usher people his way. I hasta keep my silence cause it wouldn't take much to make me look like an overdose."

Troy jerked her arm again, causing her to lean her head against his. "You can't guarantee what you say in your drug-fueled rants," he barked into her ear.

Janice shook her arm free and threw both hands in the air and shrugged dramatically. "I said what I said. If I screw up, I'm as good as dead."

Cabel, who had been watching the display in the rear-view mirror, finally turned in his seat. "We just have a misunderstanding that needs clarified. I need to find Brian."

"Brian lives in Colorado," Janice revealed.

Cabel started to feel defeat before she continued.

"Yer in luck, though. Buck season starts Monday and he always brings a huntin' party with him. He usually comes to town the Thursday before, so you oughta find him 'round town as early as this evenin'."

"I see you're still keeping tabs on him," Troy joshed.

"Damn right," Janice shrieked proudly. "He was the love of my life. Just 'cuz he married that Roman lady don't mean I can't still stalk my man online."

"Shoulda put a hit on her through his dad if you loved him so much," Troy egged on Janice. "I'd like to see what he'd done in that case."

Janice chortled contemptibly. "Oh believe you me, old man Randolph favored me over that hussy. That was part of the reason they had a fallin' out. Pap didn't approve of this Roman girl. I think it got even worse when they had a kid together."

"Falling out?" Cabel intervened. "Are we talking a sizable rift?"

"Oh yeah," Janice confirmed. "They don't speak. Brian don't want nothin' to do with 'em. Use his land fer hunting and that's about it. He was pretty engrained in that family business, too."

"Which business? The chicken business or the 'other' business?" Cabel inquired.

"Both," Janice replied simply.

"You think he could give us details of the 'other' business?" Troy questioned, mimicking Cabel's use of air quotes while saying "other."

"Oh hell yeah, he could tell ya 'bout every inch of it," Janice replied confidently. "Sure he would, too, if he thought he could bring down his pap without bein' held accountable."

Cabel looked to Troy with a devious smile and back to Janice. He reached into his jean pocket and pulled out a crumpled up twenty-dollar bill.

"Great information. Have a couple rounds on us," Cabel thanked.

"Preciate it," she answered and snatched the money from his hand. She then shuffled awkwardly before finding the handle to exit the car.

Troy moved back into the front passenger seat and watched Janice reenter the bar before turning back to Cabel.

"So what's your plan? You've got something on your mind."

"If we can locate Brian, he'll tell us everything about their operation," Cabel answered.

"How does that help us?" Troy wondered. "I'm still going to go to jail in the end."

"Maybe," Cabel answered, the devious smile returning. "But you've got nine-thousand dollars you can put towards a good lawyer. In the meantime, we can strike back and strike back hard."

Troy put up a suspicious smile and cocked his head.

Cabel continued. "It's the only way I'm going to feel at peace again. I'm not going to spend the rest of my life huddled in my laundry room while these Appalachian mobsters are still running free."

"See what I did there?" Troy mused. "You're turning into me."

Cabel wanted to deny this, but said nothing in the difficulty in doing so. Something inside him had been unlocked and his sensibilities were being overtaken by a slow-burning desire for retribution.

10

CAMO

Three pickup trucks pulled up to the York Café just after night fell on Chancy, some not looking to be in much better condition than Troy's old beater. In contrast to his truck, these were vehicles clearly marked for hunting. All the older model trucks had camouflage patterns of green and brown spray-painted across their rusted bodies. Toolboxes in the bed and fully stocked gun racks in the back window completed the picture.

Cabel insisted Troy wait across the street while he sat on a bench just outside the restaurant. Since Cabel was not a suspect in Adriane's murder, he secretly worried that spending too much time in public with Troy would arouse suspicion.

Once parked along the streets, two men exited from each of the single-cab pickups. Cabel didn't have a good idea of what Brian looked like and deferred to Troy to alert him to who he was within the party.

Troy motioned wildly from across the street, signifying that this was the correct party. Cabel tried to understand the flailing hand gestures to more specifically identify Brian, but realized he would get it wrong no matter whom he chose. He quickly decided to approach identification broadly as he stood up.

"Brian?" Cabel called out towards the group about to enter the cafe.

A man near the front in an orange hat whipped his head around. "Yes?"

"Hey man, I haven't seen you since high school," Troy jumped in, having just dashed from across the street. "What have you been up to?"

Brian motioned for the other men to go into the restaurant and approached Troy and Cabel as the group complied. "I'm sorry I don't recognize you."

"Troy Mason, I was a few classes back in high school."

"I'm Caleb," Cabel added, unsure about giving the actual name he used. After a moment's hesitation, he expounded, "Caleb Walsh."

"Again, I'm sorry," Brian apologized with a shake of his head.

"We need to talk to you about your father," Cabel admitted, seeing that the plan was going nowhere.

Brian smirked suspiciously. "Are you associates or adversaries of my father?"

"Let's just say we're on the wrong side of his ire," Cabel answered.

"Huh," Brian expressed, clicking his tongue off the roof of his mouth. "Never run across live ones before. This makes me unsure of the best way to proceed."

"Well our time is running out," Troy noted. "Anything you can give us would help."

Brian laughed. "Oh no, don't get me wrong. I'm willing to

help as much as possible. My father is a blight that is eroding away the purity of these parts. His undoing would be in the best interest of the God-fearing people who remain."

Brian looked as if he was about to say more, but remembered the party of fellow hunters waiting for him inside.

"Why don't you meet me tonight at the motel?" he suggested. "Room 125 at Medea, preferably before midnight. I don't think we need to do any incognito nonsense. Dad isn't interested in tracking my movements."

"We'll be there," Cabel confirmed, trying to contain his exuberance in getting such a great lead.

* * *

Motel Medea sat on the east end of town, on the opposite side of Chancy as the funeral home. It was after eleven and Troy had been impatiently waiting for Cabel to arrive.

Standing outside his truck, Troy kept swiveling his head around in all directions, nervous about being there alone. He probably should have stayed in the truck, but he'd gotten bored sitting and decided to make a few laps around the lot. A light drizzle dampened him and he began to shiver, but refused to reenter his vehicle, not liking the confined space.

As his anxious gaze panned around again, he took in the two-story motel wrapped around an empty parking lot that faced the main road. All the guests had enough parking in the spaces along the building, leaving the middle of the lot barren. A service station once sat in the middle, but was demolished in the late 1990s, not long after the town's only factory was shuttered. After the closure, there was no longer enough need for three gas stations to exist. Large discrepancies in the color and levelness of the asphalt could be seen where the underground gas tanks had been removed a generation earlier.

Troy knew it well. His father owned the station in those days and its closure is what forced Troy out into the world. In his youth, he had dreamt of being the station's manager, but that dream was extinguished along with the factory jobs. His dad, Mitch, took a job as a mine inspector. And since O'Brien was one of the few counties in West Virginia not to claim a coal mine, this put his dad on the road quite a bit and left Troy to his own devices. He didn't like being alone and spent his days running with a rough crowd. The rowdy nature of his friends fueled his propensity for recklessness, and ushered him to his most regrettable choices.

Troy forced those memories away when he noticed that Cabel had finally arrived.

"What took you so long?" Troy asked Cabel as he approached.

"Sorry, I was finishing a story," Cabel expressed. "The news doesn't rest or write itself, so taking a day off means little."

"Well let's go in, I'm freezing my ass off," Troy griped.

The two took off in the direction of where they believed Brian's room to be located.

"Supposed to be warmer this weekend. Almost like summer they say," Cabel mentioned as they huffed along.

"I'm cold now though," Troy grumbled. "Wish you would have gotten here faster."

Troy pulled open a rusted screen door to knock on the closed wooden door to Room 125. The exterior design of the motel caused the room entrances to become weathered over time. The grimy stucco that covered the building gave it a worn-down look as if it had seen better days but didn't care to recall them.

Brian pulled the door open and inspected the two. He was wearing basketball shorts and a West Virginia University t-shirt, which clashed with the University of Colorado ball cap on his head. In the background, a 24-hour news channel aired the days' events.

"Come on in guys," Brian finally invited as he pulled the door the rest of the way open.

The two entered quietly and were fast to take a seat on a couch near the door.

"So tell me. What has my father done to you?" Brian cut to the main topic straight away.

"I paid him to do a hit job, a percent up front. He didn't do it, but still wants the rest of the money," Troy complained.

Brian then looked to Cabel as if he was expecting him to answer as well.

"I'm just an accessory to this," he finally admitted and shrugged apathetically.

"As much as I would love for you to take my father down, there's no good way to do so," Brian admitted. He paused briefly and cracked open a sweating beer on the end table. "He covers his tracks very well. Burns any paper trail, gets his insulin and other medications from the pharmacy he traffics opioids through, only takes cash, launders it through the poultry operation – which I'm annoyed to find is still in my name, by the way. Every property he occupies in this county is in my name."

"Troy first met him at a cabin up Turkish Knob," Cabel revealed. "Do you know anything about it?"

"Yes," Brain answered. "Turkish Knob is actually where we'll be doing our hunting this Monday. Dad's got – or, I guess, I have – 150 acres up there, and doesn't care about people using it as long as they keep a wide berth from the cabin."

"It seems like he would pretty well be unprotected up there," Troy noted, otherwise deferring questioning to Cabel.

"Well, no one thinks he lives up there full time. That is to say, the ones who know that he's still alive. To the general public, he's just a ghost. To the criminal community, he's just an old crippled man who has no place but a shack in the middle of the woods. No one who has challenged him has thought to check there after hours. Even so, he's got a pretty extensive surveillance system hidden in the brush. His hired help is always on call if one of the sensors is tripped."

"I noticed some of those out there," Cabel confirmed. "Tell me, does he have a lot of people challenge him?"

Brian laughed. "Not anyone in his debt. Like I said, you guys have made it further than most. His empire is built into a network of illicit activities across West Virginia. Copper theft is a big deal in the state, but he doesn't allow it here. He'll help traffic what's stolen elsewhere, but he won't let any group come in to take what's here. There are a lot of people in the network who would love to change that, but they're not sure how to undermine my dad's control of this region."

"For a three-person operation, that's pretty impressive," Troy remarked.

Brian nodded and took a drink.

"Tell me about his help," Cabel requested and leaned forward on the couch.

Brian drained his can of beer and hopped off the bed. He went to the mini refrigerator and got out a full one. He offered one to each of the men, but both declined.

"Len and Frank are pros at what they do," Brian stated, reseating himself on the bed. "Neither live in the county. Len comes from two counties over and Frank has a swanky place in Stonewall County."

"Len lives in Huntsville?" Cabel asked for clarification.

Brian nodded. "He does everything in his power to lie low. Even takes a desolate back road through farm country to keep from being tracked."

"I know which road you're talking about," Cabel revealed and cracked a smile. "I've taken it a few times on the way from work just for the hell of it."

"If it's a confrontation you're looking for, I can give you specific times and places to find them alone," Brian offered. "You'll never get to my dad unless you take them out first. Even if you managed to take dad out first, they have directives to hunt down and slaughter everyone involved and their families. So, taking them out first is priority."

The two sat in silence of Brian's presence, pleased with how helpful he was being. Brian took this opportunity to chug his beer before continuing.

"Friday is key because that day they do money pickups in Baker and Stonewall Counties respectively. That day Len leaves at about four in the afternoon to head back to Huntsville. He does a pickup at the park there, but you could probably catch him easier on the back road if you played your cards right. I'm not telling you how to do your job though."

"No, I think that's a great idea," Cabel commended. "Isolating them is our only chance. Just to be thorough, where is the money drop at the park?"

Brian struggled for a moment to spit out the name. "Virgil. Victor. Ver... Vernon! Vernon McGuire Memorial Ball Field. There are three fields there, but go to that one. If you follow the third base line straight back, there's a tree a hundred meters away in that direct line. At the base of that tree, there is a memorial plaque. If you slip the plaque from its base there's a false bottom that they store the money in."

"Smart," Cabel said simply.

"Frank is a little trickier," Brian continued. "He's a hide-in-plain-sight kinda guy, so he's a little more difficult to get the drop on without anyone noticing. His money pickup is at Antaeus Park outside of Westland."

Brian paused, looking to the ceiling in thought, and polished off his can before continuing. "Actually, this may work to your advantage. Have you ever driven by that park this time of year?"

"Yeah, they have an ungodly amount of Christmas lights set up there," Cabel answered.

"Right!" Brian exclaimed, pointing at Cabel. "And they start putting them up just after Halloween. Unless it has changed, his drop is in a compartment under the seesaw closest to the parking lot. Once night falls any other time, it's an easy grab for him, but the lights blow his cover at this time of year."

"Not to mention all the passersby gawking at the lights," Troy added.

"He usually pushes the retrieval to late at night," Brain continued. "We're talking two in the morning."

"Friday sounds like a good time to me," Troy commented, looking to Cabel. "I say we each take on one of them."

Brian put his hands in the air. "I don't want to know nothing about how you're going to do it," he expressed. "Just do it, and I don't want to hear from you again after you hit the door here."

"You basically just handed us the game plan," Cabel noted.

"Listen, if I'm willing to go after Dad, he's even more willing to go after me," Brian replied. "If he catches wind of me conspiring with you, there will be nothing to stop him from gutting all of us. I've made a new life as a professor in the Centennial State and quite enjoy my life apart from his disapproving gaze."

"Aren't you concerned about him seeing us here?" Troy wondered.

"Nah," Brian replied casually as he put his hands behind

his head. "I heard that a woman was murdered last night. I'm assuming that was their handiwork."

Cabel and Troy both nodded hesitantly.

"That's too close an interval for them to kill again," Brian speculated. "If they murder someone on back-to-back days, it will look like there's serial killer on the loose, and the dots will more easily connect back to them."

Cabel was relieved that he wouldn't be spending the night in his laundry room again, until Brian added one last note.

"That is, unless they make it look like an accident."

Cabel chuckled nervously. "Well with that, I think it's time we take off."

The three men stood.

"I hear you have a kid," Troy blurted. "A son?"

Brian seemed suspicious of the question and hesitantly nodded.

Troy puffed his chest. "I have a son, too."

"Oh yeah? How old?" Brian inquired.

Troy's pride deflated as quickly as it had ballooned. "I'm not completely sure."

"Oh," Brian replied as if he regretted asking the question. "Well, mine just turned ten."

"You've been at odds with your dad for that long?" Cabel inquired, putting together this information with what Janice had told them.

"It's true," Brian confirmed. "Where did you get your information about me from?"

"Janice," Troy swiftly replied.

Brian cocked his head back. "Ah. I don't guess she'll ever let that go."

He then walked to the entrance and pulled open the door. The others followed.

"I love my wife and dad hated her just for who she was," Brian admitted. "I had to choose between love or hate."

Cabel passed him and pushed open the screen door, letting Troy move beyond him.

As they stepped outside, Brian continued, "I mean, between love and hate, why is that even a choice you need to think about?"

Cabel nodded in agreement and Brian, seemingly satisfied with his response, closed the door. Outside, a cool wind blew, and with it, the light drizzle continued. Both men now seemed unfazed by the dampness as they moved through the lot.

"What do you think?" Troy asked with an unlit cigarette clamped between his teeth.

"Any number of things," Cabel answered vaguely as he inspected the sprawling motel.

"Listen, you can bunk with me tonight if you want," Troy offered as he fumbled with a lighter. "My dad is out of town until Saturday so I'm going to crash on his couch."

Cabel ignored the offer as he continued to look around. "Do you think there are any cameras out here?"

Troy joined him in searching the roof lines, corners, and crevasses above the motel walkways.

"I'm not seeing anything," Troy declared.

Cabel looked towards a small building attached to the edge of the motel's short side. It was the farthest section from them, but he could make out a crop of dark hair peeking over someone's seated position behind a counter.

"Do you know anyone that works here?" Cabel asked Troy.

"Not that I know of," Troy answered, midway through his smoke.

"Main offices usually have a wall with monitors on them, if there is a surveillance system," Cabel noted. "Go in there and see if you see one."

"Why don't you do it?" Troy shot back.

"I do know people who work here," Cabel answered. "Ask them where the ice machine is or something."

Troy flicked his cigarette. "What if I know them?"

"Ask them out on a date," Cabel flipped back, half joking. "Come on man, you got this."

Troy turned, grumbling something incoherent as he made his way towards the small office. Its neon vacancy sign illuminated the misty night while the damp ground bore its reflection.

Cabel waited until he knew Troy had committed before slowly approaching the camouflage trucks he saw on Main

Street earlier. Still checking for cameras, he made his way to the passenger side of one he believed to be Brian's truck.

Troy reemerged a minute later, shaking his head as he approached. Once Cabel was sure he understood the signal, he jerked the latch on the door to discover that it hadn't been locked. He slowly pushed the squeaky door open as Troy arrived.

"What are you doing?" Troy whispered frantically.

"Anyone from this town knows it's the only place in the world where you have the luxury of unlocked car doors," Cabel, pleased with himself, replied.

Cabel searched for a latch that could fold down the single cab seat back. He found just that, and with a few hard pulls, the vertical portion of the bench tipped forward. Behind it they discovered a pile of clumped work shirts. Moving some of these around revealed what they had been hiding – three additional shotguns in addition to the two in the back window.

"You see," Cabel stated smugly, motioning to his find. "If my father was a country crime kingpin, I would be packing some extra firepower, too."

Troy chuckled under his breath. "Well, I'll be damned."

Cabel pulled out one of the guns and handed it to Troy as he balanced a second on his foot. A little more digging revealed a box of ammunition.

"We'll leave the third gun here," Cabel stated before he covered it back with the shirts. "It'll be less obvious these are missing that way."

Troy, eyes darting around, tucked the shotgun under his jacket and Cabel did the same, stocks of both remaining exposed below their waste line. Nevertheless, Cabel quietly closed the door and the two hobbled off into the night.

"Do you think the night clerk saw us?" Cabel asked as they reached his vehicle on the far side of the property.

"No," Troy answered flatly. "She's busy watching TV." He paused. "And probably thinking about our upcoming date."

* * *

Later that night, as Cabel curled up with his appliances, he began going through his plan of attack in confronting Len. His imagination ran away with him and he began subconsciously punching and kicking under the blanket. He didn't know it, but he was slowly drifting to slumber. This was interrupted by his dreamscape providing him with a nightmare scenario. What happens if he loses?

The sensation of being tossed to the ground was too real and his body jolted violently in response. Wide awake, he sat up on the floor and rubbed his face. He then checked the clock on his phone.

12:34.

Armed now with the growing concern of his demise and the fact that he may never get another shot again, he decided to give Miranda a call. The phone hummed more times than usual before she finally answered.

"Hello," a sleepy voice whispered.

"Hey Miranda, it's Cabel," he spoke softly, trying not to rattle her too much at the onset.

There was a pause, Miranda obviously checking the time before responding, "Cabel, it's a school night."

"I know," he answered regretfully.

"Are you in trouble?" she asked, becoming gradually energized by concern.

"No."

"Is your friend okay? Did he survive the other night?" she was fully awake now. "Ooh, ooh. Did you hear about the woman who was murdered?"

"I know everything," Cabel responded reluctantly. "My friend is fine, too. For now."

"Are you fine, too?" she asked again, but in a different way – more softly this time.

"For now," he answered more honestly. "I'm in deeper than ever, though."

"Oh dear," Miranda commented, trailing off.

There was a slight pause as Cabel struggled with what to say next. He finally decided to speak up when he feared Miranda was falling back to sleep.

"Hey, I have to be honest," he started. "I really like you and wanted to know if you would like to go fishing with me on

Saturday."

"Fishing?" she balked. "This time of year? It's deer season. I don't think the fish are out."

"Fish are out year-round," Cabel replied smoothly. "It's supposed to be in the mid-seventies on Saturday and it will be on my family's property in Tipperton. My granddad has tons of farmland along the river, so you won't need a fishing license or anything. Just bring yourself – I'll provide everything else."

Miranda paused. "Okay. But you'll bring yourself, too."

Cabel choked in joy of her response. "I hope to, but keep praying just in case."

"Will do," she replied.

Minutes later he was off the phone and sleeping soundly on the cold tile, no longer thinking about the unsavory things that had to be done to regain a place in his own bed. *At least now,* he thought to himself, *I have a reason to live past Friday.*

DOWNHILL

Since the end of the year was growing near, Cabel was running dangerously low on the vacation days he could take from work. He had to work Friday, as much because of the deadlines as the threat of unpaid leave. Knowing what was planned for later in the day, and not wanting to involve his SUV in those activities, he reluctantly offered Troy a vehicle trade for the day. Troy agreed gleefully and promised to return it in one piece at the end of the night.

Cabel, despite drowsiness from the continued inability to sleep well in his laundry room pile, arrived at work early. He didn't feel it was a good idea to be noticed driving a murder suspect's vehicle, so he made sure to get the vehicle out of O'Brien County before daybreak. Cabel parked Troy's truck in the overflow parking lot of a poultry processing facility, located within walking distance to the newspaper and far from the surveillance cameras of the main facility. In addition, Cabel would need to leave early in order to prepare to implement his plan to confront Len and wanted to make sure he got in a full day of work beforehand.

Throughout the day, Cabel grew paranoid that his coworkers were onto him. Being journalists after all, it was natural for them to ask a simple question and uncover vast conspiracies if the answer didn't land in a straightforward way. It was a bloodhound sense and all they had to do to pick up a scent trail was to be given that first whiff of something pungent.

"Where's your car today?" Wes, one of their newer stringers asked as he entered the building. Cabel could feel his blood pressure rise as one of their most green writers already detected that something was out of sorts.

"Oil change," Cabel replied plainly. He kept his head down and calculated the many ways he could accidentally blow the lie wide open.

"Cool," Wes answered. "Need a ride to pick it up after work?"

Cabel waved him off. "Nah. I'm leaving early, so I can just walk up and get it."

Wes simply nodded and walked off, seemingly satisfied with the answer. Cabel felt fortunate that he wasn't asked what service station his vehicle was located. Any answer he gave could easily be verified as a falsehood. Cabel breathed a sigh of relief and pushed his office door partly closed in an attempt to minimize further interactions with staff.

He plopped down in the green office chair, which creaked and popped with all the signifiers of its years of use. Cabel leaned back and crossed his arms, trying hard to keep his mind off the evening and ward off the associated nervousness.

The week's edition of the newspaper sat in front of him and he stared at his front-page blurb about the passing of Floyd Alan. The small paragraph served as a teaser to the obit further in the paper, but Cabel was pleased it sat well above the fold.

The story about Floyd's death being ruled a murder was primed to run in the next edition and Cabel was further happy that his efforts would result in more front-page real estate.

It was juxtaposed with the story about the string of robberies written by others on the staff that sparked a notion. Were all crimes in their small community connected by something larger?

Could Oscuro have a hand in these crimes too, Cabel wondered.

He picked up the edition and scanned the story for anything that could signify a connection to the country crime lord. Nothing jumped out at him, but there were a lot of questions that had answers that could not be published on the record.

Cabel grabbed his office phone and punched in the 728 extension for the office phone in the corner of the building where the stringers worked. After a short pause, Wes answered.

"Hey Wes," Cabel began. "You worked with Kelly on the robbery story, didn't you? He's not in now, is he?"

"No," Wes responded swiftly. "I think he's back at the courthouse. The arraignment was yesterday and he was trying to get some follow-up answers."

"Uh-huh," Cabel mumbled, already knowing the answer he asked.

"Hey, listen," he continued. "I was reading over the story and I wondered a couple things. Maybe you have the answer and I won't have to bug Kelly later."

"Sure," Wes allowed.

"These robberies. We know it was a multi-person job, but there is only one person named in the article." Cabel placed a finger against the newspaper article to find the name. "A John Rianson. What can you tell me about him?"

"Dumb kid looking for meth money," Wes stated bluntly. "Age twenty, from Huntsville. He was in my youngest brother's high school class and graduated near the top, too. His life has really gone down the tubes since high school."

"I know a few like that," Cabel remarked before moving on to a more pressing question. "Is he connected to any other groups of people who would commit crimes? I mean, we know there were other people involved with the break-ins."

"Kids mostly," Wes noted. "There were at least five involved in the crimes, but only three have been apprehended."

Cabel scanned the article again. "I see that the other two that were caught are under eighteen. Do you think the rest are juveniles, too?"

"Yes," Wes answered curtly again before expanding. "Rianson was the mastermind, and he recruited these juniors and seniors to carry out his deeds with the promise of drugs and money."

"Damn," Cabel murmured under his breath away from the telephone receiver.

Wes continued, "We don't know anything about the juvenile arraignments. We can't publish their names and they don't allow us into those hearings even if we wanted that information."

"I know," Cabel acknowledged. "Well it sounds like there's one less kingpin want-to-be off the streets."

"Sure, sure," Wes agreed. "But there's always a kingpin. Where one falls, another rises in their absence, and that's news for another day."

Cabel sighed. "Keeps us in business I guess. I wish that wasn't true, but it's painfully obvious that it is."

* * *

By the time Cabel was ready to leave for the day, he thought he had escaped the worst of coworkers noticing his changes in routine. He packed a brown messenger bag and headed for the hallway to the back door. He made it halfway before being called by Chris, the editor.

"You're leaving without saying goodbye?" Chris observed from the opposite end of the hall.

Cabel turned slowly and shrugged. "Sorry. I didn't get much sleep last night, so I'm kinda out of it."

He took a few steps towards her to not look so eager to leave.

"What you got going on this weekend?" she asked colloquially and embraced grammatical inaccuracies with her question.

"Nothing much," he answered dismissively. "Lazy weekend I guess."

Chris cocked her head. "You've seemed distant all week. Is everything alright?"

"Ah, yeah," Cabel replied, snapping back to reality. He rubbed the back of his head nervously as he scanned for a suitable reply. "I've just been thinking about this Alan murder. I mean, he owned the drug store in Chancy, too. I've been doing some digging in my neck of the woods and I'm not liking what I've found."

Chris straightened her posture, interest piqued. "Oh yeah. What are you seeing?"

Cabel shuttered to think of an answer that would not expose his involvement. He winced visibly before responding.

"Let's put it this way. You came from the D.C. area – and were damn glad you got out of there and could resume a normal and more peaceful life in a small country setting."

"Right," Chris agreed.

Cabel continued, "But what if it's only peaceful on the surface? What if under the facade was the same old crime-infested world you left behind? You would be disappointed to know that, wouldn't you?"

"I would," Chris confirmed and seemed to understand where he was going with the example.

"Let's just say I am disappointed," Cabel admitted.

Chris responded by sternly locking eyes with Cabel. In his tired eyes, she appeared to glean the sadness of a genuine response and broke away when it had become uncomfortable.

"I think we ultimately come to be disenfranchised with the world in which we grew up," Chris stated as she took a few steps backwards and leaned a shoulder against the wall. "It's like a child. If you're with the kid at every moment of every day, you never notice them growing until one day you say to yourself 'oh shit, they're fully grown.' I guess what I'm trying to say is that you've just come to realize that your world is fully-grown. The crime has always been there, growing, but now you notice it."

"Then what?" Cabel asked, more downtrodden than before.

"We have to fight it," Chris replied with vigor, pumping an arm slightly. "We're journalists. We fight back against the injustices of the world in a way that no military or police force can. So that's what I want you to do. It's our calling to go fight!"

"Fight is what I'll do then," Cabel answered in a more upbeat tone, beginning to feel inspired with the unlikely pep talk. "Have a good weekend."

On the way to the back door, Cabel passed through the print shop. It was a cavernous room that once housed the newspaper press before printing duties were moved offsite. Nevertheless, the room was now packed with smaller presses that were used for printing flyers, posters, and other jobs contracted out by local businesses.

Towers of paper boxes lined the walls, filled with reams of paper in a multitude of colors. Walking past the stacks, Cabel noticed long pieces of cardboard that were used in the shipping of the paper products to the shop.

Cabel scanned the room and found one of the shop workers meticulously filling out paperwork. He stood still until he got the short man's attention.

"Are you using these?"

* * *

The sun was approaching the horizon as Len sped down the dirt road towards Huntsville, kicking up a cloud of dust as he rolled along. The desolate road was the only one that connected O'Brien County directly to Baker County, though the two were widely considered to be two counties over from one another. The road was mainly used for farm access, but was oftentimes utilized by motorists wanting to take a scenic route across the bulging landscape.

Len was a regular to this road and paid little mind to the beauty in his peripherals. Perhaps once taken in by the rolling fields enclosed by wire fences – rounded mountains towering in the background – he paid no mind to the sights now even as twilight ushered away the daylight.

As he motored on, something did catch his eye. He crested a hill, then dipped into a straight stretch and noticed that something looked different in the low point of the stretch, like it had been disturbed. Moving closer, he couldn't quite figure out what changed. *Ditch work,* he thought, but couldn't recall any place along the road that had a visible culvert.

Driving over the questionable area, it suddenly became apparent to Len that there was no road there at all.

The black Chrysler bobbed violently as it passed over the spot, still moving at an excessive rate of speed for what a dirt road was conditioned to handle. Len cursed and slammed on the brakes, which caused the car to fishtail. His arms stiffened as his hands squeeze the wheel to demand control. After a beat of this, the Chrysler skidded peacefully to a halt.

Composing himself, Len calmly exited the car and looked back at the site of the incident. Through the thick dust illuminated in the sunset, he could see two panels sticking out of the ground on what appeared to be a ditch running across the road. Suspicious, Len reached into the backseat of the car and removed a sawed-off shotgun before proceeding.

The car had stopped about a hundred feet from the ditch, but Len paid no mind to that. His immediate thought was to check the tires and bumper for damage.

The tires looked fine. He inspected the two on his side before rounding the back of the car to the passenger side. Those tires were fine, too. The front passenger side, however, had visible damage. The bumper was smashed upward and had a slight wobble to it when Len gave it a kick.

"Damn," he grumbled under his breath and turned his attention back to the ditch.

He cradled the shotgun under his right arm and sighed. After a brief hesitation, he began to move towards the ditch, crunching on the gravel and sand that made up the roadway while he marched. The sky, orange now, was darkening quickly, but still allowed enough light for him to see the makeshift ditch.

He considered it the work of a negligent farmer when he approached, but still kept the inkling of something else at play in his mind. The suspicion quickly formed into a hunch when Len picked up one of the panels, discovering that it was just cardboard that had been covered with road dirt.

Len dropped the cardboard and swung back in the

direction of his car. All this time, there had been a low hum in the distance. He thought it was his car until now, when he was far enough to realize that there were two sources of the engine sound. His suspicions were confirmed when he spotted an old pickup truck that now sat at the top of the next hill.

* * *

Cabel could see Len standing next to his handiwork. He was never one to be good with a shovel but, with adrenaline pumping, managed to carve out an adequate crevasse the width of the road.

"I can't believe I'm doing this," Cabel uttered to himself as he put the throttle to the floor.

Before Cabel was ever on the gas, Len was lining up a shot at the windshield of the pickup. There was no scope or sight on the modified gun, so he first lined up the shot with the barrel. The first shot fired as Cabel accelerated towards Len. The shot pinged the top of the truck cabin's roof. It did not hit the glass, but still caused enough force to crack the windshield from the top down.

Cabel heard the metal ricochet and saw the glass splinter, flinching automatically even as he kept a firm grip on the wheel. He knew it was only a matter of seconds until Len fired the next round. Hastily lining up the truck with where Len was standing, he ducked down just as the second round blew out the windshield completely.

Expecting a third round, but not hearing it, Cabel peeked his head up to see that Len had taken off in a sprint. He ran off the road and attempted to scale the closest wire fence. Nearly on him, Cabel cut the wheel in Len's direction. A victim of his own trap, Cabel hit the corner of his ditch, which made the truck bobble crookedly as it bounced into the fence that Len had just cleared. The metal wires stopped the truck dead in its tracks. Cabel's lack of seatbelt and already precarious position on the seat caused him to fly into the dashboard chest-first.

The impact knocked the wind out of Cabel, but he was able to recover quickly, knowing danger still existed outside of the cab.

He pushed the door open gently, but it still made its typical loud, creaky whine. The truck was now level with the ground, but firmly wedged between the side ditch and the mangled fence. Cabel stumbled out and kept low to the ground as he searched the area for Len's whereabouts.

He rounded the back of the truck and noticed the shotgun lying near the edge of his ditch. It was a double barrel that required reloading after two shots. Cabel knew now that Len had opted to run rather than reload. Closer inspection of the weapon also revealed that the wooden stock looked shattered, which indicated to him that it had been crushed in the incident by the tires.

When he straightened to his full height, Cabel heard a groan from the front of the truck. As a precaution, he picked up the damaged shotgun with his gloved hands and cautiously approached the front of the truck.

Len moaned again as he came into Cabel's view. He was trapped beneath the front of the truck – the wire fence under it pinning him firmly to the ground. The driver-side tire had just missed finishing the job by about a foot, but looked to be crushing Len's right hand. When Len noticed Cabel, his audible agonizing stopped and he regained his tough demeanor.

"If you kill me, Oscuro will spare no expense in hunting you down," Len barked through labored breath.

Cabel continued to examine the scene, making for certain that his opponent was firmly immobilized. He noticed a gun in Len's shoulder holster was peeking through the wire and quickly removed the gun from the hitman's possession.

"Is that not already happening? Oscuro is already hunting me down, is he not?" Cabel answered, trying to sound as tough as the hitman. "This way at least brings me some satisfaction."

Having no need for it, Cabel tossed the broken shotgun to the ground. He wondered why Len hadn't used his sidearm instead, but answered the question when he discovered the clip was empty.

"Keep the loaded clip in my opposite pocket," Len admitted. "It's so pricks who beat me in a fight can't off me with my own piece."

Cabel furrowed his brow and looked at Len. "I just beat

you in a fight. Why would you tell me?"

Len said nothing, but the answer quickly came to Cabel. The clip pocket was tucked under Len's side. In order to get to it, Cabel would have to loosen the debris that was pinning the killer.

Cabel stashed the empty handgun in his jeans. "I'm not interested in your clip. I'm not a killer like you."

"Yet here you are, primed to kill," Len observed with a taunt.

Cabel ignored the comment and paced to the back of the pickup, unsure of what to do next. He would have to kill. To make matters worse, he had just used the truck as a weapon and it was now just as much a part of the crime scene as anything else.

Putting those thoughts out of his mind, Cabel grabbed the shovel out of the truck bed and quickly began filling back in the ditch, glancing periodically over at Len while he toiled. The few minutes of physical labor gave him time to devise the next part of the plan.

With daylight just a remnant, he tossed the shovel back into the pickup bed, but suddenly caught sight of the other items in the back – three milk jugs full of gasoline.

Cabel lowered the tailgate and climbed on the back to retrieve the jugs. As he hopped back down with two of the three, he considered removing Troy's license plate. This would leave only the VIN plate as proper identification, but with the windshield broken, he could easily access it and remove it with some pliers.

Then Cabel had a new thought. Troy was already a suspect and even if he told the truth about being framed, it would still reveal his true crime, which could be deemed just as damning in a court of law.

Troy will have to go down for the crime I'm about to commit, too, Cabel thought to himself, and in a moment of pure selfishness and self-preservation, decided to leave the evidence in place.

Cabel took one of the jugs and placed it directly under the truck's fuel tank. He then opened a second jug and poured it around the first jug, making a trail in the dry grass that led to where Len was still trapped.

"Still with me?" Cabel asked almost mockingly.

"Go to hell," Len spat back in a weakened voice.

"You first," Cabel mocked before taking the third jug and splashed it coldly over Len's body. He continued to pour around to the passenger side of the truck, making sure there was enough left to pool in the soil where he stopped.

He tossed the empty jug under the truck and had a moment of panic as he realized that he had no way to ignite the fuel.

"I bet there's a cigarette lighter," Cabel muttered under his breath, remembering Troy lighting a smoke with it the other day while on the way to Cucumber Hollow.

He opened the passenger door and slapped the lighter into the socket to give the coils a moment to heat. While he waited, Cabel pulled open the glove box to discover a stack of old documents and a hidden pack of cigarettes.

It had been years since he had last smoked, so he decided it was the best occasion to give it another temporary pass. Cabel pulled a cigarette from the box and retrieved the car lighter. He pressed the red-hot metal coil to the cigarette, cautious not to expose it to the building fumes around the vehicle.

He started to exit the cab when another, larger, thought came to him. He leaned to the edge of the door and grabbed the handle for the seat release. Cabel pulled the lever and the seat's back swung down, revealing a pile of musty clothes.

Cabel balanced the cigarette between his lips as he began to dig, but didn't have to burrow long to find a shoebox buried at the bottom of the pile. He pulled off the lid with shaky hands to discover the $9,000 still hidden in the truck.

Stunned, Cabel walked back to Len with the wads of cash in one hand, the cigarette in the other, and a sudden feeling of remorse in his heart.

"You know, I'm sorry," Cabel stated sincerely to the gasoline-soaked man. "If I had realized the money was in here earlier, things might have ended differently. I would have just given it to you."

"Damn lotta good that does me now," Len replied, unimpressed and resigned to his situation.

Cabel considered tossing the money in with the imminent pyre, but thought better of it. The money may still get them out of trouble yet.

"I'm afraid this is your last moment, so say something nice if you have it in you," Cabel offered in a steely voice while he struggled to tuck the money into his pocket.

Len mouthed expletives though the words never fully manifested into sounds.

Cabel grimaced, reading the curses on his lips. "Disappointing last words," he replied. He tried to sound tough, but found the remarks fell flat. Not thinking further, he flicked the burning cigarette onto Len's chest, which ignited the gas almost immediately.

Cabel ran from the field and back into the road as the heat from the building flames began to reach unbearable levels. He took the remaining cardboard from the road and tossed it close to the truck and waited for it to ignite with the rest of the evidence. Satisfied that his tracks had been covered, he stumbled back to Len's car. The view of the truck's gas tank exploding lit up the rear-view mirror as Cabel adjusted the seat. He looked up to see a ball of flames reach to the heavens in the reflection and extend well outside of the limited view of the skinny glass.

* * *

Frank arrived at Antaeus Park at two in the morning as he always did near the holidays. It was late enough that he could park in the main lot without fear of being seen. Even better for him, Stonewall County was famously understaffed and police officers were only on call after two a.m., with none being on patrol in those late hours.

The park was over-the-top with its Christmas decorations. Lights that flashed green and red wrapped around the fence that ran along the perimeter of the park property. Every tree in the eight acres was adorned with ribbons and lights, and a giant inflatable Santa Claus bobbled in the wind as other electric iterations of St. Nick illuminated the public area.

Walking casually, Frank ambled down a gravel path

framed by wooden beams raised off the ground about a foot. At the end of the path was the playground area, with the first piece of equipment being the seesaw.

He approached the play set and knelt at its base. Digging away the wood chips revealed a sealed panel clipped tightly in place, held closed by one screw. Frank casually retrieved a small screwdriver from his coat pocket and made short work of opening the casing.

Inside was not the money he expected, but a note.

MEET ME IN THE PARKING LOT. THIS ENDS TONIGHT.

-TM

Frank crumpled the paper and stood. He scanned the parking lot with piercing eyes and found no one present, nor any other vehicle in the lot.

* * *

Troy was there. At the end of the parking lot, a boat ramp sloped downhill and disappeared into the water. He sat crouched at the bottom of the ramp, rifle in his lap, and watched the starlight reflection dance in the waves. He had been there for hours, taking time to contemplate life and reflect on all the poor choices he had made throughout.

"Troy!" Frank shouted angrily from the parking lot. "Now's not the time to puss out! If you want to take a crack at me, now is your chance!"

The yelling startled Troy and he lost his balance, falling back onto the cement ramp. He lay there just long enough to regain composure and then slowly rose to his feet.

* * *

Frank was watching for movement in the park when he saw Troy rise from below the hillside. Seeing that he had a gun, Frank reached into his coat and pulled a handgun from a shoulder holster.

"Let me tell you how foolish this is," Frank started as he began to close the distance. "Gunfire here only gives you a limited amount of time to cover your crime. We're a mile outside of Westland, but someone is awake and close enough to phone it in to the police. There's a state trooper who lives just inside town limits and he can get his pants on pretty fast. That gives you less than ten minutes to clean up and run."

Troy weighed the possibility of that being true and decided not to risk it. "It seems we are at an impasse then," he admitted. "What do you suggest?"

"Melee," Frank suggested, coming to a stop just a few feet from Troy. "Let's duke it out like real men."

* * *

Troy considered himself a pretty good fighter, but was unsure he could take on a seasoned killer. Nevertheless, he decided getting beat to a pulp was better than taking a bullet.

"Fisting cuffs it is then," Troy answered and set his rifle on the ground.

Frank did the same with his handgun and raised his fists. "Okay then. Let's do this on three. One. Two. Three."

Troy charged the hitman, flailing his arms as he struggled to keep them clinched. Frank barely moved as he took a defensive stance. He effortlessly pulled back to deliver the first punch.

12

REEL

"It's supposed to be a beautiful day," Miranda noted to Cabel, though the evidence was made clear by the warm sun beating down on them.

Cabel was leading Miranda down a dirt road along the river near Tipperton. An offshoot of the Potomac River, the local streams were well known for their stocks of trout, which was one of the big draws for out-of-towners to visit. Though November was a clear offseason for the sport, the unseasonable weather made for one last opportunity.

This part of his family's land was gated off, but Cabel had

loved to walk this road in his youth. In the summers, the surrounding fields were filled with infinite rows of corn that would grow as high as ten feet with the right application of fertilizer. It was like a maze and Cabel loved to run through the thick stalks in those days, playing hide and seek with his cousins.

The landscape was a stark contrast to those summer days. By late fall, all the corn had been shaved away by a harvester, leaving only the stubble of the once-leggy plant.

Cabel felt good and had managed to sleep in his own bed for the first time in a while. After returning home, he'd sent a text to Troy, letting him know he had Len's car and that he could switch it with Cabel's SUV when Troy returned from his mission. That was a few hours before midnight Friday and Troy replied in the affirmative. As they walked, Cabel glanced at his phone to again read the last message received from Troy.

"WHERE DID MY TRUCK GO?"

Cabel wanted to post a snarky reply about how his predictions about the truck had come true, but decided it was better saved for a conversation in person. Tucking the phone in his pocket, he turned his attention to the woman beside him.

"How's your friend doing?" Miranda prompted, not knowing it was exactly the thing on Cabel's mind. "Is he still kicking?"

"Believe so," he answered lightly. "He's staying at his dad's house on the other end of town. I reckon I should meet up with him later."

Cabel thought a moment about the Mason dwelling and realized he had only been there once before, but not because of Troy. It had been a few years earlier when Troy's father, Mitch, had him deliver a truck part from Huntsville. He recalled a beautiful, two-story brick structure that had only been built the year before. The grass seed planted in the yard had yet to fully take hold, giving the estate somewhat of an unfinished appearance. Cabel imagined a lush yard of grass had taken hold by now. The inside was just as glamorous, with hardwood floors stretching from end to end, beginning and ending at walls untouched by picture frames or any other wall hangings that required making holes. Cabel had only taken a step inside the door at the time, but he could get the sense of how immaculate the interior was just from the precipice.

"So why didn't you ever try to talk things out with your old boss at The O'Brien Times?" Miranda asked after they wandered along in silence for a while. "I mean, Huntsville is a long way to drive every day."

Cabel shuffled his feet as they kept moving, a backpack of bait and tackle on his back and fishing poles draped over his shoulder. "I've always had a personal directive to keep clear of the Paxtons. I've had a few pleasantries with his son here and there, but I've made it a goal to generally stay away from the old man."

"But why?" Miranda pressed.

Cabel smiled and worked to suppress his frustration with the subject. "You would have made a great journalist."

Miranda smiled back. "Being a teacher isn't so different. You still need to get to the bottom of things when spit wads are constantly coming your way."

"True," Cabel relented and chose words carefully for what he was about to say next. The sinister events of the evening before now began to weigh on his mind.

"I can be vengeful," he started hesitantly. "I'm slow to anger, but once I've been crossed, my creative sensibilities combine with my desire to bring ruin. As long as I keep my distance, no one has to suffer that."

Cabel looked to Miranda to see her staring at the roadway as she walked.

"I know that's not a great thing to admit while on a date," he added uneasily.

"No," Miranda agreed softly with a flutter. "I just have to note not to get on your bad side."

The two made eye contact and Cabel feigned a smile before attempting to put away his thoughts to focus on the present.

"I don't think you ever could, the way I mean. Like I said, I'm slow to anger. I don't expect you'll ever see it," he replied carefully. "My fuse is long and not easily lit."

At the end of the road was a steep bank that led down to the fishing hole. In dry summers, Cabel's family would use the inlet to pump water into the field, irrigating the crops with a large water canon that ejected arches of water deep into the field.

Cabel and Miranda set up shop on this side of the river, but it became apparent after a half hour that the fish weren't biting there.

"Maybe the fishies are on the other side," Miranda suggested. "Is there an easy way to get over there?"

"We'd have to go clear out and around, but even then, the access land on that side isn't owned by us," Cabel admitted.

"What about that?" Miranda asked, pointing at a rope swing further down river, at its most narrow part.

"That would work, I guess," Cabel admitted hesitantly. "That rope has been there for years, though. Not sure if it's still in great shape for swinging."

Miranda stood up and dusted off the seat of her jeans. "At least it's not a terrible day for getting wet."

She skipped playfully to the dangling rope and left Cabel to hurriedly gather the fishing supplies. By the time he had reached the pass, she had already swung across to the rocky outcropping on the other side.

"Seems sturdy enough. Held up pretty good for me," Miranda stated proudly, placing her hand on her hip while the other hand wiggled the rope at him tauntingly. "Your turn."

Cabel didn't feel great about the prospects of making it across. Not only was he carrying the weight of the equipment, but he had a huge weight disadvantage to her smaller frame. Nevertheless, he put on a brave face and caught the rope when she swung it back to him.

Giving it a few tugs beforehand made him feel better about the rope's sturdiness, but as he swung across, Cabel could feel the rope begin to give.

"Crap!" he shouted as the rope broke loose from its knot from the branch above. He had mostly cleared the water, but one leg still went into the drink. The other foot planted firmly on the rocky bank, which helped him quickly pull the other leg from the river. Through the ordeal, he still managed to keep a grip on both fishing poles. Despite the swift save, he focused on his wet leg, soaked through his jeans up to the knee.

Miranda couldn't help but laugh and she held her sides as

Cabel attempted to wring and shake the excess water from the denim.

"Clearly I weigh a little more than you," Cabel joked to show that he was not upset at the situation. "Getting back just got a bit tougher, though."

* * *

An hour later, the fish still weren't biting, but they no longer paid mind to those concerns. The two reclined against the rock cliff, enjoying the warm breeze that meandered through the trees. The fishing poles were wedged in crags near the water's edge and continued to be ignored by the underwater inhabitants.

"You never wanted to be a farmer?" Miranda asked after a respite in their conversation. "This seems like a pretty sweet lifestyle."

"It's hard work any other day and my family busts ass constantly to keep up this much acreage," Cabel stated. "Besides, it is my family's farm. Could you imagine working with your family on a daily basis?"

"Both my parents run a law firm together, so I can understand," Miranda admitted. "Most days, I don't think they can stand to work with each other."

"I just look at my dad. He's the fourth generation working this land and my grandad was always hard on him," Cabel revealed as he glared downstream. "Because my dad had that type of father figure, he became one in that same mold and was pretty hard on me in my early days on the farm."

"But you got out. How did you dodge being a fifth-generation farmer?"

Cabel sighed. "I think my dad recognized that history was repeating itself and made the conscious decision to break those chains." He added after a pause, "I'm thankful for it."

"I can tell you don't care for your grandfather," Miranda noted and shifted upright so she could get a better look at Cabel's face.

"I only really knew him as my dad's boss. He was more like that to me than a grandfather."

Miranda chuckled. "Maybe you just don't like old people."

Cabel jerked his head at the statement as if he'd never considered it before.

Miranda giggled at his dumbfounded face. "Well, you don't like your grandfather and you don't like this old guy that kicked you out of the paper. I'm detecting a pattern here."

Cabel drilled down on this idea in his mind and came to the conclusion that she could be right.

"I had never thought about it, but I'm going to give you that one," Cabel conceded and gave a shrug. "The old folks in these parts tend to be resistant to change - resistant to progress more than anything. And progress is the thing that is needed to help the younger working class get by here. Blocking the progress blocks the prosperity of the next generation. So, I think if I do, in fact, despise old folks, then that would be the reason."

After another twenty minutes of relaxation and more idle conversation, Cabel's pants leg was nearly dry and they decided to head back to town. A few yards up the outcropping, the river became shallow between the two water holes and Cabel rolled his baggy pants legs up to see if he could make the trek without rewetting himself.

"That's great and all, but it doesn't help me much," Miranda complained. "I could either get my pants wet or take them off."

"My vote is on the latter," Cabel joked coyly. "But if you do decide to go that route, I won't look."

Cabel started into the water when he heard a zip behind him. "Okay, I'm going to do that," Miranda announced.

Though tempted, Cabel kept his promise and continued on without looking back. Instead he kept his focus on the slippery rocks of the riverbed in front of him, holding unpacked fishing supplies above his head.

He had nearly cleared the river when he looked towards the bank. It startled him to see a man standing firm on the highest point of the bank. Cabel's immediate reaction was to turn to see if Miranda had noticed. She hadn't, and fortunately didn't notice him peeking, either. He jerked his head forward quickly.

"We have company, Miranda," he warned.

Cabel heard a gasp and imagined she was probably trying to figure out how to cover herself while keeping her jeans above the water line. Climbing the bank, he stood next to the man who stared like a hawk to the field on the opposite property – the top of the bank elevated enough to see beyond the rock wall.

"Hello granddad," Cabel greeted with an air of contempt in his voice.

His grandfather did not respond, only continued to stare off into the distance. A distant generation of the Walsh family once had Native American ancestry mixed into the gene pool, and though there was little evidence in the current generation, it certainly manifested itself in Cabel's grandfather's stoic temperament.

"Stop up and see your parents before you leave," he finally spoke, unblinking. "They want to make sure you're alright."

"Alright?" Cabel replied, confused.

His granddad finally turned his head to look at Cabel. "Do you remember Troy Mason? He was a friend of yours in grade school, wasn't he?"

"I know him," Cabel answered with a building unease.

"Mitch found him dead this morning."

Cabel's ears began to ring and a sudden wave of numbness began to vibrate through his core. Weakened, he dropped to his knees into the sandy bank, but could only hear the muffled thud of the soft silt. He exhaled loudly, knowing not of what other emotion to express.

"I'll give you a ride back to your car," his grandfather offered. "I brought my truck down through the gate."

Cabel slowly pulled himself together and stood up, taking a shaky step forward. He could feel a hand press against his back and turned slightly to see a redressed Miranda next to him. The small group crested the bank and could see his grandfather's truck sitting where the dirt road ended. The mountains in the distance seemed blurry and out of focus. His mind was racing as it took power from his other senses and the world seemed deadened. The only other sensation he could compare it to was the absence of sound after a long winter snow, but his thoughts only blipped on this notion. He could only wonder about Troy and about what happens next.

Cabel's grandfather reached the truck and lowered the tailgate. He gave it a few taps to indicate that was where he wanted them to sit. Cabel and Miranda pulled themselves up on the edge of the bed with no words. Words were failing him as he slumped in a stupor.

The pickup rattled alive and started down the bumpy path. Cabel sat and stared straight ahead. He could feel pressure building behind his eyes and knew that tears were imminent. He didn't quite understand it since this was someone he had only gotten to know again so briefly. Still, he held back the emotion as long as he could until he felt Miranda place an arm around him and a head on his shoulder. This served as a release lever to the dam of emotions held back and Cabel finally had no choice but to let loose.

* * *

It was late afternoon – well past lunchtime – but Cabel's mother stood at the stove in the kitchen frying bacon. His senses had slowly returned as they arrived at his parents' house, and the pop of bacon grease and the smell of burning fat triggered a Pavlovian response in Cabel's stomach. Hunger had taken over his feelings.

"We thought we would have breakfast for dinner tonight," his mom announced gleefully. "Is that alright, Caleb?"

Cabel listlessly sat down on a stool near the kitchen counter where Miranda joined him.

"We always had pizza for dinner on Sundays," he explained flatly.

"Well, you and your siblings don't live here anymore," his mom answered. "We kinda took it upon ourselves to change the menu, seeing as how we're the ones eating it."

"Thank you," Miranda inserted graciously. "Breakfast sounds wonderful."

"Who is your friend, Caleb?" his mother quizzed.

Cabel scowled with embarrassment, too wrought with emotions to take on another. "Mom, this is Miranda."

"Miranda. Lovely name," she complimented.

"Thank you," Miranda replied with a building smile. Turning to Cabel she asked in a low voice, "She keeps calling you Caleb. What's that about?"

Cabel's mother, overhearing the whispered question, responded, "Oh that. He hates his name. Ever since grade school, he tried to rebrand himself as Cabel, even purposely writing his name wrong on schoolwork. After a while, we just kinda gave in and let him do it because he was dead-set on keeping it anyways."

Miranda nudged him and smiled. "Is that true... Caleb?"

Cabel decided to give in to the mockery and cracked a smile.

Cabel's mom seemed to realize he was still downtrodden from the news about Troy and sympathized. "I'm sorry to hear about Troy. You two were so close as kids – had many a sleepover under this roof. Many birthday parties..." she trailed off, realizing how the years had passed. It seemed to be getting her down, too.

"Anyways, had you seen him much in recent years?" she finally finished, focusing her attention back to the stove.

Cabel shrugged. "Not really."

Miranda shot him a look that clearly said, *"don't lie to your mother,"* and Cabel tried to think of more to say to that.

"I did see him recently, though," he finally added.

"They think it was a drug overdose," Cabel's father revealed as he entered the kitchen. "His dad found him on the couch this morning. Didn't even realize he was dead at first because he looked like he was sleeping so peacefully."

"I guess he never really recovered," Cabel's mom added. "He had that other one a few years ago, didn't he?"

"Illegal immigrants are bringing in drugs," Cabel's dad interjected. "They're bringing those in from Mexico."

Cabel pushed his stool away from the counter as he observed his mom nodding in agreement. "Excuse me a minute," he grumbled as he turned and started down a nearby hallway. Miranda, unsure of what to do, followed.

"Stay out of the basement! It's a mess," his mom shouted.

Cabel instead went to his old bedroom, which was kept in

a mostly undisturbed condition since his college days. Rock posters still adorned the walls and the dresser drawers contained socks that he hadn't worn in almost a decade. From the bottom row, Cabel pulled one of the drawers completely out, revealing a time capsule of relics from his younger days. He reached into the hidden compartment and pulled out a shoebox.

"Do you see your parents differently as an adult now than when you were a kid?" Cabel asked Miranda while he sat on the bed and removed the box lid, revealing a stack of pictures.

Miranda looked to the ceiling and thought before shrugging off the question. "They're a little less passionate about their work, but the outlook seems unchanged."

"My parents from twenty years ago would be ashamed of who they are now. They aren't the parents I grew up with, that raised me and loved me. These are creatures of judgment. They seem to hand down verdicts about what everyone else is doing wrong – me especially. Troy died and it was the Mexicans. It's so easy to condemn someone you don't know – someone so far away that the problem can't possibly be yours. He wasn't killed by a drug overdose and Mexicans didn't kill him."

"What was he killed by?" Miranda inquired, curiosity heavy in her voice.

Cabel realized that in his anger he'd said too much and tried to rewind the topic.

"Maybe I didn't notice it as a kid. As a kid you're meant to be corrected, meant to be told you're doing wrong. Not in your late twenties. We are all supposed to be finished products by now."

Miranda sat on the bed next to him as she stared at him quietly. Cabel realized that maybe his emotions were accentuating all his grievances with the world and he stared back in silence for a beat before offering an apology.

"I'm sorry. This is just a lot."

Miranda curled her lips weakly and nodded, reaching out to stroke her fingers through his hair in a sympathetic gesture. Taking a deep breath, Cabel turned his attention to the shoebox and rifled quickly through the stacked pictures.

"Here it is," he alerted. He set the photograph face down on the bed next to him and put the lid back on the box. Rising,

Cabel carefully put the box and drawer back exactly where they had been, as if he were trying to cover the evidence of the items ever being disturbed.

"What's the picture?" Miranda asked carefully, recognizing the emotional distress that Cabel was encountering.

Cabel remained standing as he picked up the picture and stared at it intently for a moment.

"We were maybe eight or nine," he started quietly. "We were pretending to be explorers who were traveling the world in search of riches. Once we found the gold in each area of the map, we crossed it off and moved on to the next. We had such great imaginations. It's a shame you can't carry that youthful ignorance into adulthood."

He then handed the picture to Miranda and she focused on it under the dim light. There were two boys with arms around one another. A map of the world was taped to the wall behind them, with locations on different continents marked out in red crayon.

"He didn't have to die," Cabel continued, sitting cross-legged on the floor. "He could have just paid that money and no one would have been the wiser."

Miranda slowly lowered herself to the floor next to him and tried to defuse the frustration Cabel was feeling.

"Listen to yourself, though," she countered. "You said that your parents were nothing like they were twenty years ago. Was Troy?"

Cabel closed his eyes and took a deep breath. "We were seven, twenty years ago. You can't hardly expect us to be the same as when we were children."

"But that's what you want," Miranda noted gently. "In Troy, you were looking for the person he was then. You were looking for your childhood friend. It's something that can no longer exist. He was already dead in that way."

Choking back more tears, Cabel ran his fingers over the picture of the two friends. "I knew that... in a way," he admitted. "But he needed saving – from himself, and from the people who killed him."

Miranda was confused and repeated her earlier question. "Who killed him? You're sure it wasn't an overdose?"

"Yup," Cabel worded deliberately. "In the last week I spent with him, at no point did he mention drugs or show any indication that he was using. In fact, a lot of signs pointed to him avoiding it all together. Lot of alcohol, though, obviously."

Miranda was quiet for a minute and he could tell there was a deep concern growing inside of her. It appeared as though she was beginning to piece together the situation as a frown marred her facial features.

"Are they coming for you next?" she asked softly.

"I've kept my personal information out of it so far," Cabel answered with confidence. "They know my name, but that's about it."

"Names seem to carry a lot of weight in an area like this," Miranda argued.

Cabel stood and placed hands to his hips as he recalled Oscuro's obsession with family names. "You're not wrong. At least they don't know where I live or what my vehicle looks like."

As soon as he said it, a new realization struck him. How did his SUV get back to his house? If Frank killed Troy, he would have had access to the GPS system in his vehicle, which included saved directions to home. It was entirely possible that Troy survived the attack and was killed later after he dropped off the vehicle; however, there was no way to know for sure – which was an unknown he wouldn't be able to live with.

Cabel sighed heavily. Miranda stood and wrapped her arms around him in a comforting fashion. Holding her close, he softly admitted, "On second thought, maybe I'm not as safe as I want to believe."

13

PEW

Deer season kicked into gear Monday morning. Shots rang out from the woods and reverberated hillside-to-hillside, echoing in stereo through the populated hollows. Buck season was its own holiday and the forests were full of diligent hunters who wasted no time in bagging the first males. The impressive racks were destined for a place on the walls of their homes and the meat would find a spot in their deep freezers. Where most states only allow a few days off from school for Thanksgiving break, West Virginia took the whole week. There were far more important meats on the minds of people here and venison trumped turkey any day.

Keeping school bus drivers from preoccupation was an impossible task as well. Years earlier, one West Virginia county tried to hold school during this particular week, but was forced to close when all the bus drivers called in "sick." The woods were calling, and the allure of a meal and a trophy were too much to pass.

It wasn't about who dropped the first one, but how many points were on the antlers; however, those getting the first kill were no less excited as they hauled their prizes into the game check-in stations. These stations were usually a convenience or hardware store, and it was there that someone from the newspaper would come down to take a picture of whomever had their buck available at the time. No matter the point-size, the paper just wanted the shot for illustrative purposes. It was something that old Harry Paxton would have called filler back in his prime – text being all that mattered to the antiquated publisher.

"Looks like Dawn is on picture duty this morning," Cabel noted to himself as he watched the older lady, a former coworker, approach from across the street to greet some elated hunters.

Cabel took a few moments to watch the typical scene play out from the window of the courthouse where he'd been asked to stop in and talk with the sheriff. After communicating with Dawn, the two hunters walked to their pickup and lowered the tailgate, revealing two bucks. Cabel spotted a mighty rack on one of the deer, but the other appeared to be much younger and had spikes that had yet to branch into a more acceptable prize. Regardless, the two hunters took a position around the dead animals, blood still dripping from their mouths and pooling in the bed. Dawn squatted and aimed the camera at the two as they each smiled and brandished a thumbs-up as the flash snapped. Dawn then scrawled some notes on a folded piece of paper and began to speak with one of the hunters. It was then that Cabel lost interest.

Turning his focus to the reason he was here, Cabel sat down on a long bench that looked like it had once belonged in a church. It was a dark-stained wood that perfectly matched the dark, mahogany hallway. He wondered how his Monday morning was going to turn out. The sheriff's office had asked him the night before to come in as part of the investigation into Troy's death. That told him they suspected more was in play than just another overdose.

Concerned after receiving that phone call, especially since Frank had access to his vehicle for several hours, Cabel had meticulously searched for traces of evidence that Troy had been in his car. He had found nothing, but made sure to vacuum out the SUV in case there was something he had overlooked.

As he had cleaned, Cabel realized that the authorities would not be able to legally search his car without probable cause, so he had shifted his attention on to another concern. Could Frank have planted evidence on Troy's body like he had with Miss Knotts? Fortunately for Cabel, he kept his ride in pristine condition and could mentally inventory any items he had left in the SUV that night.

After going down the checklist, the only thing that had come up missing was a baseball cap. It was one he had bought late last year when the O'Brien County High School football team went to the state playoffs. It was a gray cap with a Viper - the school mascot - embroidered in the center. It was a hat he rarely took out of his vehicle, but Cabel made a quick sweep of his house just to make certain.

Turning his focus to the present, Cabel checked the time again. He'd come to the sheriff's office early enough with the hope that he could make it to work at a reasonable hour. However, he'd arrived too early because he ended up beating Sheriff Sam Diggle to his office by forty-five minutes.

Cabel didn't see this as a problem though. It gave him time to formulate an airtight answer for any question that could be thrown his way. He stood for a moment and briefly paced before sitting back down on a long bench, staring at his feet while mentally fabricating potential statements. In most lines of the mock conversation, Cabel could find issues where he could be exposed as giving false witness. He also knew Sheriff Diggle enough to know that he could sense nervousness in interrogating suspects and witnesses. He was a veteran of the county sheriff's department, only deciding to run for the top job when he was past his prime. With retirement looming, the good sheriff made sloppier work of open cases and let many easy arrests slip past his attention. When Sheriff Diggle finally entered the room, Cabel decided that there was only one good option available and he put on his figurative journalist hat.

"Sheriff Diggle," Cabel greeted as he stood and extended a hand.

The sheriff eyed Cabel over before reciprocating. "Yes. What can I do for you?"

"Oh. I'm Cabel Walsh. One of your deputies called me last evening and asked me to come in for an interview. I assume as a witness for something."

Sheriff Diggle thought for a second and chuckled lightly when he remembered. "Ah, yes. Come into my office."

The sheriff was an African American man in his late sixties. He had a slumping posture and walked with a limp. True to small town form, Cabel was classmates with one of his daughters. In fact, she was the first friend he made in junior high, after escaping the unpleasantries of Tipperton Elementary. They were lab partners in science class and her captive audience sprung into a solid friendship.

It was odd to Cabel, looking at it now, that he realized he never considered race back in those days and wondered if racial awareness was something that came with age. Even among the intolerant, Cabel could only think of one time the daughter had been harassed at school. She had been on a pay phone in the school's common area when one of the good ole' boys came up to her and hung up the receiver. Though she was known to not put up with anyone's nonsense, she didn't respond to the torment. Instead, she simply retrieved another set of quarters and dialed the number again. "Buncha redneck assholes," he remembered her saying calmly after the person on the other line answered again.

Cabel thought about that moment a lot and questioned more and more as he aged of whether there was something he could have done other than stare in stilted silence. More than ever he wanted to live in a world where those hidden barriers of race no longer existed. The barriers were slowly being chipped away, but he hoped to do more to chip away at his side. That was for another time, as Cabel knew he needed to focus on the task at hand.

"How's Jenny?" he asked. "I was in school with her and haven't seen her for years."

Sheriff Diggle sat down at his desk and tucked a bag he had been holding into one of the desk drawers. "She fine, she's fine. Jenny doesn't get this way much anymore. She's been working as a bank manager in the Memphis area the last couple years. Um, Bartlett. Just outside of Memphis."

"Oh," Cabel responded with diminishing interest. "Well tell her I asked about her."

"I'll do that," the Sheriff replied calmly and motioned for Cabel to sit.

"Reason I called you here today," Sheriff Diggle transitioned. "What can you tell me about Troy Mason?"

Cabel took this as a question he wouldn't get wrong and didn't hesitate to answer. "He was a childhood friend of mine. We hadn't spoken for years until the other week. He had been running with a hard crowd and seemed to be in a good bit of trouble."

"I've had several people tell me you've been seen with him the last several days," the Sheriff pressed. "What was that about?"

Cabel paused this time. He knew he had to use his key move sooner than planned. "I'm a writer with the Huntsville Herald now and I'm working on an investigative story about the death of Floyd Alan. It's being published this week, actually. The trail led me home and I don't like the things I've found and am still finding. This area is not my jurisdiction of reporting, so anything from here on is in the O'Brien Times' jurisdiction. I'm trying to tie up my loose ends now with the Huntsville angle."

The Sheriff smiled with surprise. "Oh, I thought you were still at the Times. Well, perhaps it is lucky that our paths have crossed."

Cabel nodded, seeing an opportunity to command the situation. "It is. There's still meat on the bone for Huntsville, but I'm in a position where I can't move forward until I know what you know."

Sheriff Diggle bit his cheek and shook his head. "Whoa. I'm the one asking the questions. Also, I can't comment on ongoing investigations, so you're questioning of me is moot."

"Fair enough," Cabel replied, knowing he took the bait. "Troy Mason is dead, this we know. Word is it was a drug overdose, but the fact that I'm here being questioned about him tells me that there's more to it than that."

"Well there certainly is meat on the bone for Huntsville," the Sheriff interjected. "It might be of interest to you then that Baker County law enforcement found Troy's burnt-out truck sitting along the side of a deserted road with a charred corpse under the wheels."

"That is of interest to me," Cabel replied and failed to suppress a smirk.

The sheriff continued, "What I want to know is how Troy got home from there. It was unlikely he did so on foot."

The slight smile Cabel had melted away as he chose his next response. He knew this one could be the most critical of any.

"I gave him a ride home," Cabel fibbed. "But I picked him up at Antaeus Park in Stonewall County. I have no clue how he got to there from his truck."

Sheriff Diggle, surprised by the answer, flipped open a small notepad. "What time was this?"

"After dark, probably nine or ten."

The Sheriff scribbled as Cabel continued. "He didn't seem drugged up at that point, but he didn't talk much either. Seemed exhausted and cold. He asked me for a hat and I gave him one, but other than that, there was mostly no conversation."

Sheriff Diggle slowly lowered his pen and pulled open the drawer with the bag inside. He reached into the bag and plopped the hat, encased in its own plastic bag, on the middle of the desk.

"That looks like the one," Cabel divulged. He reached for it, but it was yanked away by the sheriff.

"In addition to a lethal combination of Heroin and Fentanyl, Troy had a broken left cheekbone," he revealed.

"That's new information to me," Cabel admitted with sincerity and scrambled to fill the gaps. "That could explain why he didn't say much, and maybe why he wanted the hat."

"Where did you take him?" Diggle asked quickly.

"Home," Cabel answered just as quick, but realized his mistake and corrected. "That is, to his dad's place."

Sheriff Diggle rubbed the stubble on his face, as if sudden frustration had come over him. "We shouldn't be doing this before coffee," he grumbled. "Why don't we cut the crap. If you're doing an investigation let me know what you know?"

"I can't comment on an ongoing investigation," Cabel quipped.

"Bullshit," the Sheriff barked. "Tell me off the record."

"Off the record doesn't work like that," Cabel replied confidently. "You can tell me things off the record, though, and I can reciprocate with what I know."

The Sheriff leaned back in his chair, mulling the offer. "Quid pro quos aren't my thing."

"Come on, sheriff," Cabel nudged. "These are your last days in office. You have, what, a little over a month before retirement? Why not give it to me straight? You have my word this is all off the record. Quid pro quos are my thing."

"El Oscuro," Sheriff Diggle simply muttered before he leaned forward and cupped together both hands.

Cabel eyes widened, which was exactly what the sheriff was hoping would happen.

"Yeah. I see it in your eyes, too. Every time I mention that name, the person I'm interrogating puts on that face. Every. Damn. Time. What do you know of him?"

"I think he's responsible for Mr. Alan's death, as well as Adriane Knotts, and now Troy."

"Why?" Sheriff Diggle practically yelled, banging his fists against the desk. "What is the connection between these three?"

"Like most everything in West Virginia, the answer is drugs," Cabel answered in a defeated voice. "Miss Knotts got involved because she recently fired Troy, Troy had an outstanding debt with Oscuro, and Mr. Alan was about to find out and blow the whole thing wide open."

Cabel realized that he had mostly made up the part about Mr. Alan, but the sheriff didn't seem too concerned about it as he continued.

"What about the body under the truck?" Sheriff Diggle questioned.

"I suspect Troy got one of Oscuro's men before they got the better of him. That would also explain why they doctored it to make it look like an overdose when they have already murdered two others this month. I mean, these parts rarely see one murder in a year, let alone three in a week's time."

"But who are these men?" the sheriff asked with a break in his voice. "We've been chasing these goons for the whole of my tenure and we've not uncovered so much as a lead. These men are ghosts."

"Do the names Frank Bombardi and Len VanHoven come up in your investigations?" Cabel asked.

"Both ghosts," the sheriff replied dismissively. "They must all be using aliases because we can't find records of these names anywhere. If they're here, they're hidden good."

In that moment, Cabel knew he could blow the case wide open if he just mentioned Chester Randolph. Not only was he El Oscuro, he was the only name that Cabel knew not to be an alias; however, that moment was brief as a more selfish motive took hold and Cabel decided that helping the sheriff's investigation would impede his own.

"Are we done here?" Cabel asked as he stood. "I've got a busy workday ahead of me."

"So do I," Diggle replied with a resigned tone. "You got any other leads you can give us? I'm not someone who wants to remain ignorant, though you would be surprised at the lengths that some people choose to do so."

"I understand that," Cabel agreed, walking to the door. "I'm someone who needs to know everything."

"You'd make a good sheriff," Diggle complimented.

"I'd make a good publisher," Cabel corrected after a pause. Cabel cracked the office door and glanced to the floor as he decided to part with some information.

"If I were you, I'd canvas that pharmacy. Bet you'd solve the county's drug problems in one fell swoop."

* * *

Troy's visitation night at the funeral home was later that evening. Cabel wanted to skip the whole thing, but Miranda talked him into going and even offered to accompany him in the event he needed comforting. With her there, Cabel managed to play it macho as he entered the funeral parlor, but upon seeing Troy's open casket in the front of the room, he quickly hit the brakes.

"That's about all the further I can go," he admitted quietly after moving three pews forward. Cabel quickly darted to the right and took a seat about halfway down the row. He moved swiftly enough that Miranda had no choice but to follow, calmly taking the spot next to him.

"They shaved his head," Miranda noted as she peered towards the casket. "His hair wasn't like that before."

Cabel refused to look and instead watched his right hand brush the felt of the bench cushion.

"They do that when autopsies for overdoses are performed," he explained in a low voice. "He's probably got a scar on his head from where they stitched him back up. Probably a couple wicked scars across his chest as well."

Taking a deep, steadying breath, Cabel finally looked up. He could see Troy's mother and father at the front. They greeted mourners who lined the aisles. Cabel could not think of a time he'd ever seen the two in a room together. They had divorced when Troy was in the first grade and, even before then, only one or the other ever seemed to go to school functions. Even now, in a room with their son's lifeless body, they faced away from one another and embraced mourners from opposite aisles. They were a couple that had long been broken, and their son – the only thing left that they shared – was broken too.

As his eyes traveled between the two parents, another person caught his eye in between them. It was the woman who he and Troy had the unpleasant exchange with the week before in The 33 Restaurant. Cabel could not remember her name, but her appearance remained the same.

She departed from the casket and started towards the back when Cabel caught her eye. She immediately changed her stride from purposeful to a cocky swagger. She passed Cabel's pew, sliding into the row behind him. In a moment, she was leaning over behind Cabel.

She whispered, "There may not be lanes on these country roads, but you should always know which side you're driving on."

Cabel clinched his jaw and turned his head slightly to set an eye on her. "Did it take you a week to come up with that?"

The lady made a self-satisfied grunt, straightened her posture and disappeared from the room as quickly as she had passed through.

"I'm beginning to understand drugs," Cabel stated after a minute. The lady's comment did land as hard as intended and Cabel could feel himself sinking in defeat. "I've seen what Troy had to go through, what he had to put up with in this town. People wholly turned their backs on him. Why wouldn't he reciprocate? Drugs always appear to be on your side in lieu of anyone else. And befriending drugs always widens the gap between society and pariahs."

Cabel sighed and felt the weight of the situation pressing down on him.

"Have you known someone to die from a drug overdose?" Cabel asked Miranda, feeling as if he were hogging the conversation.

"No one close, but I know a few classmates that are gone," she responded somberly. "It's everywhere, but I find your analysis of it astute."

"There's probably no way to fix it," Cabel concluded and said no more. The grim summary lingered in the air for several beats more.

"We were four-years-old when we first met," Cabel reminisced spontaneously, his voice choking out as he spoke. "We hadn't started school yet, but we went to the same church in Tipperton. It musta been a Halloween party because I remember he was dressed as a cowboy."

Miranda took his left hand and caressed it comfortingly as he continued, "My mom was a housewife, so I never had a sitter – never had a chance to interact with other kids up until that point, so I was enamored when I first saw him. He was shy though and didn't want anything to do with me. I remember chasing him around the room all night, trying to get him to play with me."

Cabel let loose some tears he had been holding back and Miranda stopped stroking his hand and gripped it tightly.

"My childhood is gone," he struggled to say, his words breaking at their ends. He thought about what Troy had said the other day about Cabel being the only good thing left from his childhood. He realized now that Troy had been the only good thing left about his. He realized too late, and all that was left were the ceremonies at the conclusion of a life lived not long enough.

He repeated his last words again, this time in a whisper to mask the distraught nature of his voice.

"My childhood is gone."

Miranda sighed, seemingly unsure of how best to approach the man sobbing next to her. She switched hands so she could put an arm around Cabel.

"Childhood doesn't last forever," she reminded him empathetically. "Ultimately we smack into a wall of unavoidable changes. It's just a matter of how hard the impact is when we encounter it."

"It stings quite a damn bit for me," Cabel admitted. He looked up again and around the room, unsure of what he was looking for. He then turned his attention to Miranda.

"Has that happened for you?" he inquired.

"I spend most days with kids," she answered after a shrug. "There's no better way to know your childhood is over than to realize you no longer view the world the way a child does."

She paused and scanned the room as Cabel had.

"I guess to put it in the form of our analogy, I may not have hit that wall yet, but I'm sure as hell applying the brakes," she added.

Cabel searched the parlor again, this time remembering for what he was looking.

"She's not here," he said cryptically. "Her sister was here not a week ago, and she's not here now."

"Who?" Miranda asked and leaned forward to get a better look at Cabel's face.

"Troy's wife," he answered disdainfully. "The mother of

his child. She's not here. She was Adriane Knotts' sister, who they buried the other day! Could she not be bothered to stick around one extra day so her son could see his father one last time?"

Miranda massaged his shoulder in an attempt to calm him. "It's okay."

"It's not," he thundered, a roulette of swirling emotions.

"Her heart is already broken," Miranda replied assuredly. "I couldn't imagine burying loved ones on back-to-back days."

"She didn't love him. That's how this whole mess got started," he retorted, but trailed off once he realized he was in danger of revealing something he shouldn't.

Miranda was about to say something, but an elderly woman suddenly approached the two. She was a short, white-haired woman who had a hunch in her back, which made it all the more striking that she had appeared so suddenly.

"Hello Caleb," the lady greeted.

"Hi Mrs. Olin," Cabel replied, as he turned to Miranda. "She was our kindergarten teacher."

"Oh," Miranda nodded in surprise.

"You and Troy had some great times back in those days," the old woman mused, seemingly unmoved by the sadness around her.

"We did," Cabel replied and forced a smile.

Mrs. Olin continued, "I remember Troy used to come in on Mondays and tell me about how you and him played laser snipers in the woods behind his house. He was always so proud of himself because you could never find him when he hid."

Cabel offered a slight smile. "I had forgotten about that," he stated, even though he had just talked about it with Troy several days earlier.

"He told me his secret," she continued. "He would get down on his stomach and slide across the forest floor. That was how he went undetected."

"That would explain a lot," Cabel replied, the memories flooding back to him. "The front of his shirt was always so dirty when we came in for snacks. He never told me why."

Mrs. Olin smiled and stared deep into Cabel's scarlet-rimmed eyes. "I'm glad I could give you a little closure to that mystery."

Cabel smiled further, doing it sincerely for the only time that night. "I'm glad you could too."

With that, Mrs. Olin nodded and disappeared back into the crowd.

"That was random, but I needed it," Cabel eventually admitted after a long pause.

"Good," Miranda answered, sounding relieved.

Cabel sat quietly a little longer when someone else at the front of the room caught his eye. A tall man in a long coat stood over Troy's body. It was an outfit he'd seen before. He gazed at the man as he put a fedora to his head that was previously held to his chest. The man then turned towards the back of the room.

"Frank," Cabel uttered under his breath.

Cabel watched as Frank started towards the back of the room. He found himself unable to look away, even when Frank locked eyes with him. Cabel's pulse began to race when Frank gave him an exaggerated wink, which said everything about what had led them to this room.

Once Frank passed, Cabel made the conscious decision not to turn around, in hopes that Frank would disappear out of his life as soon as he disappeared from Cabel's periphery.

He was not that lucky.

"Good evening," Frank's voice boomed from directly behind them. Cabel turned his head to glance at the hitman as he sat down in the pew behind them.

"Did you enjoy my handiwork?" Frank added, his voice almost sounding elated.

TAIL

In an evening of emotions, Cabel had checked many from the list. Sadness, joy, fear, guilt – all of these he could mark off; but anger was one that had not fully taken hold until now. It was more than anger, in fact. As he sat quietly with Miranda, Cabel could feel a well of rage bubble up inside of him and he knew that his only hope was to channel it. If not, he would be in danger of doing something drastic and stupid. The same could be said for acting in rage, but doing so would at least deaden the feeling of the consequences.

"Did you enjoy *my* handiwork?" Cabel repeated back Frank's question as he held his gaze, referring to his final encounter with Len.

"So you took Len," Frank replied, nodding slightly as he pursed his lips. His voice sounded as impressed as it was threatening. "I thought it may have been Troy, but I guess I shouldn't be surprised. The boy couldn't fight worth a damn. An old man could have taken him."

Curiosity on her face, Miranda started to turn around to see who was behind them when the man growled, "Face forward, both of you, and stay that way. If you want to live, you'll do as I say."

"Who is that?" Miranda stiffened and whispered to Cabel, worry heavy in her question.

"That's Troy's killer," he answered flatly, refusing to take his eyes off Frank.

"You're damn right. Now face forward," Frank interjected, overhearing the answer. Cabel ignored the order to face forward and watched as Frank took out an old cellular flip phone and punched in a phone number with a thumb. Once he finished dialing, he held the cell to his ear until someone answered on the other line. He mumbled something unintelligible and handed the phone to Cabel.

"It's for you," Frank stated and Cabel took the phone.

"Hello?" he answered, his tone cautious.

"What did you think of our handiwork?" El Oscuro asked over the line.

"I'm getting sick of that question," Cabel answered disrespectfully. "I'm in the funeral home, so this isn't exactly tactful."

"You're in some deep shit, so let me lay it out for you," Oscuro bellowed in his gravelly voice. "I'm sure you've been interviewed by the police by now. Being a friend of Troy, your name registers pretty high on their suspect's list, but won't be enough for an arrest. We nudged that along by extracting a hat my associate found in your car the other night. That hat, for whatever reason, ended up near Mr. Mason's lifeless body. My estimate gives you a few days until the authorities find out it is yours. Now here's what you are going to do to ensure that you are not the next guest of honor at the funeral home."

Cabel cut him off, talking quietly to make sure none of the

mourners could hear. "You are right that I've been interviewed by the Sheriff, but where you're wrong is about the hat. They've already figured out it is mine and I've already admitted to giving Troy that hat. I am essentially off the hook in that regard."

Oscuro did not reply right away, to which Cabel felt he had the upper hand, so he continued, "I will tell you what I told them about you."

Frank must have heard what Cabel said because he slowly put a hand inside his coat, a popping sound indicated he had unclipped his shoulder holster.

"Now listen here," Oscuro barked back. "I realize you are new to this crime thing, but I will tell you with absolute certainty that snitches are not welcome in the underbelly. If you've compromised us, Frank will not hesitate to put a bullet in your head right now. He'll have nothing to lose if you've fingered him."

"No, nothing like that," Cabel corrected immediately, "but the sheriff will be investigating Alan's Pharmacy."

"How did you know about that?" Oscuro barked over the receiver loud enough that Cabel had to pull the phone away.

"I'm a journalist and Floyd Alan's death led me to uncover the scheme there."

"I thought we were off the record?" Oscuro seethed. "I thought you worked two counties over?"

Cabel shook his head. "That investigation had nothing to do with you. It started two counties over with Mr. Alan's death. The fact it led to your doorstep was not my intent."

"Well, it's all off the record," Oscuro mumbled quickly, almost to the point of belligerence.

"You come to me while I'm at a wake for my childhood best friend and try to threaten me to conceal information. I don't care if you're a crime lord, you treat me with some respect," Cabel demanded, growing louder. "You get nothing more from me."

The phone was silent for a moment and it appeared that Oscuro cooled down before continuing, "I want you to take a look back at Frank and nod," he requested.

Cabel complied, turning to the hitman and dipping his head. Frank, understanding this as some signal from Oscuro, removed his hand from his concealed weapon and reached into a hidden pocket on the opposite side of his coat. Cabel winced with the uncertainty of what was happening, but felt a sense of relief when Frank removed a small squirt gun from his pocket.

"You are most likely going to die by my hand," Oscuro started once he felt Cabel had delivered the unspoken message. "I didn't want it to be an unfair fight, so I asked Frank to bring some weaponry suitable for a little squirt like you."

Cabel snapped back, trying to speak vaguely as not to clue Miranda in to what he had done. "How easily do you think I'll go down? I hear Len is under a truck somewhere in Baker County."

Oscuro grumbled to himself for a moment before fully returning to the receiver. "I'll wager that you'll be dead by Thanksgiving. Survive any longer than that, then you may start to notice folks you care about and members of the Walsh clan dying suspiciously."

"You're giving me three days?" Cabel retorted. "I'm not a genealogist like you, but in that much time I can know everything about you."

"Try me," Oscuro dared.

"Sure thing, Mr. Randolph," Cabel replied before clamping the phone closed.

Frank continued to hold the bright green squirt gun out for Cabel to take, but ended up tossing it in Cabel's lap after growing impatient of him ignoring the gesture. Cabel, enraged, turned and tossed the phone into Frank's lap. Even though the hitman may have kill orders once unmasked, Cabel suspected he would try at all costs to prevent being exposed before exercising his last resort.

"Turn back around," Frank ordered, to no avail.

"Get out of here and don't you dare come at me again," Cabel ordered back, this time loud enough for everyone in the back of the parlor to hear. "You've got five seconds to get out of here before I tell everyone what you are."

"I..." Frank started.

"Five!" Cabel started counting over top of him.

Frank threw his hands up as he stood and edged towards the end of the row.

"Four!"

He swiftly rounded the pew and took off through the back entrance.

Half tempted to break the ridiculous toy gun, Cabel gripped it tight as he turned back to the forward position on the bench and stared motionless for a moment, the adrenaline continuing to pump.

"You just shooed off a trained killer," Miranda pointed out finally, finding her voice as the shock of the encounter seemed to wear off.

"That was certainly something I never expected to do," Cabel replied as he continued to stare blankly.

"What's next then?" Miranda asked. "Do you think he's waiting for us outside?"

Cabel thought briefly and sighed. "He knows what my vehicle looks like, so it's extremely likely."

Another pause transpired, this one long enough for Cabel's heart to stop racing. Already, he was formulating a plan – one in which Miranda's safety was the top priority.

"It's Thanksgiving week. Are you planning to see your family?" Cabel asked as he turned towards Miranda.

"Yeah, I hoped to leave after the funeral tomorrow."

"You don't need to go to his funeral," Cabel insisted. "I'll be fine there on my own."

Miranda began to object to the notion and Cabel realized this was no time for beating around the bush.

"Listen, this guy has seen you with me, so now you're in just as much danger as I am. These men have a way of punishing their victims by hitting their loved ones first."

"Aw, I'm a loved one," Miranda fawned in spite of the situation.

Cabel reached into his back pocket and pulled out his wallet. "I want you to take this and get a hotel room over in Harrisonburg for the night," he requested, handing her two one-hundred-dollar bills. "From there I want you to go on to your family. Damascus is on the way from there, right?"

"Yeah, but I need to pack first," Miranda answered, realizing how serious Cabel was.

"I tell you what," Cabel compromised, "stay in

Harrisonburg tonight. Then you can come back in the morning and pack. Give me a call when you get back to town and I'll keep you company while you do it."

Miranda tilted her head in confusion at Cabel.

"I just want you to be safe," he stated in concern.

Realizing that several mourners were giving them the eye after the ruckus with Frank, Cabel tugged on Miranda's arm, indicating they should go. The two slid out of the pew and made their way to the parlor at the end of the room. Cabel turned for a moment and stared towards the front as Miranda went for the exit. He could see part of Troy's face from where he was standing, but it was enough in that moment. He exhaled deeply and knew once he looked away, he would never see his first friend again. There could be no closure tonight. Troy had been murdered and his killers were still out there, threatening Cabel and all the people he cared about.

He sighed once more and broke his gaze, turning to catch up with Miranda, who was waiting on the outside stairs. Once beside her, the pair made their way to the parking lot. Cabel's eyes darted around the area in search of Frank. Miranda's vehicle was parked much closer to the front door than Cabel's, which made for a shorter search than he had hoped.

"My ride is in the lower lot," Cabel shared as he entered her passenger seat. "Make a circle around to the back of the lot to check if the area is clear."

Miranda slowly put the car in drive and drifted to the lower part of the parking area, which was downhill from the funeral home. The bulk of the mourners had filed out and were making their way home, which made the sweep much easier since Cabel's vehicle was one of the few remaining in the lower lot.

"Looks clear. Give me a call when you're ready to come over in the morning," Cabel requested again of Miranda. He opened the car door and then hesitated a moment before leaning over and giving her a peck on the cheek.

She pressed her hand to the location his lips had been and smiled. "Be careful."

Cabel nodded and closed the door before realizing he was still holding the toy gun. Unsure of what to do with it, he finally tucked it into his jeans like a normal gun.

Cabel turned his attention to his vehicle and unlocked the doors with the remote key fob, which activated the lights. He peered into the back seat to make sure there was no one lying in wait.

Empty.

He did the same to the hatch, but lifted the gate afterwards just to make certain.

Watching Miranda drive away, he got into the SUV and started it, letting it idle for a minute to give time for the air to heat. The unseasonable warmth from a few days ago was gone and the bitter cold had crept back to its rightful place in the season. Snow flurries meandered in the breeze and Cabel watched them flutter in the headlights.

His eyes then gravitated towards the exit to the parking lot, where he caught sight of Miranda's car ready to pull out onto the main road. Behind it was another car waiting to pull out too, which he felt was suspicious the second he laid eyes on it.

"They're going after her," Cabel growled to himself as he watched Miranda's car pull onto the main road, the trailing car following closely. Seeing this made Cabel's heart rise to his throat.

He immediately put the SUV in drive and flew down to the exit, paying little attention to his surroundings. He swung out into the road with limited checking as well and nearly cut off an oncoming pickup truck. Undeterred, he sped onward in an attempt to catch up with the two cars. Cabel finally picked them up again as they were turning right at the stoplight in the center of town onto the road that would take them over the mountain and into Virginia.

The three vehicles were running back-to-back-to-back by the time they reached the base of the mountain. The front most car was running slower now, as if the motor had trouble making the climb. Regardless, it would be a longer journey for all since there were no passing lanes and barely any pull-off spots.

This gave Cabel time to retrieve the stolen shotgun from under the seat. It had been loaded since the night he killed Len, but had yet to be fired. In fact, Cabel hadn't even brought it with him that eventful evening. Unwilling to use his personal vehicle as a weapon, the shotgun was the only option he had for this scenario.

The convoy crested the mountain about ten minutes later and started downhill, crossing into Virginia at the summit. The red sandstone slopes that the road was carved from were unusual for the geology of the area, but it was something Cabel hadn't considered before. He was born in Harrisonburg, and his family made regular trips to the area for supplies and better grocery options, so the odd coloring was just something engrained into his regular life.

Downhill went faster and the trio of vehicles hit the bottom of the mountain five minutes after reaching the top. This side of the mountain led into the George Washington National Forest, where the road cut through a continuous corridor of trees – sycamores and pines interspersed – with an occasional creek breaking up the monotony.

Because of the abundance of passing lanes in the forest, Cabel felt that this would be the real test to see who was in the middle car. Since the front car was moving more slowly, common sense would dictate that the following car would pass it, unless it had ulterior motives for remaining where it was.

To Cabel's surprise and trepidation, the middle car pulled off to the side of the road not long after entering the forest. Cabel realized then that he had been so engaged in who was following Miranda that he was careless in not tipping off who he was following.

His options were to continue on with Miranda or to stop there and find out the identity of the pursuer. He chose the latter against every fiber of his being and pulled off behind the other car, being sure to leave as much space between them as possible. If nothing else, it gave an opportunity for Miranda to flee into the night, even though it potentially put his life in peril.

The shotgun leaned barrel-up against his passenger seat and Cabel was quick to grab it with one hand as he put the other on the door handle. He was sitting where he had a clear enough view of the car to know when anyone exited from either side.

For a few minutes, nothing happened and Cabel's thoughts raced while he ran through the possible outcomes. Was he a good enough shot? What if he missed? Could he flee quickly if needed? The questions were abruptly put on hold when he saw the driver's door swing open.

Cabel clutched the gun tightly and flung his door open. He started to raise the gun, but dropped it to the driver's seat when he realized that it was Miranda running towards him. She had a baseball bat clutched tightly with both hands and was charging towards him with a loud grunt.

"It's me!" Cabel shouted and placed both hands in the air.

Miranda had not paid mind to what was in front of her and continued to charge, but broke her stride when she heard Cabel's voice. She looked up long enough to confirm it was him before slowing her charge to a trot while lowering the bat to her side.

"Was that you this whole time?! Holy crap, you've had me freaked out clear across the mountain," Miranda exclaimed a little breathlessly when she reached Cabel.

"I thought you were the front car and someone was following you," Cabel replied simply. "I'm sorry, my mind is getting the best of me. Paranoia is setting in."

Miranda peeked around Cabel to see the gun sitting next to him. "I'd say."

Cabel laughed to himself. "At least I know you're safe now."

"Doubly safe," Miranda added as she watched Cabel move the shotgun back to its hiding place.

"Why don't you come with me?" she asked when his attention returned to her.

"What?" he responded with surprise.

Miranda looked to the gravel at her feet and made circles in it with the head of the ball bat. "I mean, you've already come this far, and you're just as in need of refuge as I am."

"Are you sure?" Cabel asked cautiously, realizing this could be a large step forward in their relationship.

Miranda grinned and tapped Cabel's shin with the bat. "You won't sleep well in your place tonight with all that has happened."

Cabel nodded in agreement, thinking of the laundry room floor.

"That settles it then. Do you mind following me there?" she asked.

Cabel smiled and cocked his head, unsure if that was joke or not. She was already heading back to her car, the bat swinging idly. So he got back behind the wheel and then continued on into Harrisonburg.

At the hotel, the two were settled into a room, both laughing when they realized they had no toiletries or extra clothes to otherwise change into. Cabel sat, hunched over anxiously on the sofa at the edge of the room while Miranda got ready for bed with what supplies she could muster.

"What are you going to do tomorrow after you see me off?" Miranda asked, stepping out of the bathroom.

Cabel looked up at her before he took a more relaxed posture on the sofa. "I'm going to have to play their game. If I don't, they could come after you again later, or they could start hunting down my family. They know who they are and they aren't hard to find in Tipperton."

"Could you just pay the money Troy owed them?" Miranda asked as she inspected the empty dresser drawers at the front of the room.

"I'm on the hook for one of their associates being killed," Cabel answered, careful again not to give away the fact he did the killing. "As perverse as it may sound, these people have a code they live by and that's not the kind of infraction that can be paid with cash."

Miranda seemed to be growing frustrated that there were no other options and her head began to bobble as she considered a final solution.

"What if you went to the police?"

Cabel shot off an exasperated chuckle. "I talked to the sheriff this morning. He's investigating, but he's got a few months left before retirement, so I doubt he's going to push too hard. You know that cliché in cop movies where the veteran officer dies right before retirement."

Miranda nodded.

"I'm sure he's seen those movies, too. Can't blame him really."

"Yeah..." Miranda replied disappointedly.

"He had the perfect opportunity to ask me to elaborate about Adriane Knotts' death, but didn't bother to do that,"

Cabel criticized. "On top of that, he only has two deputies, and the local state police detachment only has three officers that work an area that's seven-hundred square miles wide. Too many times I've seen crimes go unpunished. Violent one's, too. I literally watched someone get their skull cracked at the tavern one night and that guy didn't even see a magistrate's office. The only justice in this world comes from good reporting and that's something the county sorely lacks."

Miranda exhaled, unsure of what to do from there. "Give 'em hell I guess," she resigned herself to saying. "You got to do what you got to do."

"I guess we do the best we can with the lemons life gives us," Cabel sighed in a defeated tone, standing up from the sofa.

"Life doesn't give us lemons though," Miranda stated.

"What?" Cabel replied in confusion, his voice up an octave.

Miranda clarified as she sat down on the bed. "Lemons are actually the hybrid of a sour orange and a citron. They were crossbred by man – genetically modified, which means life didn't give us lemons."

Cabel paused for a moment, his eyes drifting towards the ceiling as he considered the implications.

"We create our own lemons," he finally surmised.

"We still need the lemons, though," Miranda added as Cabel sat down beside her. "Without them, we never would have had lemonade."

She paused as she looked lovingly at Cabel. "The more bitter the beginning, the sweeter at the end."

"I think if we apply that analogy to our situation, the best we can hope for is lemon juice in all its sour glory," he droned as he looked again to the floor. It was a few moments before he became aware that she was staring at him and he looked back up at her questioningly.

"I think there's some sweetness to be had," she countered with an eager smile.

He smiled back and leaned in to meet her waiting lips. The kiss was as promised, sweet and warm. The obvious question was in his eyes as they separated.

She grinned broadly and pointed to the couch.

HINGE

Cabel followed Miranda back to her home in the morning and the two were pleased to discover her small, second floor apartment undisturbed. Cabel was concerned at first when Miranda had trouble pushing the front door open, though she assured him that this was a persistent problem with the entrance.

With a renewed sense of safety and fresh clothes at her disposal, Miranda took an opportunity to shower while Cabel waited patiently in the living room. Reclining on the couch, he looked around at the rustic decor and family portraits that lined the walls of the small room. Normally he would have inspected the elements more closely, but his mind was pre-occupied. He fidgeted with the squirt gun given to him by Frank as he made an inventory of items he would need to fight back against their operation. It was some time before he recognized that he had been staring blankly at the same spot in the room.

Cabel heard Miranda exit the shower and rustle around in the adjacent bedroom for a minute before emerging in the doorway, covered by only a towel.

"I would have invited you in, but I hear you like to shower in the dark," Miranda teased.

Cabel laughed lightly at her teasing before looking away, a little embarrassed at her suggestion. She smiled at his obvious discomfort and then quickly disappeared back to the bedroom.

"You say you're not going to the funeral?" she asked in a shout, her voice muffled as if she was in a closet.

"Frank knows I'll be there," Cabel replied loudly as he returned his gaze to the same spot opposite from where he was sitting. "The next time he approaches me, he will be a lot less merciful."

"Huh?" Miranda grunted. "Why don't you come in here so I can hear you better?" He slowly stood up, tucked the squirt gun in his coat pocket, and walked to the doorway leading into her bedroom. She was fully dressed now and he watched as she hurriedly shoved necessities into a small luggage case.

"You're devising a plan," she guessed as she continued to pull clothes from drawers. "You're always quiet when you're working things out."

Cabel leaned against the frame and spoke broodingly, trying hard to act cool as he spouted his stream of consciousness. "It's me against an unseen world right now. I didn't ask for this. I didn't ask for any of this, but it's mine now. I inherited it from Troy. I feel I inherited his troubles, his darkness."

Miranda finished packing and zipped the suitcase up in an awkward fashion, falling over onto the bed as she followed the zipper track around the edges. Much like a cat, she bounced to her feet and brushed it off like nothing unintentional happened. She regained her composure and stared at him intently with a serious look.

"I want you to promise me this," she requested. "I want you to promise me you won't let his darkness become your darkness. It's his, and you don't need to keep it as your own. Turn it loose so it can wither into nothing. That kind of thing can put a person into a nosedive that they never pull out of. Troy was a perfect example of that."

"I agree," Cabel replied and noticed that Miranda shot a stern look in response.

"And I promise," he added hastily.

"One more thing," Miranda continued, her expression softening. "I want you to promise me we'll go fishing when I get back."

"I definitely promise you that," Cabel answered more enthusiastically. "It may have to be ice fishing though as it seems that winter is upon us."

Miranda smiled and picked up her suitcase, following him out to the front door, stopping only to get a heavy coat from a closet near the door. Cabel took the suitcase while she put on the coat and carried it downstairs to her car, putting it in the back seat.

"Drive careful and watch out for the other fools on the road," he warned as she joined him at the car.

"I will," she promised. "And you be careful. I want my fishing date with you."

Cabel nodded and hugged her tightly, enjoying the closeness of her body against his.

After a shared smile and kiss, he watched her drive away. *Definitely something to live for,* he thought.

* * *

With Troy's funeral at one o'clock, Cabel had to hustle through the itinerary he had set forth for the morning. His first stop was the one he dreaded most, but knew if these were his last days of life, the outcome wouldn't matter anyway.

Cabel walked into the front door of The O'Brien Times with all the fanfare he expected. Tuesdays were production day for the weekly and the three employees in the single-room building were too busy at their stations to greet him.

He continued to stand at the front desk for an uncomfortable amount of time until the woman at the computer closest to him looked up from what she was typing.

"Hi Cabel," she greeted passively.

"Dawn," he answered back.

"What can I do for you?"

Cabel cut right to the point. "I need to look at some of your archive books. Probably sixteen years ago."

Dawn sighed and pointed to a large bookshelf halfway down the room. "Help yourself," she offered, returning to her screen.

Cabel hoped that would be the bulk of the interaction with her. He suspected that Dawn had been vocal in his dismissal all those years ago and felt wary of trusting her.

At the bookshelf were large books organized by year. He reached up to the shelf just above his head and pulled out the volume from exactly sixteen years ago. It was cumbersome to remove and he wrapped his arms around the giant tome, struggling to keep from dropping it.

Dawn discreetly looked up from her computer to watch him juggle the volume.

"Be careful with that one," she warned, breaking her silence when she noticed which book it was. "The papers are detaching from the spine."

Cabel nodded in acknowledgment and leveled the book to his hips. With the difficult part over, he walked it over to a slanted table once meant for newspaper pagination. The book landed with a loud thud that Cabel did not intend to make. He looked around the quiet room to see if anyone was watching him and saw that Dawn had returned to her task and the other two employees at a desk further back remained unfazed. That was when Cabel made a curious observation. Not counting the Paxtons, there were usually four employees hard at work; however, one was absent on that busy day.

"Where's Andy?" Cabel asked, his intrigue getting the better of him.

"Yesterday was his last day," Dawn revealed. "He took an editor's job at the daily down in Beckley."

"Oh," Cabel replied in surprise. "He was the editor. Who is going to replace him?"

"Not a damn clue," Dawn replied, her passiveness now with a touch of aggression. With that, she returned to her work and said nothing more.

Recalling that he was on a tight timeline, Cabel got to work, too. He carefully opened the book, which contained bound editions of every newspaper published in that particular year. Flipping it open to the middle, he could see the pages detach from the spine, as Dawn warned; however, the copies continued to remain together with the adhesive that once kept the book whole.

Cabel breathed a sigh of relief that he hadn't destroyed the volume and continued on to the second week of June, where he expected to find what he had been hunting. Sure enough, the article was the lead story in that week's edition.

RANDOLPH WINS MAYOR'S SEAT IN CLOSE RACE

The byline from the year 2000 bore Andy's name. Cabel was surprised that Andy had left the paper. He had been a long-time writer for the publication, a career that spanned more than two decades, as was evidenced by the article Cabel was reading. As he perused the political piece, he noted that Randolph defeated challenger Brent Ashfield for the open mayoral seat by only thirteen votes. He read on, but the remainder of the article only covered the councilmen races.

This wasn't what he was looking for. Flipping ahead three more months to the last week in September, Cabel confirmed what he had only vaguely remembered hearing people talk about around him at age eleven.

It was the lead story of that week, too, a headline that spanned the width of the paper and was printed in their boldest type available.

ASHFIELD FOUND DEAD, RULED HOMICIDE

Cabel read:

> *The community was shocked*
> *last Friday by the death of Brent*
> *Ashfield,   former   Chancy*
> *Councilman and one-time mayoral*

*candidate. The death is being ruled
a homicide.*

*Ashfield was found at his
home on Cherry Street with a
gunshot wound to the back of the
head. His wife discovered him
when she returned from work
around 4 p.m. Authorities say that
the crime took place around 10
a.m., perhaps the result of a
botched robbery.*

*The murder is the first to take
place in O'Brien County in more
than eight years...*

"Are you looking for anything in particular?" Dawn asked
as she finished her work at the computer.

Another veteran of the paper, Dawn had worked at the
paper for nearly thirty years. Cabel was reluctant to prod her for
information, but knew she was flush with it – especially the
recent history of the county.

"Brent Ashfield's murder sixteen years ago. Did they ever
find the murderer?"

"Yes," Dawn answered quickly, eager to show off her
knowledge. "It was Frank something. I can't remember what the
last name was."

"Bombardi?" Cabel offered.

Dawn sighed, knowing he had a leg-up on what she knew.
"Yes, that sounds right."

"Did they ever find him?"

"Yeah," she chirped. "They found him dead in the woods
about a year later. His body was burnt to a crisp, but they
identified him with dental records."

"Huh," Cabel expressed, floored by the revelation. "I
didn't know that."

Dawn chortled with satisfaction and moved to the front
desk to shuffle paperwork for filing. Cabel watched her as she
swiftly straightened the disheveled pile, breaking it down into
three separate piles. She was a master of her domain, a highly
organized person who kept mountains of paper records despite

the fact she could do it all from memory if needed. But as with all things, what she was doing was gradually growing obsolete. Computers were slowly taking over the filing process, as they had layout and circulation. She fought these changes tooth and nail, fearing she would be the next thing to go, but she remained. However, the battle-weary nature of sustaining such fights turned her bitter in these later years and she wore that resentment like a badge of honor.

"What do you know of Chester Randolph?" Cabel asked her when she didn't seem busy, going all-in with his questioning. "The guy who beat Ashfield out for the mayorship."

"He's dead, too," she answered as if she were unsure. "They found him dead in his home a couple years after he decided not to run for a second term."

"Dead?" Cabel replied with unrestrained shock. "How?"

"Diabetic complications," Dawn answered, somehow more sure of herself on this question. "They cremated him and spread his ashes up on Turkish Knob."

"Are they sure it was him?" Cabel pried, unsure of how Oscuro could have switched his body with a double that would have had identical fingerprints and dental records.

"Absolutely," Dawn replied. "He was a good friend with the coroner. I'm sure he would have identified him on the spot."

"Good friends," Cabel repeated softly to himself. "They really are ghosts." He was satisfied how quickly that nagging question found an answer, but wondered what became of the coroner.

Cabel would have continued with the questioning, but Corey Paxton abruptly burst through the door. Upon seeing who it was, Dawn stopped what she was doing and returned to her filing.

"Sorry I'm late. I had a couple phone calls to take this morning," Corey apologized as he charged through the room. He stopped in his tracks when he spotted Cabel off to the side of the room.

"Cabel! What brings you in today?" he asked, surprise warring with curiosity in his tone.

Cabel closed the book. "Research on a story."

"For us I hope," Corey remarked in a softer voice so Dawn wouldn't hear. "As you can see, we're sorta short-staffed these days."

"Dawn told me Andy is gone," Cabel informed. "That's too bad."

"It was surprising," Corey responded quickly. "Folks in this business, if they can make it five years in the same place, they tend to go for thirty or more."

"I'm getting there," Cabel reckoned. "I have two more years before I hit that sweet spot in Huntsville."

Corey rubbed his head for a moment and leaned in close. "Can I try to court you back before it gets to that point?"

"You would want me as a writer?" Cabel asked with a tone of unbridled hope. He spoke at normal volume at first, but quieted when he noticed Dawn's ears perk.

Corey lowered his head further, going into full whisper. "I'll tell you what. Let me get through Thanksgiving first and we'll talk next week. Wednesday next week sound good?"

"Sounds perfect," Cabel replied with guarded excitement.

Corey smiled and nodded. "Great, I'll see you then."

* * *

Cabel returned home for the first time since the afternoon before. He suspected Frank had likely paid a visit during the night. His fear was confirmed before he could even enter the house. As he unlocked the door, he noticed that the latch felt differently from how it usually had. Further inspection found that the metal plate around the latch had been pried loose. When he pushed the door open, it swung lower than usual, scraping the rug inside the house in a way it never had before.

After he entered, Cabel moved more cautiously and slowly swept every crack, cranny, and closet he could find until he came to the laundry room. The lightly soiled laundry that he had been using as a bed much of the last week was no longer in the center of the room, but tossed about all over the room, with some hanging from the cabinet top above the washer.

"Guess it wouldn't have done me much good sleeping there after all," he conceded before he moved back through the house to the kitchen.

As he passed through, Cabel noticed that the largest knife was missing from the woodblock on the countertop. He tried to recollect the last time he had used it and realized it had not been any time recently. Now even more cautious than before, Cabel removed the second-largest knife and wielded it while he completed the canvas of his house. Finally arriving in his bedroom, he easily located the missing knife, plunged straight down into the lone pillow on the bed.

Feeling confident now that Frank had been there the night before, Cabel went to work gathering up the things he needed. Spending little time in the house, he collected a few pairs of dark clothes from his closet and moved on to his game room. In the back corner of the room was a large toolbox with a tote bag sitting on the lid.

Cabel hurriedly dumped the clothes into the bag and set it aside to focus on the contents of the toolbox. From inside, he removed duct tape, a flashlight, a lighter, and a headlamp that could be clipped to a hat.

Lastly, he removed the squirt gun, which he had kept tucked in his coat pocket. Holding it thoughtfully, he stared at it briefly and felt that it had some kind of hidden potential that could serve as a middle finger to the gangsters. With a grim nod, Cabel tossed it in the bag with the rest of the items and headed out the door.

The last item on his list was a five-gallon gas canister that was tucked away under the back porch. It had been depleted at the end of yard mowing season, which made it easy to carry with the other items in his grasp.

Stowing the items in his vehicle, he pulled the key from his pocket and paused, remembering one thing he had forgotten. Cabel reluctantly went back into the house to the bedroom. He had declined to remove the knife from his pillow, but chose to on this pass. Instead of taking it back to the kitchen, he opened his top dresser drawer and placed it inside.

Inside the drawer was the handgun that Cabel had confiscated from Len on the evening of their encounter. The clip was still empty and he did not possess the correct ammunition for that type of gun, so it remained unloaded.

Cabel stared at it for a moment and an idea came to mind that he hadn't thought about before. He decided the idea was worth pursuing and tucked the weapon into his belt. He then picked up a nearby permanent marker before he went in search of a sheet of paper to finish what he had returned to the house to do.

The last stop for preparation was the gas station at the intersection in the center of town. Cabel had briefly clerked at the mart before and knew that the milk in the cooler was often returned for being sour. Despite this knowledge, he carried out three gallons of the most generic whole milk they had in stock. He also purchased a five pack of small candles that caught his eye by the register. They weren't quite as small as tea candles, but were large enough to provide a temporary burst of scent to a stale room.

Cabel also prepaid for gas while inside. Returning to his vehicle, he retrieved the gas canister and sat it on the ground next to the pump. He removed the nozzle, which caused the display screen to ask if he wanted a car wash. He pushed No – the lettering on the button barely visible, worn from scores of people who made the same choice in the past.

Cabel began pumping when he happened to look up at the intersection. At the stoplight, waiting for it to change, sat Frank in a burgundy Town Car. The large windows of the late model land yacht made him clearly visible and he paid no mind to his surroundings as he stared intently at the red light. He had a look of disdain towards the traffic signal, as if it was the only thing in the world that could halt someone as unstoppable as he.

"Shit!" Cabel yelped, realizing that he had been studying Frank so closely that the gas canister overflowed. He quickly returned the nozzle back to the pump and locked sight again with the Town Car, which was now moving through the intersection.

He was headed south – the direction of the funeral home.

* * *

Cabel didn't attend Troy's funeral. He felt guilty, but knew that Troy would have much preferred he stuck to the plan he was about to enact. He instead made a pass through the funeral home parking lot after the funeral started to confirm by the sight of the Town Car that Frank was in attendance.

He was.

Cabel knew that Troy would be buried at the Pine Garden Cemetery on the eastern outskirts of town and returned to the gas station at the intersection to wait for the procession. Normally, a sheriff's deputy would direct funeral traffic at this intersection and this occasion was no different.

Cabel removed the cap he was wearing when the hearse passed and he felt a well of emotion under the surface, but had no time to address it now. It was Troy's last trip through the town he despised, cussed, and lashed out at; but couldn't help but call his home all the same.

Cabel swallowed hard and watched the hearse disappear from view. Then he quickly turned his attention to the back of the line.

To Cabel's advantage, the burgundy Town Car was the final vehicle in the procession. Putting the SUV into gear, Cabel lined himself up with the gas station exit and waited for Frank to approach.

When Frank was nearly through the intersection, Cabel hit the gas pedal. With a squeal of tires, he skipped across the uneven pavement and slammed into the passenger side of Frank's car, bringing both vehicles to an immediate stop.

Once Cabel reversed his vehicle slightly, Frank pulled forward into a lot just above the gas station. Cabel followed behind him, but parked a safe distance away in case he needed to make a quick escape. By the time both parties came to a stop, the sheriff's deputy from the intersection was already on the scene.

Frank exited his car and immediately rounded to the passenger side to survey the damage. As sturdy as a car that size appeared, the door looked like it was smashed in with little effort. Frank grabbed the door handle and tried to pull, but the warped metal kept the latch from being engaged properly.

"What just happened?" the deputy asked Frank, approaching him first.

"I don't know, I was just driving," Frank answered

sincerely. "It did a number on my door, though. Think it's busted up the hinges." He had his license and registration at the ready and handed it to the officer as he looked downhill, over the officer's shoulder.

"Are you hurt? Do you require medical assistance?" the deputy continued to question Frank.

Frank ignored the question because he caught sight of who had hit him and his head jerked to stare down Cabel.

"Sir?" the officer prodded.

Frank snapped back to attention. "Ah no. No. I don't think I'll need any help at all."

UPHILL

"I'm sorry guys," Cabel apologized to the two men while he approached with license, registration, and insurance cards in hand.

"What happened?" the officer asked, turning towards Cabel.

"I thought the funeral line had finished going through," Cabel responded convincingly. "I thought he was going straight through the light and I didn't check again to see him turn."

The officer took possession of both the men's vehicle information. "Let me go and pull my vehicle up here." He turned back towards the patrol car, which left the two men in the precarious situation of being alone.

"What the hell you doing?" Frank snarled once the deputy was out of earshot.

"Having a conversation without you getting all trigger happy on me," Cabel replied with an air of coolness in his voice. His disdain for the situation was growing into indifference to the outcome as he treated his response to the dangerous man's question like any other conversation.

Frank snorted with indignation and reached a hand into his suit jacket. "Don't think it is not still a possibility."

"How was the funeral?" Cabel asked in an attempt to steer the conversation away from violence.

"Not as satisfying as yours will be," Frank quipped back.

"At least I'll have one," Cabel retorted. "Word on the street is you're already dead."

Frank turned his head and furrowed his brow, unsure of how Cabel gleaned that information. "Law don't look for a dead man they already put in the ground," he responded dismissively.

"Nah," Cabel answered back calmly. "If that were actually true, exhumations would be kind of pointless."

Frank craned his neck to see the sheriff's vehicle approaching. "Is this what you had to talk with me about? You're running out of time to tell me something meaningful."

"This is fine," Cabel assured, crossing his arms. "I'm just curious to see if ghosts put their date of death next to their date of birth on their driver's license."

Frank smiled in silent reply as the deputy returned.

"Here you are, Mr. Walsh," the officer addressed and handed the documents back to Cabel. He then turned to Frank.

"Here you are, Mr. Stewart."

"Please," Frank replied with a grin, "call me Michael."

Cabel wasn't necessarily surprised by the revelation and decided to turn to his backup plan. He jerked back quickly.

"He's got a gun!" Cabel shouted and pointed to Frank.

The officer had briefly turned away and instinctively pulled his gun as he turned. Unfortunately for Frank, it was his instinct to do the same. Frank realized his mistake and quickly halted the motion of his arm, but it wasn't quick enough to keep from exposing the concealed weapon, still holstered under his coat.

"I need you to remove the weapon and lay it on the ground," the officer ordered firmly with gun drawn.

Cabel watched in hidden delight as the situation unfolded. Frank carefully removed his gun, placed it on the ground in front of him, and took a hesitant step back from it.

"I have a conceal carry permit," Frank explained to the officer.

"That's fine, but it's not concealed at the moment. Turn and place your hands against your vehicle," the officer demanded. "We'll get all this sorted out in a moment."

Frank nodded in compliance and did as he was told though Cabel could see fumes of rage billowing under the surface. As the officer approached Frank to frisk him for more weapons, Cabel marveled at the lack of procedural caution the officer displayed and peered down at Frank's discarded handgun, which was basically within Cabel's reach. He stared at it and took note that it looked identical to Len's.

"The paperwork is in my wallet," Frank told the deputy once he finished patting him down.

Cabel, satisfied with the outcome, returned to inspect the damage he inflicted on his once-pristine vehicle. The grill and bumper were smashed, but he managed to hit Frank squarely enough that both headlights escaped unscathed.

"Mr. Walsh," the officer called out, "we're done here if you would like to go ahead and trade insurance information with Mr. Stewart."

"Yes sir," Cabel answered, then approached Frank one last time as the deputy got into his car, in sight but out of earshot.

"I don't really need any of this information. I have it all already," Frank shared in a baritone's whisper.

"I saw what you can do with a pillow and I'm not real impressed," Cabel responded unflinchingly. "Why don't you come up tonight and take another crack at it? I'm curious if you can handle yourself when the victim knows you're coming."

Frank smiled suspiciously, though a twitch of his lip made Cabel believe he had succeeded in throwing Frank off-kilter.

"We're on then," Frank finally proclaimed confidently. "Throw whatever you want at me. Troy sure did."

"You keep missing the part where I'm not Troy," Cabel replied, turning to head back to his vehicle. "I've proven to land a blow."

With the most potentially disastrous hurdle out of the way, Cabel only had two more stops to make. Pulling away from the scene with a polite nod to the deputy, his next destination was the body shop, which turned out to be the largest hitch in his plans.

CLOSED THANKSGIVING WEEK, a sign on the Superfix Collision Center door read.

"Buck Season strikes again," Cabel expressed under his breath while he punched the doorjamb in small knocking strokes. He didn't stop as he considered other available body shops in the area. Only one came to mind and Cabel sighed loudly before he returned to his vehicle.

Ralston Auto Body was a shop way up Creek Mountain, which divided O'Brien County into east and west factions. Cabel always spent his time on the Eastern side and rarely ventured past the divide. The western side was the gateway to most of the state's outdoor interests. Ski resorts were dotted along the continental divide, just past where Spruce Knob and Seneca Rocks jutted from the ancient mountains. It was a different world that was a treat for hikers and rock climbers from all walks of life. It had been on Cabel's mind on occasion to explore the nooks and crannies of those mountains, but time never seemed to allow for the adventure.

The detour threatened to throw off the timeframe Cabel hoped to stick to, so he raced up the mountain to try and recover some of the dwindling time. He was thankful his vehicle still operated with no issues from the accident, taking the mountain turns as expertly as it always had.

Cabel pulled into the gravel driveway of the body shop and was relieved to see people outside. There were two men speaking, and as Cabel drove close, one hopped into a car and began to drive away. The other, a man in denim coveralls, stood with hands in his pockets and watched Cabel pull up to the battered metal building that served as the shop.

The man was Lucas Ralston, another figure from Cabel's childhood. Lucas did not inspire the same feelings of nostalgia that Troy had. This guy had been the king of bullies, the kid that everyone feared at Tipperton Elementary School. He had once put a kid in the hospital after a playground altercation. He surely would have been suspended if he'd not gone to every witness in the class and threaten to do the same to them if they didn't lie about what happened. The intimidation worked and Lucas managed to scrape by without any severe punishment. In fact, the only punishment that Cabel could recall was the one where he framed Lucas for breaking the teacher's car window.

"I can tell why you're here," Lucas assumed while he stared at Cabel's front bumper. "How've you been Caleb?"

"Cabel," Cabel corrected, barely out of the vehicle. "Haven't been too bad. Can't say the same for the ride."

"Hit a deer?" Lucas guessed. "Or hit a man?"

Cabel shrugged. "Last one's more right than the first."

Lucas pushed back the brim of his cap. "Let me get my estimatin' sheets and we'll go over it."

He disappeared into the shop for a moment and reemerged with a clipboard and a pen. He immediately squatted down in front of the damage and began prodding and taking notes.

"I was sorry to hear about Troy," Lucas stated as he pulled debris from the cracked bumper. "I wanted to get to the funeral today, but we're trying to get caught up since we were closed Monday."

"Did you get anything?" Cabel questioned blandly. "I'm assuming you were closed for buck season."

"Yep," Lucas stated proudly and hopped back on his feet. "Eight point in the first hour. I'm glad cause we have a lot to do here, so I was able to at least get laundry finished yesterday."

"Will it be a problem to work on this?" Cabel questioned. "I can leave it as long as you have a loaner I can use."

Lucas finished with the inspection and scrawled some notes down on the clipboard paper.

"Yeah, that will be fine. I've got at least one more loaner you can use." Lucas pointed, "That red one over there. I can call your insurance company and get things rolling. Should be able to get the parts ordered today."

Cabel smiled and, for a moment, put his thoughts behind

him on whom he was speaking with. "Thanks. I would appreciate that a lot."

Lucas forced a smile and looked to the ground. His cheeks appeared pink, but Cabel thought that could be from the cold air blowing across the mountainside.

"By my count, it looks like around $2,800 in damage," Lucas estimated. "However, I want to give you a discount. Let's say $2,000 even. I was terrible to a lot of kids back in our day, and I was especially terrible to you. I've had a good bit of time to reflect and I promised myself that I would make it up to any of my victims that needed my services."

"Have you had a lot of former victims take up your services?" Cabel genuinely questioned.

Lucas returned his gaze to the ground and nodded side to side. "No. You're the first."

There was a respite as a huge gust of wind blew across the two and rattled the forest of trees around them.

"I am truly sorry, though. You don't realize when you're a kid what an affect you can have on people. I deeply apologize. I'll never get to apologize to Troy now. Not that I was as bad to him as I was to you. I just want to try and make it right all around."

In the midst of all the things happening in his life, Cabel found himself suddenly moved. This was not a sentiment he ever expected from the king of bullies. But as he peered at the former classmate, he could see an authentic look of remorse on his face.

Cabel smiled big and slapped Lucas on the bicep, instantly aware that the man was still as much muscle as he was when he was a child.

"Lucas." Cabel expressed. "I don't want your discount. My insurance is good and they'll gladly pay full price. But I will accept your apology. I can tell you it means a lot."

The big man nodded and smiled. Cabel turned and began to look out to where the red loaner car was parked in the grass. Another idea came to him, which required him to add another stop to his list. He would also need a favor from the redeemed Lucas.

He turned. "Actually, Lucas, I think I'll keep my vehicle

for one more day, but could you deliver the loaner to my house?"

* * *

There was a narrow-wooded area below Cabel's house that Frank traversed to stealthily creep to the front door of the home. It was eleven o'clock and the moon was just bright enough through the clouds that the killer could see Cabel's battered SUV in the driveway outside the dark house. Frank had only brought along his sidearm and a guitar string for a garrote, confident that was all he would need to subdue Cabel for good.

It was a starless night, which made for deeper cover when he approached the door and slid a custom tool into the crack in order to work the latch free. He found himself curious when the door proved to be already unlocked.

All the lights in the house were out, which was different from the night before when a bright hall light illuminated the interior. Still not putting much stock into Cabel's ability to fight back, Frank simply switched on the light once he made sure the curtains were drawn.

Nothing had changed from before. Frank moved into the kitchen and flipped on the lights. He noticed that two knives were missing from the block now, which put him a little more on the defensive when he inspected the laundry room. There had been signs that Cabel had slept there, but a quick inspection found that the clothes were mostly where Frank had strewn them.

On to the back room, Frank continued flipping on the lights as he moved through the house. Every dark and hidden place came up empty before he finally moved to the bedroom in the back corner. The knife in the pillow was gone, which Cabel had already mentioned, but in its place were pillows and sheets piled under the blanket to imitate a sleeping body. Frank didn't buy the rouse for a second.

"You're going to have to do better than that," Frank announced loudly. "Pillows under a blanket? Really?"

Frank stood patiently and waited for a response – waited

for Cabel to leap out of the closet and do some sort of pathetic and amateurish attack, but nothing came.

Finally, Frank pulled back the blanket, revealing the pillows and sheets he expected, but also the missing knives and a note scrawled in red ink. He picked it up and read:

YOU'RE ABOUT TO HAVE A BUSY NIGHT.

-LOVE CABEL

Frank dropped the note to the floor.

"Come on, I just want to get this over with," he bellowed at the empty house. "I'm sure you do, too. Are you here or not?"

Frank slid to the closet and slowly opened the door with one hand while placing the other hand to his holster. When he was confident the closet was empty, he swung the door the rest of the way open and kicked at the pile of unused shirts that took up residence on the closet floor.

Frank stared at the pile and sighed, wiping a nervous sweat from his brow that he would never admit was there otherwise. As he decided what to do next, he felt his phone vibrate in his pocket.

Frank removed the smartphone and saw the number for the poultry house on the caller ID. He quickly answered the call to listen to the automated message.

"Safehouse Security Systems has detected a fire alert for your property, Chicken House. To send this alert through to 911, press 1. To deactivate alarm, press 2..."

Frank immediately pressed 2 and hung up the phone. He then went to his apps menu, where he had several apps dedicated to alerting him when someone tripped the sensors at the chicken house and the cabin. None of them had been triggered, but he noticed that every listed sensor leading to the chicken house had a red dot next to it. He pushed the dot to find more information, which popped a warning prompt on his screen.

DEVICE DISABLED

Frank growled loudly and made his way to the exit. Because of the illicit activity, the chicken house alarms only went to him. With Len gone, he was now the only one left to oversee the operation. Len's death had left Oscuro distraught. Frank and Len were professional criminals willing to fake their deaths in order to secure the anonymity of the operation. With their dedication, the operation had expanded far more than two able-bodied men should be able to handle. That workforce was now cut in half and Frank would have to deal with a potential 36,000 square foot inferno on his own.

He quickly made his way back through the narrow woods to his car, rustling through the trees since there was no longer a need for stealth.

Once back in his vehicle, he sped down the road to Tipperton, trying to keep his speed down when he blew past known speed traps. For fifteen agonizing minutes Frank clinched the wheel and locked eyes on the road while he ran through the possible scenarios that awaited him. At the absolute worst, the main financial driver of their operation would be found in ashes.

The worst was realized when Frank turned onto the narrow gravel road and saw a ball of orange flames making silhouettes of the trees that kept it hidden. Not concerned with speed now, Frank floored his car, which kicked gravel in every direction, pinging in loud knocks against his undercarriage.

Frank finally came to a stop at the base of the twisting road that led up to the poultry house. A wind had pushed the smoke downhill and, even in his car, he could detect the smell of burning marijuana.

It was over for their drug operation.

Frank exited the vehicle and stood, hands on hips, as he stared at the flames for several beats before his mind snapped back to reality. He wasn't sure if it was a coincidence or Cabel had been involved in the arson. There wasn't any evidence he was there now so Frank moved on to check to see why the motion sensors failed.

The first was just a few feet up the incline, strapped to the base of a tree. It wasn't well hidden and anyone who had previously been to the location could have spotted it. Frank located it with his flashlight and instantly knew something was amiss. The plastic casing on the bottom had been melted, as if someone had lit a flame underneath it. Additionally, he spotted darkened spots in the tree bark that had been recently licked by flames.

He also noticed a shiny substance in the gravel, which he was able to pick up in a hard, flat clump. He eyed it for a moment before crumbling it between his fingers. He then sniffed the waxy residue the remained on his fingers and found it smelled of vanilla. He looked up the hill at where the other sensors were, but didn't inspect any further. It was clear that the same had happened to them all.

Cabel had been there, but Frank became more concerned with the question of where Cabel was now. If he had attacked this location, then there was no reason that he wouldn't attack any location in which he was aware. He then recalled Troy telling them Cabel had been with him in that initial meeting on Turkish Knob.

Now with his calm demeanor completely abandoning him, he rushed to open the smartphone app that gives a live video feed to one of the trail cams near the road on Turkish Knob. Panic set in when he noticed a missed alert from a few minutes earlier. What he saw when the feed opened was the normal trees and foliage; however, Frank was able to discern one thing out of the ordinary. Scrawled in marker on a piece of paper tacked to a tree opposite the camera was a single word: HURRY.

* * *

Twenty minutes later, Frank pulled into a driveway down the road from the cabin. His cool manner had returned to him, girded by the underlying anger he felt towards the situation. The road turned into a forest path that led deep into the woods, but Frank only followed it part way, turning at a hidden road that hugged against the hillside leading to the main road.

Even though he was in a hurry, El Oscuro deemed it protocol to always park in a concealed culvert below the road and Frank always made it a point to comply. He drove through the thick overgrowth, careful not to disturb it too much as he pulled inside. From there, a narrow path led to the parking area designated for guests.

Leaving his vehicle and moving quickly along the path, Frank checked the lot carefully and found no signs of vehicles having recently parked there. He was trying to piece together how Cabel could have made it here when his vehicle was still sitting in the driveway back in Chancy.

As he cautiously moved towards the cabin, he wondered if he should alert Oscuro to what was happening. Frank took out his phone and began to compose a text, but decided part way through that it would be unlikely a text chirp would wake his boss. So he deleted the text and punched in Oscuro's number instead. He was about to hit the call button when a sound crackled through the timbers. Then a sharp pain reverberated through his right shoulder, causing him to drop the phone.

The sudden jolt sent Frank down on one knee. He reached over with his left hand to investigate the wound, finding that a bullet had hit the edge of his clavicle and ricocheted away without entering his body. Finding that he still had mobility in his arm, Frank retrieved his sidearm and got back on his feet.

"Coward!" Frank shouted into the night. "Why don't you come out and face me like a man?"

* * *

Cabel hunkered down behind a tree after firing the shot, the shotgun he stole from Brian tucked vertically between his legs with the warm barrel resting against his forehead. He laid his head back against the tree as he considered honoring Frank's request.

"How 'bout we have one last conversation before ending this?" Cabel finally shouted back.

"Come out where I can see you and we'll do that," Frank agreed.

Cabel stood up slowly and moved to where he could see Frank's dim outline in the country dark. He noticed Frank's posture was slanted, perhaps slouching from the pain, but also from fighting the harsh angle of the slope.

"I don't want to be part of your world," Cabel yelled to his opponent. "But you forced my hand without knowing how much force my hand possessed."

Frank raised his arms as much as the pain on one side would allow. "I'm not seeing it. I'm not seeing how you walk

away from this. It's home-field advantage for me. The upside
for you is that I don't have to drag you as far to find a good
place for your grave."

"I would agree with that point about you as well," Cabel
replied, raising his gun. "No one's going to come look for a man
who already has a grave."

Frank sighed and reciprocated by lining his gun up with
Cabel. He raised it gingerly, which let Cabel know the pain was
intensifying.

"Really? You barely grazed me," Frank countered despite
the fact the agony could be heard in his voice. "Besides, I'm still
a crackshot – flesh wound or not."

The standoff continued. As Frank stood firm, Cabel took
the time to better line his shot up with the hitman's vital area.
He had been in the freezing forest for half an hour and the front
of his dark clothes were wet and filthy from crawling through
the rotting vegetation that made up the forest floor in order to
dodge the sensors. The exposure to the elements was taking its
toll and a shiver had become noticeable when Cabel struggled
to align with the gun site.

"So tell me about this grand plan?" Frank asked
mockingly, growing impatient. "If these are, in fact, my last
moments, then surely you can give me that much."

"Never cross an honest man," Cabel answered in a broken
voice. "Maybe Troy was guilty of his crimes, but his crimes are
not mine. I was a reluctant accessory to all that has happened.
I'm not someone who deserved any of this. That's the thing
about honest men – we have a duty to dispel the ghosts that
come into our lives."

"You killed Len! How is that honest?" Frank asked,
growing more irritated. "Quit lying to yourself."

"He was a ghost, too!" Cabel shouted back. "And you all
will be actual ghosts soon enough!"

Frank shook his head at Cabel's attempts to sound tough
and spoke in a soft, condescending tone. "Listen, that's enough.
I am the master killer – just tell me plain and simple. What do
you think you have that I don't?"

Cabel tightened his grip on the shotgun. A sudden surge of
confidence came over him as he placed a finger on the trigger.

The knowledge that he had switched Frank's gun with Len's at the traffic stop fluttered through his mind as he answered grimly.

"Bullets."

* * *

The first gunshot that rang out roused Oscuro. Unsure if he was hearing things, he rolled flat in his bed and rubbed his bearded face. In a drowsy state, he nearly dosed off again, but voices he wasn't sure he was hearing from further down the mountain were enough to keep sleep at bay.

When the second gunshot sounded out, Oscuro realized he hadn't been dreaming and struggled to shift himself upright in bed as quickly as a man his age could. He listened for a few minutes more, but the noises had all but silenced.

Oscuro reached to the nightstand and grabbed his phone. He punched in Frank's number on the speed dial and held it to his ear. The tone buzzed on the receiver and, after two rounds, Oscuro thought he could hear ringing in the distance. Curious, he hung up the phone and dialed the number again, getting the same result. This time, however, the sound of the tone was growing louder. He hung up and tried one more time.

He could hear the ringing again, but this time it chirped right outside the cabin.

Oscuro jumped in fear as the phone smashed through one of the windows in the front of the cabin. It took a few bounces and came to rest at the back wall, near the bed.

Panicked, Oscuro hurriedly reached for his wheelchair, but in doing so, made it roll away as he tried to climb into it. He fell to the floor headfirst and shouted out in anguish as his body bent weirdly upon impact.

This was not the end of his troubles as a flaming block of wood flew through the broken window. It made a similar bounce as the cell phone and came to rest on a stack of clothes, making little effort in igniting the pile.

"No!" Oscuro shouted and chose to abandon reclaiming the wheelchair. Instead, he began crawling to the door, his footless legs frantically flailing as he pulled himself forward.

Another flaming log came through the opposite, unbroken window and banked off the wheelchair seat before coming to rest on the floor. That projectile would not have done much to ignite the concrete floor if not for the milk jug full of gasoline that followed.

It hit the hard floor and split open, gushing the volatile liquid across the cement. Oscuro had almost cleared the area, but the rapidly spreading liquid managed to soak the empty legs of his nightclothes as he continued to scramble forward.

The fiery log eventually ignited the floor and caught Oscuro's pants leg as he finally reached the front door. Before he could pull himself up to the knob, the door swung open on its own and Oscuro looked up to see Cabel standing above him.

"Help me!" he shouted, abandoning humility in the face of death.

"You're in some deep shit, so let me lay it out for you," Cabel replied calmly. "All the records I can find on you say you're already dead – Frank too – which means when your remains are found smoldering under this heap – they'll never think to cross examine dental records with someone they've already laid to rest."

El Oscuro's legs were now fully engulfed and were burnt too badly for him to even feel. The doorway was all the further he was going to make it.

Now crying out, Oscuro watched through the pain as Cabel pulled Frank's lifeless body onto the porch, a gun still dangling from his hand. The impact of the thud broke it loose and it slid within Oscuro's reach, though he didn't immediately notice.

"Please help me!" Oscuro screamed again as he watched Cabel pour a second jug of gasoline across Frank's body and down to the corners of the porch. "Please! There's so much I could give you."

* * *

Cabel stopped and looked around. He had one more jug of gas left, but felt there was a good enough inferno going that it wasn't necessary. He picked up the shotgun and jug and stood in front of the crime boss. He first tossed the jug inside the burning cabin, which exploded in a fireball and intensified the blaze.

Cabel took the shotgun and pointed it at Oscuro. For a moment, Cabel considered the fleeting satisfaction of ending his life. He lowered the gun when he realized that he did not grant Troy the same opportunity.

"This is your son's shotgun, so if anyone is going to go down for these crimes, it will be him," Cabel revealed before tossing the gun into the burning building. He then pulled out Frank's gun that he had switched with Len's empty one and did the same.

"Please!" Oscuro screamed in a final plea just before he took notice of the empty gun in front of him.

"I burnt your chicken house down earlier also," Cabel answered. "I suspect your son will burn for those crimes too."

In a final act of desperation and anger, Oscuro retrieved the handgun and pointed it towards Cabel. Cabel responded by removing the bright green squirt gun from his belt. Oscuro fired first, but the snap of the empty chamber revealed its depletion of ammunition.

Cabel returned fire. He pumped the water pistol wildly. The tiny sprays of water splashed Oscuro's face with fleeting comfort as the flames overtook his body.

He tried to scream again, but the smoke and heat from the flames choked out his voice.

Cabel removed all the incriminating items from his possession and tossed them into the flames along with the squirt gun while he waited for Oscuro's body to stop moving. Once satisfied that the job was done and evidence was being ushered away by the flames that encroached onto the porch, Cabel turned and started back down the mountain.

The porch combusted much more quickly than the rest of the structure and Cabel could feel the heat to his back intensify significantly as he retreated. The hotness dissipated rapidly as he strutted away from the scene and the coolness of the country air refreshed him as he reached the winding road on Turkish Knob.

17

RECORD

Cabel Walsh had used up most of his vacation days in a weeks' time, but he still had one more to take and insisted that Miranda take it with him. She did, without question, despite just returning to work after the break two days prior.

It was Wednesday the following week and Cabel was eager to tie up the loose ends that Troy had initially unraveled. Appropriately enough, the first stop was to visit Troy.

The cemetery looked macabre under the deep gray clouds that intermittently gave way to beams of light. The shifting shadows angled over the forested hills that now bared the skeletal structure of the trees – their summer coat of leaves now all but gone.

The two traveled in a new rental car up a freshly paved cemetery pathway to the first turn in the road that circled the perimeter. Just past the turn, a fresh mound of dirt gave away Troy's location. Cabel exited the car and confirmed the spot by a small, metal marker put in place in lieu of a proper headstone. The metal plaque simply read "T.L. MASON."

Cabel and Miranda stood in silence, Cabel staring helplessly at the brown pile as the two placed an arm around one another. Cabel's inquisitive nature grew frustrated and he began to spout off a series of questions in which no one would ever have an answer.

"We hadn't spoken in so long. Do you think if I had been his friend the whole time things would have turned out differently? Do you think he could have been a better person capable of making better decisions? Would drugs have been his only friend in those dark days? Would he have not been on his downward track if he had not had the original overdose?"

Cabel lowered his arm from Miranda's back as he turned to face her. "Do you think my continuous influence in his life could have made a difference?"

Miranda cocked her head as if she were giving it thought. She frowned as she did so.

"I don't know. I don't dabble in alternate outcomes," she finally responded. "You did what you could in the time you had. Though it wasn't enough to save him, you couldn't have done more on your own."

"He never did give me a clear answer if he accepted Jesus into his life," she added lightly after a bit.

"I reckon he was a bit like me," Cabel stated thoughtfully and crossed his arms. "When I was young, there used to be these three wooden crosses outside of town on top of a bare hillside. Being a dumb kid, I always thought that was the place where Christ was actually crucified. I know better now, but those crosses did serve a good reminder to faith."

"What happened to them?" Miranda inquired curiously.

"Oh, they're still there," Cabel clarified. He moved his hands to his hips and turned towards Miranda. "In the years since, the hillside became overgrown with shrubs and brush. You can't see them anymore, but they're still there."

Cabel paused, closed his eyes, and let out a reassured sigh.

"And that's what I think mine and Troy's faith was like. The crosses are still there, but the overgrowth makes it hard to see from the perspective of others. Maybe I'll cut back that thicket of cynicism one of these days," Cabel replied with a titter. "If this month has taught me anything, I need to at least take a crack at it."

"How about your faith in this community?" Miranda wondered. "Do you still believe in O'Brien County after all that's happened? A group of assassins came after you..."

"Assassins? What are you talking about?" Cabel brushed off coyly.

"Come on, tell me what you did?" Miranda begged dramatically. "There were trained killers after you and now they are not. They ain't in jail, so what happened to them?"

Cabel laughed. "'Ain't.' Listen at you. What kind of school teacher are you?"

"One spending too much time in rural Appalachia," Miranda replied jokingly.

Cabel chuckled a little longer until he needed to face where he was and what Miranda was asking him.

"There are some loose ends, but I heard their drug operation in Tipperton burnt down last week. If Sheriff Diggle plays his cards right, he'll retire a hero."

The levity continued to melt back into somberness and Cabel began thinking about what it meant to be in this part of the world.

"West Virginia, what has become of you?" he spoke analytically. "Even before these events, I've always kinda felt at war in the heart of Appalachia. But now I know I'm at war with the drugs, the poverty, the desperation, and the fatalism. The fatalism is the worst of all because it breathes life into the other afflictions. Regardless of that, regardless of our need to break free from those generational binds, in the end we are nothing here but the sum of our family's intentions."

Miranda didn't say a word, but placed an arm around Cabel. Because she was from the outskirts of D.C. he thought maybe she didn't get all that. Maybe she saw it as a warning that if she stuck around – if she raised a family in these parts – she would ultimately do the same to her children. She didn't say as much as held him tighter when a cold breeze blew around them.

The gray clouds continued to roll through the valley, sweeping over the mountains and swallowing up what sunlight was left on the peaks.

"When we were seven or eight or so, Troy killed his neighbor's dog," Cabel reflected and Miranda pulled back in disgust of the initial statement. "I don't know why he did. Just wanted to, I guess. We were at his house at some point while his parents were away, and he just picked up a shovel and said he was going to beat the dog to death. I followed him out as far as the carport, but refused to go any further. I couldn't see from where I was, but I heard barks and growls and squeals, then nothing. He came back with blood on the shovel, which he rinsed off with the garden hose. Over the years, I thought it was Troy playing an elaborate trick on me, but I don't know. We never spoke of it again until recently, but even then he wouldn't talk about it. I never knew if he was ever suspected of the killing, if that's what happened. He never gave me a straight answer."

"Why are you telling me this?" Miranda wondered.

"I guess I just realized, too, that I was also an enabler of his life choices. The dark things he wanted to do seemed to be barred from him without my presence to help absorb the horrors. And like a fool, I went along with all of it."

A gust of wind rattled the couple's ears before Cabel could continue, "I won't do that to you. You asked me what happened to those killers. The things I had to do to be free of it. Those were bad things too that I'm going to save for my deathbed or the deathbed of those who need to hear it."

Miranda smiled modestly to show she had a sympathetic ear. "I'll respect that and not ask you about it again. I'm not going to stop thinking about that poor dog, though."

"Yeah. It's bugged me for around twenty years now," Cabel responded.

"Friends are weird," Miranda commented lightly.

"I agree," Cabel admitted. "But I think with friends, I see in them versions of myself who made a different life choice and went down a different path. I like to see where their paths lead. They are my tour of a road I didn't travel and never will."

"Huh. Am I that to you too?" Miranda questioned half serious.

"No," Cabel smiled. "You're a great new road I'm excited to follow."

Cabel then remembered what he came to the cemetery to do. Without saying anything to Miranda, he walked over to the pile of dirt and began digging with one hand into the elevated soil.

"What are you doing?" Miranda asked, aghast.

Cabel ignored her and kept digging until he hit a large rock a few inches down. Stopping, he stood, and with his clean hand removed a photograph from his coat pocket.

"What do you have?" Miranda asked as she absently swiped at her blowing hair.

"That picture I showed you," Cabel revealed sternly, referring to the photo he took from his parents of him and Troy in their youth. He placed it down in the hole, then refilled it by pushing in the loose dirt with his foot. He then reached down with his dirty hand and smoothed over his footsteps as he stepped off the pile.

They stood together in silence once more, only the wind moaning its goodbye to fall. With one last hug, they separated and started back towards the car.

"What now? Do you want to go fishing sometime soon?" Miranda asked after a few steps.

"Too cold for it now, and that probably won't change for some time at this point," Cabel answered after a moment. "Besides, I've got a meeting with the newspaper here in a little bit."

"Do you think they'll give you your job back?" Miranda inquired as she moved to the passenger side.

Cabel dismissed the notion. "I hope they'll at least give me a free paper so I can read Troy's obit." Then, after getting into the car, he asked, "How about we still have that fishing date when the weather warms?"

Miranda smiled and nodded as they drove back towards town.

* * *

It was almost time for Cabel's meeting with Corey Paxton and Miranda decided she wanted to pay a visit to the public library while he was away. As they passed the funeral home, Cabel noticed someone leaving the building and turned his head enough to see that it was Troy's ex-wife, Ginger.

Hitting the brakes, he veered off into an empty parking spot along the street.

"What's wrong?" Miranda questioned, but not quickly enough to catch Cabel's ear. He was already out of the car and into the back seat.

"I've got one more thing I need to do," he announced hurriedly and grabbed a black rucksack tucked along the floorboards of the back seat. "Sit tight, I'll be back in a minute."

Cabel had overshot the mortuary by several yards and needed to hike uphill to reach the upper lot. He realized he was approaching too fast and slowed down to a casual pace upon drawing near her, trying in vain to mask his heaving breaths from the trek.

Ginger caught sight of Cabel closing in and stopped dead in her tracks. She was holding a large pot of lilies and struggling to keep them level while she remained motionless.

"Please continue. I'm sorry if I startled you," Cabel apologized and inched closer. "Do you need help?"

Ginger stared at him for a moment longer, her brow wrinkled and lips pursed into a disapproving pucker. She continued on with what she was doing and placed the large plant into the trunk of her car, angling it sideways to make it fit in the space.

"You're a friend of Troy's, ain't ya," she guessed in a garbled rush. "I don't want nothing to do with his life."

"I was part of his early life," Cabel reassured, though he was unsure of how to proceed with the dialogue.

Ginger shook her head as she brushed dirty hands against the hem of her dress. "So why you here at the end? You missed the middle."

"I'm here to make amends," Cabel spoke cautiously.

"Amends to who? Him or my sister? They're each a ghost now, so it don't really matter."

Cabel looked sincerely into her eyes and was surprised to find she held contact. "I'm making amends to everyone I possibly can," he answered. "On his behalf."

"That man was a human deathtrap," she ranted. "He was a garbage can containing all the horrible things of the world. He could be emptied out just to get filled back up again." She leaned forward, growing more trusting of Cabel. "And you know what? Even trashcans got to be thrown out eventually."

"He didn't kill your sister, if that's what you're thinking," Cabel stated with renewed tenacity, realizing he wouldn't get to his point if he couldn't penetrate the hatred over Troy's former spouse.

"Who did?" Ginger asked bluntly.

"Hitmen," Cabel admitted with a swift honesty that surprised even him.

"Did he hire them?" she pressed.

Cabel didn't answer, but his hesitation told her enough.

"I could punch him," she growled with fury on her breath. "I could punch the everlivin' shit out of him."

Before she could expel her rage, a young boy ran out from the funeral parlor holding a toy tractor.

"Mommy, can I have this?" the boy asked, lifting the replica over his head.

"No, Dixon. Go put that back on the pew where you found it," she replied and gave Cabel a side-eye before reaching up to grab the trunk lid. "We're leaving soon."

"He loved you and he was desperate to see you," Cabel shared softly once the boy disappeared back inside. "I had a moment to talk with him a couple weeks ago and all he could think about was you."

Ginger let go of the trunk, the springs near the hinge squeaking as it rose back to the topmost position. "I was nothing but a piece of tail to him. That's what he was thinking about. That's a page right out of his playbook."

"Maybe you're right," Cabel admitted and resigned himself

to the woman's pent-up animosity. "But what I saw was love. Love for you and the boy." He sighed, "It was just love broadcast through a channel familiar to him."

"All I got was static," Ginger spit before she turned to go back into the funeral home to collect her son. "You made a grand attempt at polishing a turd. I'll give you an A for effort in that regard, but you aint gonna reel me into agreeing with you."

"I accept," Cabel replied nodding.

Ginger sighed and walked back through the white double doors, letting them fling shut behind her. With the trunk still open, Cabel speedily unzipped the black bag around his shoulder and pulled out several wads of cash totaling $5,000.

This wasn't the $9,000 of what Troy refused to pay El Oscuro. That money would find its way to Troy's mother to pay for funeral expenses. It was hers to begin with anyways.

The $5,000 was from the money drop that Cabel raided the night he killed Len. He had considered keeping this sum for himself, but in a fit of guilt, decided that he hadn't suffered as much as Ginger.

Cabel took a final glance at the double doors before he reached into the trunk and tucked the stack of money next to the sideways lilies. He then pulled the truck lid closed himself before heading back to his waiting vehicle.

"How'd it go?" Miranda asked Cabel once he plopped behind the steering wheel.

Cabel looked to Miranda and smiled ear to ear. Regardless of the uncomfortable meeting, he had still uncovered the closure that he sought.

"She named him Dixon."

* * *

A half hour later, Cabel stepped through the doors of The O'Brien Times, but a swamped Corey asked if they could meet at the York Café across the street in a few minutes. Cabel agreed and headed to the restaurant to have a cup of coffee and wait.

Buck season was now in its final week and continued to remain at a fever pitch for such a tiny town. The small eatery was filled with camo-clad men who chowed down on greasy comfort foods and discussed loudly about the trophies that got away.

Upon discovering a fresh pot of coffee was still minutes away, Cabel opted for a glass of ice water while he waited for the hot beverage to finish percolating. He sat down at the same table he had been at the other day, facing away from the door. Shortly after sitting, the waitress arrived with the ice water and a complementary lemon wedge split across the rim of the glass. Cabel stared at it longingly and recalled the recent conversation with Troy about his disdain for the sour garnish. He retrieved it from the rim and tucked it inside a napkin.

Corey didn't take long and burst through the door just as Cabel was taking his second sip. Cabel looked back to see Corey first go to the waitress at the register and then locate Cabel. He finally seated himself on the opposite bench.

"Sorry, I just didn't want Dawn to hear. She can be pretty damn nosy," Corey admitted.

Cabel laughed. "Oh, believe me, I've worked there."

"That's actually what I wanted to talk with you about. I would like for you to come work with us again. I know that you and dad had a falling out a few years ago, but he's not really involved with the business anymore."

"How little is he involved?" Cabel asked bluntly, making sure the one who wronged him was out of the picture.

"He's in the nursing home. With dementia," Corey answered flatly. "He doesn't do anything these days except relive his days as a bare-knuckle boxer."

"Oh," Cabel replied, realizing he may have come across too harshly. "I'm sorry to hear that."

"It's fine," Corey replied, waving off any ill remarks. "He's a stubborn old man and didn't want to leave the company for nothing. I suppose his mind had to go because no other part of his body would."

"That sounds like him," Cabel agreed, masking his criticism within the comment.

The waitress interrupted them by delivering Cabel's coffee and a large glass of iced tea for Corey. A familiar lemon slice adorned his sweaty glass as well.

Corey took a long swig of tea before continuing, "Anyway, I want you to take over Andy's job as editor. You would be in charge of the content, the layout, everything. Essentially, you'd be the publisher, though I still get saddled with the title because of the family legacy crap."

"What about you?" Cabel wondered.

Corey shrugged, "I'll write the paychecks. I've been doing this reporter thing on my own for the past week and I can tell you it is not for me. Even worse, there seems to be a surge of crime in the area. In the last month, we've had a murder, a drug overdose or two, a chicken house fire, and a huge forest fire up Cucumber Hollow that they're still trying to get under control. That's too much going down at once for me, so I'm out – if you're in. Hell, I may even let you fire Dawn if you want."

"I'm going to need to give two weeks' notice at Huntsville," Cabel answered, but immediately realized he didn't want to sour his chances. "But I would be willing to help you out with the writing until I have a chance to step in full time."

"Absolutely!" Corey replied gleefully. "I'm sure you've been getting sick of driving two counties over every day."

"You have no idea," Cabel replied, slowly leaning back in guarded elation.

"I know you've had some bad blood with my family in regard to the editorial decisions made, but I can assure you I am much more progressive than my father."

With that, Cabel realized he had a chance – a chance to redeem his disgraced career in the eyes of the county, and in the eyes of the Paxton lineage. He saw a chance to take the reins of his dreams and shape the future of the county in a way he had always wanted. He could write the love letters to the area that he always wanted. Those stories and editorials that Cabel would compose would reside in the permanent archives of O'Brien County for all-time. It would allow the county to look back and know what it was like during his time in charge.

However, he looked to the more recent occurrences and recognized he would need to write the indictments about the area as well. He would need to address the underbelly sooner or later and expose the seediness that was hidden below the surface of his community. He was game for this because in the process he would have a chance to clear Troy's name and put things on the record that dead men desired otherwise.

Perhaps most importantly to him in the moment, it was a chance to cover up his own crimes. His sins would be dealt with another day, but not with the community as judge.

It's funny how people don't really think about certain friends unless that friend happens to be right in front of them. Cabel Walsh was no exception, not putting a lot of thought towards his friends, or much of a focus on anything beyond the prospects of the work yet to come.

He stared down at his napkin, retrieved the lemon wedge, and remained silent while methodically squeezing the juice into his glass, careful not to let the seeds fall along with the bitter juice.

Corey waited for Cabel to finish before he continued. "So, do you have some stories in mind that you would like to write for us?"

Cabel brandished the twisted grin of displaced confidence after he slowly looked up from his drink.

"I can think of a few."

Acknowledgments

Early readers who provided valuable feedback and advice in the early drafts that helped hone the narrative into its final form. Arranged by order of feedback are Michael Puchaney, Angel Blizzard, Sharon Martin, Jean Flanagan, Courtney Dawson, Clara Kight, Jess Felici, and Traci Mallow.

This is my third novel published with Cressen Books, LLC, and I would like to give many thanks to Ed and Wendy Lohr for the advice and expertise that guided us through the publication process. They make production easier than it ever has a right to be.

Note From The Author

This book is fiction and the characters are my own. I had only been interested in writing science fiction, so it came as a surprise in the autumn of 2016 when I became possessed with crafting this tale. It was a potent combination of my wife, Traci's, Human Resources career, the loss of childhood friends in my 20s, and the closing of a local navy base in Sugar Grove, West Virginia.

The lost friends are mentioned in the dedication. I found out about Travis' death on Sept. 7, 2003 – the last day I ever went fishing.

Clay's passing took place five years later near my parents' home. My last conversation with him was a late-night chat about how proud he was to be a father, his daughter having recently been born.

The third I had only ever known as my dad's best friend who died in a prom night car accident. Decades later, we came to discover that not only was he my uncle, but my namesake.

Subconsciously, I insulated myself from these tragedies for years, unaware of the caverns of unaddressed pain cut below the surface. This writing was an unexpected outlet to release that hidden anguish, and also the phantom pains of a childhood bullied by both classmates and the school principal of Upper Tract Elementary.

There was a bright spot in those elementary school days. My

English teacher, Rebecca O'Brien, was always kind and always stressed the importance of stories. O'Brien County is named in honor of her and her late husband, John. John authored a book about my home county of Pendleton entitled "At Home In The Heart of Appalachia," originally published by Alfred A. Knopf in 2001. A play on his title is referenced in chapter 17.

In the time since the story's initial draft in 2016-2017, a few coincidental events have taken place in Pendleton County. The approval of a Farm Bill in late 2018 legalized the production of industrial hemp in the United States. Shortly after, a Pendleton County farmer, Mike Weaver, converted his poultry operation to produce hemp for CBD and other hemp-related products. More information about his farm can be found at redbudhillnaturals.com.

Another coincidence was a 2019 forest fire in the Smoke Hole region of Pendleton County that began on Thanksgiving eve; the same night the forest fire began in this story's conclusion.

I'm sure there are other occurrences to events and characters that mirror similar events in Pendleton County. I had worried and stressed over them for years before concluding that all I am doing by telling this story is holding up a clear piece of glass. The reflection that the reader sees in that glass is up to them and their personal experiences.

I have a young daughter of my own, and she wants nothing more in the world than to go fishing. With this publication, with the release of ghosts that I never knew haunted me, I feel I'm now free to take her.

Made in the USA
Columbia, SC
08 January 2021